SEASONS OF DISCONTENT

BOOKS BY RAYMOND FRASER

fiction
Seasons of Discontent
Bliss
The Madness Of Youth
Repentance Vale
The Trials Of Brother Bell
In Another Life
The Grumpy Man
In A Cloud Of Dust And Smoke
Costa Blanca
Rum River
The Bannonbridge Musicians
The Struggle Outside
The Black Horse Tavern

memoirs, essays & stories
When The Earth Was Flat

biography
Todd Matchett: Confessions of a Young Criminal
The Fighting Fisherman: The Life Of Yvon Durelle

poetry
Before You're A Stranger
Macbride Poems
The More I Live
I've Laughed And Sung
Waiting For God's Angel
Poems for the Mirimichi

SEASONS OF DISCONTENT

a novel

Raymond Fraser

Lion's Head Press

Cover painting by Vincent Van Gogh.

First edition.

Worldwide distribution by Ingram Book Services.

Library and Archives Canada Cataloguing in Publication

Fraser, Raymond, 1941-, author
Seasons of discontent : a novel / Raymond Fraser.

ISBN 978-1-928020-05-9 (pbk.)

I. Title.

PS8561.R3S43 2015   813'.54   C2015-900901-4

𝕷𝖎𝖔𝖓'𝖘 𝕳𝖊𝖆𝖉 𝕻𝖗𝖊𝖘𝖘
Toronto • Canada

SEASONS OF DISCONTENT

PROLOGUE

Bannonbridge is a town on the Wilawac River, population about 6,000, with a sawmill and a hydro-electric plant in the east end, a foundry and cement plant in the west end, and a Royal Canadian Air Force base on the outskirts.

The town has one all-male tavern, The Black Horse, and several drinking establishments for people of both sexes. There's a golf course, a curling rink, a skating rink, three high schools — Bannonbridge High for the Protestants, St Timothy's High for the Catholic boys, and St Cecilia's High for the Catholic girls — and one university, St Timothy's. The town is predominantly Irish Catholic.

Clifton, a chiefly Protestant town of similar size, lies five miles up the river, and has a huge and malodorous pulp and paper mill on its outskirts.

And what am I, Walt Macbride, doing here? In the summer of 1963 I returned to Bannonbridge after taking a year off from university to work in Montreal. While in Montreal I saved some money but not very much, there being too many ways to spend it in the big city; and what was left I soon drank away after I came back. When I started school in the fall I did it on credit.

Twice during that summer I landed in jail, although they were just overnight visits. When my father came to bail me out in the mornings he was naturally upset, especially the second time. I could see him squatting at the bars on the street above, looking in at me in my basement cell, his voice shaking as he said, "You god . . . damn . . . You should be in an asylum not a jail!"

The first time I was in for fighting on the street; the second for getting caught on the veranda roof of a house. I was up there talking to a girl I knew through her bedroom window and her father heard us and called the police and they charged me with "prowling by night". In both cases I was drunk.

But no matter. Regardless of unpleasantries like these I was determined to stay in town and resume my schooling. I had only one year to go to get my B.A. degree. It was no fun trying to find work with just three years of university to your credit; you weren't educated enough for some jobs and too educated for the rest. I wanted at least a little control over my future. With a degree if nothing else came up I could always be a teacher.

And so with that in mind I resolved to be quiet, inconspicuous and sober, and stay the year and graduate.

After my father paid the second fine — almost half a week's pay for him — I took a walk up the railway tracks by the river. It was early afternoon, cloudy and windy and with a feeling of rain in the air. I left the tracks for a minute to buy a pack of cigarettes. I was in the habit of rolling my own to save money, but I bought a pack anyway.

It was about a mile to the edge of town where the only houses were those along the highway to Clifton. I kept on out of town and left the tracks and walked along the shore. The tide had just gone out and the sand by the water was wet but above the highwater mark it was dry and silvery and littered with driftwood. I found a good-sized log and sat on it and smoked and looked out at the river. I was thinking of owning a boat. I often thought of that when things weren't going well. I looked to where the river bent on its way to the estuary and to me it seemed the way to freedom.

The wind blew stronger and soon rain started falling. I watched the drops form black dots on my pants. Then it came down harder. I didn't move, I liked the feel of the rain. I imagined what it would be like in my boat with the rain pelting down, sitting in the cockpit out at sea. No civilization, no people to interfere with me, no coercions. A feeling of being at home and secure, like a small boy sitting at the screen door watching a rainstorm.

But getting such a boat, one that could sail the seven seas, would take who knows how many years of steady work and rigorous saving to afford it. And all that time I'd be waiting and waiting.

I was always waiting. Waiting for this year to end, the next to start, then for that to end. Waiting for school to end, then summer to end, then work to end. It occurred to me I was never accepting how things were, and in wishing them — whatever they were — behind me I was giving away years of my life. Right now I wanted to give away the year ahead of me. A whole year! It was reprehensible and foolish wishing time gone like that. It wouldn't make the the year go by any faster anyway, more like the opposite.

The month of August came and went, and the fear I'd get into more scrapes lessened. I wasn't so dead of heart, not so much on the defensive. I decided I was here and that nothing was going to drive me away. I would not leave. I fixed that in my mind. I'd stay and make the best of things. I worked at this attitude night and day, concentrated on diminishing my dislike of people, and of the town, and my situation of being stuck with both. I repeated over and over to myself: tolerance, tolerance, tolerance. It was to be a truce between myself and the world. I won't bother you, so don't bother me. I'll live like you, look like you, converse with you — I'll give up my contrary ways, take my hat off indoors, walk quietly, criticize nothing. And in return leave me alone.

That was my compromise. I didn't stop my drinking, but I reduced it. This was made easier by the fact I had no money of my own (I wasn't long back at school before my miserable savings ran out) and I was dependent on what my father left out for me to buy groceries with, what I could filch from that. We lived together, my father and I; my mother was dead and my two sisters were living in distant places.

I cut back my drinking to two bottles of wine a week, Hermit or Golden Diana or Jordan Challenge, one of those cheap Canadian sherries, so-called. And I drank them by myself, in my room, one each on two separate nights. I never got drunk because I spread each bottle over four or five hours, and passed the time listening to records and reading poetry and occasionally writing some of my own.

So the time passed, neither slowly nor quickly, but surprisingly smoothly. Classes began at the university in September. I was admitted without incident. I hadn't been sure it would be that way, since I owed them not just for the coming year, but for the previous two years I'd been there, and hadn't a penny to pay them. Added to which there was the reputation I'd left behind as a drunken troublemaker, a disrupter of college dances and such events.

Over the summer I spent a good deal of my time reading. There was little else I felt I could do safely. I used to go for walks late at night and sit on the steps of the grade school I'd attended. The school is on a hill not far from the church and the hospital. I would sit for hours smoking, looking at the stars, imagining what I'd do when the year was up and I had my degree, trying to think of something appealing. But then I had to stop going near that part of town when a rumour reached me there was a prowler hanging around the hospital area. I figured this was me – or just as bad, that I'd be mistaken for whoever it was. I had a fear of police and jails. Hitchhiking home from Montreal in May I'd got drunk as a nit and tried in the most ridiculous fashion, in fact in front of a crowd of onlookers, to steal a car, with the result I spent a couple of weeks in a Quebec jail. So with a record now I had to watch my step. Very often my imagination pictured me getting picked up and charged for a crime someone else had committed. If I was walking along a dark street and heard a car backfire, or what sounded like a backfire, I'd think it was a shot and a shadow of fear would fall over me. I'd check my watch to know where I was at the exact moment of the bang, and desperately try to recollect if I'd passed anyone on my walk for an alibi. Then I'd make for a street where there might be people, keeping my pace as casual as possible.

Pretty much every night I spent an hour or so over a coffee in Grogan's Grill. There were two restaurants in Bannonbridge, Laurent & Josette's, where older folks with money ate, and Grogan's, where mostly young people hung out. It had high-backed booths around the walls, and a partitioned row of smaller booths down the middle of the floor. I sat in the same two-person booth every night, the last one on the side hidden from the windows, leaving me well concealed. Here I drank my coffee and rolled my cigarettes and stared at a rough drawing of male and female genitals scratched on the seatback opposite. On occasion someone would join me but not often.

I found it restful to sit obscured in the restaurant. The teenagers and the jukebox made a lot of noise but it was all blended together so that I rarely heard a word spoken. But if the place was relatively empty and a conversation intruded into my thoughts I would get annoyed and leave. I was working at tolerance but I still couldn't bear stupid talk, which it invariably was – stupid and loud, and the louder it was the stupider it was.

But as I said, I was working at tolerance, and would tell myself to stop thinking that way, even if it didn't do any good.

Autumn came and passed, and then Christmas. With only my father and myself at home Christmas was pretty much just another day. A day off work for him, an excuse for a bottle of wine or a case of beer for me, as if I needed an excuse. My father didn't drink – a virtue he'd been taught by my mother – and I tried to hide that I did, but of course he knew. With bottles clinking behind my closed door and the smell from my breath and throwing up in the night and such practices he couldn't help it. But he never said anything. Not about that or anything else.

PART ONE

———

"Much study is a weariness of the flesh."
Ecclesiastes 12:12

ONE

I woke up at nine, undecided whether to go to class or not. But I was well awake and it was a bright-looking morning so I got up and went. The air was surprisingly mild for a January day. There were clouds in the sky and the snow was clean and powdery after yesterday's snowfall. I saw a dog climb over the bank on the roadside and go wading in bounds through a field, the snow up to his chest.

After class the sun was higher and brighter, and the sky clear, a soft pale blue. I could hear birds singing and saw a horde of sparrows sitting on the crowns of two tall elms. Something startled them and they took off in a fluttering frenzy, swarming in the distance like gnats, then circling back and passing overhead before moving off again.

I'm working on a letter to send to school board superintendents, when the time comes to do it. It should go something like this, based on the ads for teachers I've seen in the past.

Dear sir:

In response to your advertisement for Catholic teachers I'm sending for further information. Concerning myself, I am to graduate this spring with a Bachelor of Arts degree from St Timothy's University in Bannonbridge. My majors are History and English, though I've taken a variety of other courses as well, such as Psychology, Sociology, Theology, Philosophy and Latin. At midterm of this my final year I averaged 80% on my exams

*with no mark below 75%. I would estimate my average over the
four years at somewhere around 75%, although it could be a
little less.*

*I haven't gone to the trouble of getting a reference from
my parish priest, as you request, since this letter is not an actual
application. However, I am sure I can satisfy you in that respect
whenever necessary.*

*I will be twenty-three upon graduating, having taken last
year off school to work. I have no teaching experience. The
specific purpose of this letter is to learn what positions, if any,
are available to me, and of course the salary involved.*

> *Yours sincerely,*
> *Walt Macbride*

I'm being careful to avoid mentioning I took courses in
French and Chemistry, for fear of getting stuck teaching those.
The subjects that I do mention – besides History and English
– aren't taught in high schools so I'm safe there. I'd really
rather just teach History (if I have to teach at all) but I can't
limit myself too much. It's not as if school boards will be lining
up at my door.

I've decided to start keeping a journal of sorts, writing
in it as the mood strikes. It will give me something to do while
I'm waiting for this year—this final year—of education to end.
What you're reading now is the first entry.

I say what *you* are reading, because I have to imagine
I'm addressing somebody. Even a love-struck teenage diarist
says "Dear Diary," as though talking to a friend. It's what you
do when you write, you talk to someone who's not there.

The insubstantial reader I have in mind is not just any
reader but one who's bright and witty and kindly and friendly.
A grateful reader with access to no other writings than these
pages of mine – perhaps a prisoner in solitary confinement, or
a castaway on a desert island; or some traveller in a foreign
land who doesn't know a soul or speak the language and
who'd otherwise have only walls to stare at in a lonely flea-

ridden hotel. A tolerant, sympathetic reader, without a nastily critical bone in his body.

A fellow mortal who's curious to see what goes on inside this curious head of mine, and what the outer world looks like from in there.

§

This afternoon I was in Sobeys Supermarket buying groceries, and as I was walking about the aisles I observed that in the toilet paper section they no longer sell toilet paper but "family tissue". I've watched this curious transition, how the item went from "toilet paper" to "toilet tissue" to "bathroom tissue" to "family tissue". One wonders what's next, "heavenly tissue"?

Come to think of it, it must be time to get rid of the "tissue" part, since people are probably catching on that it means "paper", and "paper" was once connected with "toilet". In fact "toilet" originally meant a dressing table, so you wonder what the word before "toilet" was — what horrible word so redolent of what went on there that it had to be euphemized?

All this verbal sanitizing wouldn't be going on if people didn't feel embarrassed about buying the stuff, by whatever name. You see a man go up to the checkout and put his purchases on the conveyor, shiftily slipping the four-roll pack in there in the middle somewhere so it will be inconspicuous. Meanwhile looking elsewhere and fumbling in his wallet as the salesgirl casually rings up and bags the toilet paper like it was a box of potato chips. The man buying has a strong suspicion that the young and pretty salesgirl doesn't *have* bowel movements and so never uses toilet paper. And that she's inwardly laughing at a picture of him using his.

The paper is coloured and perfumed and its name euphemized but remember, gentlemen, even the prettiest girl uses it. And kings and queens and presidents and prime ministers and movie stars and priests — even Christ had to use something. And the Blessed Virgin. And Cleopatra. Though what it was in those days I don't know; such information is hard to come by. There's nothing on it in the university library, I'm sure of that.

Christ washed his disciples' stinking feet. And Ghandi, saintly and all, went around cleaning out chamber pots, or whatever receptacle Indians were wont to crap in. They didn't run from reality or gloss it over. As Shakespeare's Juliet said,

> *"What's in a name? That which we call shit*
> *By any other name would smell the same;*
> *And so shit would, were it not shit call'd,*
> *Retain that curious perfume which it owns*
> *Without that title."*

"You can call it a rose," she added later, "but it won't smell like any rose I've ever taken a sniff of, I can tell you that."

§

Tonight I went out for a coffee at Grogan's Grill, which I regularly do. As I strolled along I couldn't help noticing how peaceful the town is in winter, especially at night when it's tucked under its bedding of snow. There's an immobility about winter; there are few colours and little noticeable change. It stays stationary week after week, like a picture stamped on the mind.

Before leaving the house I read a little about Rama-krishna and Naran, and it made an impression on me, gave me an uncharacteristic feeling of being at peace in a world that itself seemed at peace. Men of religion like these are probably right in their beliefs. The renouncing of what they call "animal activity" on the one hand and the contemplation of God and service to mankind on the other probably does bring a person to the most desirable state in life. A man living in such a way could bear all the world's blows, go hungry, be ridiculed, beaten, thrown into jail, and yet never be seriously disturbed, having as he does the sense of being on the right way.

I can't say I *fully* believe this, but I can attest that the moments of serenity I felt tonight were worth any amount of physical pleasure. When you consider the frustration, the malaise, the general havoc involved in the pursuit of sexual gratification, for instance, it hardly seems worth the effort (supposing you had a choice in the matter). The sex act itself is ecstatic, but it's short-lived. To be at peace with creation, that has duration, and if realized would seem to be the ultimate attainment.

The peace of mind I felt tonight didn't last long. It never does. But it was enough to tell me there is such a condition, that it's possible.

As I passed St Cecilia's High School, where the Catholic girls go, I saw the lights were on, probably for the cleaners. I could see that the basement lights were bare bulbs, the first floor lights were globed, the second floor were of the tubed variety, and the top floor had the very latest in flat fluorescent bars. As though the nearer you got to heaven the better the lighting was.

§

This morning a record by the Beatles, a new British rock group, mysteriously arrived in the mail. On one side is a song called "I Want To Hold Your Hand" and on the other "This Boy". I don't know why it came or who sent it. It's professionally packaged with my name and address in type. It could be some kind of introductory promotion thing by a record club, but there's no literature with it, not a word of any kind.

Anyway, it's a nice gift to get out of the blue. I've played it a few times and I like it.

I'd vaguely heard of the Beatles, but until now didn't know what they sounded like, since we don't have television and I've stopped listening to the radio.

I was thinking of how much I dream nights, and how, if I'm near waking, I'll sometimes edit what I'm dreaming, even though I'm not yet actually awake. Sometimes I run through scenes and if they're too preposterous reject them, as I did last night. I was standing by an Indian warrior and wanting to impress him with my martial prowess I snatched his tomahawk from his belt and threw it at a wall some thirty feet away. It was supposed to stick in, of course, but it didn't; it bounced off, and I thought, oh! oh! and started hurriedly editing it so it would rebound back to me and land in my hand. Then I could say, "There! Try that sometime, War Eagle!"

But I didn't like that version, it was too farfetched; so I rolled back the scene to its starting point, and when I grabbed the weapon from his belt I flipped it in the air and caught it behind my back and handed it to the young Indian maiden standing beside him. That way I showed the Indian brave how easily I could disarm him and impressed a pretty girl at the same time.

It's January 17 and the coldest day of winter so far. Fortunately there's little or no wind blowing because the frost in the air is blistering. I felt it sharply on my nose and cheeks walking to class this morning. The insides of my nose froze tight with each breath and I had to breathe through my mouth. It was like inhaling ice water.

My bedroom window is almost completely frosted over. Through a small opening I can just see the the fields of snow across the river, a patch of greenish-blue sky, and the black belt of forest dividing the two.

I went to the back porch to hang the clothes out and there was a great mass of icicles fastened around the clothesline. I had to return for a hatchet and chop the line free. The falling ice crashed onto the propane tanks below, themselves under a thick coating of ice.

A few nights ago the Anglican church burned to the ground. It was a beautiful little wooden church, gothic in style with ribbed sides and ornately carved eaves, ironwork doors, and a bell tower. There's only a corner part of one wall standing now, charred and burnt away at the top with a pointed-arched window in it, the glass blown out. A fire hose is still pouring water into the gutted cellar and steaming smoke continues to rise from the ruins. Gray icicles hang off the partial wall and the charred timbers. The ground surrounding the site is covered with little black nodules of ice, like ice pebbles. There's a strong smell of burnt when you walk by the church.

The minister's house next door is untouched. Its roof is crusted with dirty ice from being sprayed by the hoses against flying cinders. A tiny adjunct of the church, used as a recreation hall, is also intact. It looks like the church itself, having the same style of architecture and with a small cross atop its roof at the front.

§

On Friday I bought a bottle of wine. After drinking half of it I felt in a benevolent mood and went to call on Barbara, a girl I'd gone with a while back. We'd broken up at her request, but I was thinking now of perhaps taking her to the Saturday night dance at the university. I hunted all over the back shed for a flask of some kind to carry the rest of my wine in (a round quart bottle being cumbersome and conspicuous) but didn't find one, and so leaving the wine behind walked to her house. I still hadn't made up my mind whether to take her dancing or not. Bringing her back to my room seemed like a better idea, but I wasn't sure she'd agree to that. But as I said, I was in a generous mood, and if dancing it was, dancing it would be. And later we could go to my room.

She answered the bell on my second ring. I was expecting the usual black slacks and striped shirt, but she'd got herself dolled up as if she'd been expecting me. She looked fresh and radiant in her pink sweater, plaid skirt, and red lipstick.

"Oh," she said, her expression changing. A shadow came over her face. "I'm going to the dance."

I was standing just inside the door, seven-cent cigar in my mouth, my glasses beginning to fog up. "With someone?" I asked.

"Yes."

I chewed on my cigar. "There it is again, the problem of communication. You'll just have to get a phone in."

"We have one."

"Oh. Last time I was here you didn't."

Her family had been having financial difficulties at that time, with her father laid off from his job, and their telephone had got disconnected.

She waited, a faint smile on her lips now, as if conscious of having the upper hand on me – or so I imagined. My glasses were almost completely fogged and I could barely make out her face.

"Well," I said, backing out the door. "I'll see you around."

I had to stand a minute outside before my vision came back. Then I hurried home and put on some better clothes, stuck the quart bottle in my coat pocket, and went to the dance. On the way I took a drink and almost vomited. The wine was warm from sitting in my room since afternoon, and was bad stuff anyway, the cheapest there is. My stomach was probably nervous anyway, after my encounter with Barbara.

I sneaked the wine in under my coat and hid it in a classroom upstairs and during the dance made a few trips up to finish it off. I danced with a few girls, and from what I could judge didn't make the best of impressions on them. Barbara danced the whole evening with the guy she was with. I got into a dejected mood. I felt the old feeling that had been gone the past few months return, a feeling of disconnection and isolation. It wasn't just Barbara tonight; the other girls, the two I danced with – there wasn't a lot of warmth there that I could detect. It's true I'd antagonized one of them before and she hadn't forgotten, and with the other I must have sounded drunk in my babblings. She was a young thing too, only fifteen or sixteen years old, and absolutely beautiful, to make matters all the worse.

The dance floor was packed, the music loud, fast, irritating. Nevertheless I stayed to the end.

I was standing outside the door when Barbara came out. I turned away from her and didn't speak. She had a partially guilty look on her face, but also a touch of smugness, as it seemed to me. Her new friend was a boarding student at the university, a few years younger than me, clean-cut, well-dressed, the type of young man parents want their daughters to bring home.

When they were out of sight I started home, but I was too keyed up. I couldn't leave it at that; I wanted a showdown. I decided to go over to her place and have it out.

After walking around for a while to give her escort time to depart I approached the house, and seeing they weren't on the doorstep went in the yard. There was a streetlight in front of the house, and the inside lights were on. As I neared the front door I glanced in the living room window and saw them — the two of them on the sofa, the guy's arm around her shoulder. I stepped quickly away from the window and hurried back out to the street.

I cursed all the way home. I said to myself I'd grow a beard, stop taking baths, and live like the bum I was cut out to be, since living respectably bore no fruit. That gave me some satisfaction.

However, the next morning I felt better, and put away my resolutions, for the most part. I told myself if I started living like a bum nobody would notice the difference. I did start growing a beard though — not the kind I had in mind the night before, down to my knees, but a regular beard.

A beard suits a literary man, particularly a literary man who can't afford to waste good wine money on razor blades and shaving soap.

§

So much for my romantic life. As for my scholarly life . . .

Walking into Professor Murray's American History class I remove my hat and bow to him.

"I've been to see the rector, sir, and he said for me to make an apology to you. Ahem!" And in a melodramatic voice, tossing my head wildly about and pausing after each phrase for effect: "Professor Murray! I do most happily . . . and with all respect . . . all *proper* respect . . . make this humble . . . this humble, if I may say so, *apology* . . . for having intruded upon you . . ." [here an extra long pause] . . . "such valuable advice when it was neither requested *nor* desired."

I see him quivering, his mouth working soundlessly, eyes wide as an owl's. Finding his voice he stammers, "Get out − get − get out of this class − you − !" He's shaking awfully in his rage. "Out, I say! − and don't − don't come back!"

What it was that brought this about − Well, I saw it coming a long way off. Murray at the lectern reading from the History text, raising his head, removing his spectacles, staring at the back wall of the room.

"I'm not sure if I mentioned this before," he begins. "I may have said it to one of my other classes."

He's wandered into Oriental religions, and I know he's going to refer to Suzuki and Radakrishna again, in the very same words he used two weeks ago, which were the same he'd used a month ago, and the same he'd used a number of times the year before. Yes, here it comes. I turn my head aside, rest it on one hand and look bored, as a sort of protest, though he doesn't see me. He never looks at his students, always at the wall behind them. A long preamble on Suzuki and Rada-krishna, the essential unity of religious belief, and then zeroing in on Suzuki, "probably the greater of the two" − how many books he wrote in different languages, his age, his scholarship, and − "and this man," he says, "has a thorough familiarity not just with eastern scholarship, but with western science, philosophy, and religion!" He pauses, setting himself to deliver the climax, the master stroke: a sentence he composed all on his own and which almost blinds him as he says it, it's so brilliant . . . "He . . ." Swelling to his full size, set to deliver it like Zeus delivering a lightning bolt . . . "He . . . *he quotes everybody from Plato to Saint —* "

Suddenly I sing-song out loud " *— to Saint Augustine to T.S. Eliot!*"

My voice startles him — freezes his tongue in mid-flight. A few exclamations of laughter from the class. Then dead silence. Murray starts out by shaking from head to foot, then jumps about like a cartoon alarm clock. "Get — OUT! Out of — ! Out!"

I walk to the back of the room where my coat is hung. Putting it on I say, "Professor Murray, I don't know how many times I've heard that spiel of yours, and every time it's in the exact same words. Your students lose respect for you when you repeat yourself like that. You're like a recording playing over and over. We like our teachers to have some spontaneity. A record player could do what you're doing." I tug on an overshoe, zipper it halfway. "From now on," I continue, "it would be a good idea if you kept a score sheet and every time you told a little story mark down the time and place." And with that I button up my coat, pull on my gloves, and go out the door.

When I was gone — so I was told — Professor Murray stood unspeaking for several minutes. His face was pale and his lower lip trembled and came to rest under his upper lip, giving him the look of an old owl on the verge of tears. He took a kleenex from his pocket and went through fumbling motions of cleaning his glasses. At length he was composed enough to speak.

"I realize," he said, "I might sometimes repeat myself — but when you've got three different classes to teach you can't keep track of — of everything you say. But . . . but . . . that sort of thing . . . that — it's inexcusable . . . In all my years . . ." He put his glasses on, fumbled with the pages, hands vibrating, searching for the place he'd left off. "Something will be done . . . I assure you . . ."

And he resumed reading.

It was close! Fortunately I only muttered it under my breath, so he didn't hear.

" – to Saint Augustine to T.S. Eliot!"

Those two old humbugs. Who'd want to quote them anyway?

§

Going by the Anglican church three days after the fire I saw it was still smoking. The beams and parts of the wall that had been left standing had been pulled down and thrown into the basement in a heap. Out of this clutter of black boards and beams an old chimney rose very solitary-looking, standing about fifteen feet high with its head lopped off. It didn't appear to be marked by the fire, its bricks and mortar still their natural colour.

The few small maple trees in front of the church were also unburnt, and with their bare little branches seemed to share with the chimney a feeling of being out of place. The old chimney was dulled and more resigned to its exposure, but the maples were like bashful girls suddenly finding themselves naked in public.

I've had Barbara on my mind lately. She's my most recent girlfriend and so naturally I can't just forget her. I'm sure she won't get out of my head until I find another to displace her.

I don't think we were that great a match. We didn't have a lot in common – she hardly ever spoke and I wasn't the gabby type unless I was drinking. If I was sober there was a lot of dead air between us, and that made me uncomfortable. What she thought of it I don't know because she never said.

§

We're having our January thaw. It rained this morning, and the streets and sidewalks were slick with melting ice. With my leather-soled army boots I had to be cautious walking. The sidewalks *look* to be sanded but it's old sand layered over with transparent ice. To get up Victoria Street hill I had to walk on the edge of a snow bank.

The facade of St Cecilia's church, from the great gothic doors on up past the windows of the bell tower, was coated with frozen rain, giving it a ghostly other-worldly appearance.

Passing houses tonight I heard drops falling from icicles. The air was misty, the clouds low and luminous, and out towards the airport the sky glowed rose-coloured from the airport lights. By the time I reached home a wet flakey snow was falling, melting as it touched the bare asphalt.

§

It was a July afternoon when the large truck drew up to the ferry slip. The ferry was about mid-river on its way across from the north side. The truck stopped inches from the end of the down-sloping ramp and there was no chain or barrier between it and the water. I was standing with some others beside the ramp and I thought, "If he's not careful he'll roll into the river." It was a heavy van with a full load. His window was down and from where I stood I saw him apply his emergency brake and settle back to wait for the ferry. But emergency brake or not, the ramp slanted too sharply and the truck was too heavy and close to the edge and I knew it was going to slide over. The others around me could see this too. We watched, fascinated, as the large front wheels slid the remaining few inches, the driver suddenly realizing his predicament. There was a look of horror on his face as the great truck went into the water, sending up a huge splash and swell. In an instant it was gone, buried from sight.

We stood as if mesmerized, fascinated by the threshing water, watching it lash against the pilings, waiting for the driver to come up but knowing he wouldn't. It was the first drowning I'd witnessed, the first death of any kind. A teenage boy in the crowd shouted, "We can't let him just drown like that!" and throwing off his clothes he dived into the water. Another of his friends followed him. By this time the ferry was almost to the mouth of the slip and coming on fast. The slip was narrow and if the boys didn't get out they'd be crushed against the wharf. I saw two of them pop to the surface, then the third, alarm on their faces as they saw the ferry bearing down on them. The crowd on the wharf waved frantically, yelling for the ferry to backwater. With some other men I ran to the ramp's edge. The ferry was in the slip now, its front propeller churning hard, slowing its approach, but unable to fully stop. We formed two chains so as not to be pulled into the water ourselves and reached our hands to the boys and got them up in time, just barely, as the curved nose of the boat rammed against the ramp with a creak of wood against wood, shaking the wharf.

The driver was still in the cab of his truck at the bottom of the river, beneath the ferry, but it was too late to do anything for him.

That is the sort of dream I'm accustomed to having, very vivid and, unlike my life, filled with plenty of action.

§

My Romantic Life, Part II

The girl named Hilda said, "Connie, is my lip bleeding? Turn the light on, Ross, so she can see."

Ross Trowbridge, who was in the front seat of the car with her, turned on the overhead light. The black scab on her lip was running with blood; she must have bit it or picked it partially away with her fingernail. The scab covered almost half her lower lip, and was so black I first thought it was a birthmark. Her lips were blemished with blood and her chin stained where she was wiping it away with a kleenex. Seeing the look on Trowbridge's face I burst out laughing. I'd man-euvered Hilda into the front seat with him when the car got stuck, saying we might as well occupy ourselves since we were here. Do some snuggling up, in other words.

Ross and I had spotted Hilda and her friend Connie on the roadside hitchhiking to Clifton and picked them up and took them for a drive. The spot we were stuck in was miles out a backcountry road.

I knew it was the last thing Trowbridge wanted, to have Hilda in the front seat with him. He'd only agreed to pick them up because I was interested in Connie, and talked him into it. Connie wasn't bad-looking at all, unlike Hilda, who was.

When we slid on the ice and got stuck in the snowbank I climbed into the back seat where the girls were. I could see the big scab on the girl's lip and said, "Why don't you get in the front with Trowbridge?"

"Turn the light out!" the girl cried. And she laughed too. I don't know if she was laughing at the joke as I saw it. In the meantime I put my arm around Connie.

"Come on, Trowbridge, don't be so backward," I said. "Give her a kiss!"

But he'd had enough with that bloody lip. "Let's get out and walk back," he said. "We'll have to find a phone and call a tow truck."

That's what we did. And all I got from the night was a laugh, not that I'm complaining. In this world of trial and trouble a laugh is not something to be laughed at.

§

Friday night I took my bottle to the dance at the Exhibition Building. It's called the Jamboree, and the five-man band of fiddler, guitarist, drummer, pianist, and trumpeter plays lancers, jives, and waltzes. As you come in the door you can hear the trumpet blaring and blasting like a great bull elephant.

Next morning before I was half-awake my conscience was already raking my memory like an Inquisitor, sorting through the drunken night, turning things over, holding up pieces of memory and pointing an accusing finger. I felt guilty immediately, shrinking into myself with remorse and shame. I'd give anything to retract last night! Then I came fully awake, looked out the window at the gray January day, went over my night as it came back to me — and realized it had been a wonderful night! My guilt vanished, replaced by exultation as I reviewed the girls in my memory, the dances I had with them, whirling and whooping and stomping the floor. And the slow dances, cheek against cheek, thigh against thigh, breast against chest. Girls from out in the country who didn't know me and so didn't refuse me, taking me at face value. It was one of my best nights in a long time and I regretted none of it! I rolled over in bed with a big smile and sang a few lines of a song.

Now it's Tuesday. I've given myself the morning off, cutting two classes. I also failed to show yesterday morning, because it was the first of the week and I couldn't be bothered going.

It's not the subjects of study, I have sufficient curiosity about philosophy, psychology, history and theology; but to my mind I need only books and time to learn all I need to know. I don't need middlemen feeding me the information — dull professors with their tedious lectures, their tests and term papers. It's an onerous way to put in time. I'm only going to that place because at the moment I don't have a reasonable alternative — and because it's there and it costs nothing to go, if you don't pay them.

§

There was frost on my window in the morning, but when I got dressed and went out it wasn't that cold. The trees were encased in whiteness, every branch and twig, and the air had a misty fairyland look about it. Dark clouds covered the sky but for a corner where the sun was rising up. The darkness and brightness, the frost-bound trees, the rolling hills of snow in the fields, all gave the morning a strange and fascinating aspect.

On my walk to class I heard a quick slap of wings as two pigeons took flight from a house roof. A small dog came trotting down the sidewalk towards me, both ears bobbing. He ran at a three-quarters angle, his rear end swung partly round, like a prancing show horse.

Here's my father. I bought some fish for dinner today, it being Friday, but happened to place it well back in the fridge out of sight. My father thought I hadn't got any. Now I've come home from school and am in my room. He begins coughing in his room, gets to his feet and walks out to the kitchen, coughing all the way. Then he turns around and comes back and between coughs says, "You didn't get any fish today, did you?" I tell him I did, and still coughing, he mutters, "Oh, you got some," and goes into his room. He continues coughing a while and then stops.

It's hard for him to say anything at all to me, let alone something I might interpret as critical. It took having to bail me out of jail four times in the past few years for him to finally let me know what he thought of my activities in one pithy exclamatory utterance.

§

It's very still out, not a breath of wind, the trees standing as if petrified. The trees have the appearance, almost the expression of old women, some heavy and bent, some spare with sharp noses pointed to the sky, some with arms outspread matronly, others frozen in poses of fury. Others black and wasted with sparse tangled hair.

A dog barked at me and I hit him with a snowball. He yelped, and for a minute I felt maliciously better in spirits.

It hasn't been one of my better days. Not that anything has happened, other than the incident of the dog and the snowball. I wrote Barbara an eleven-page letter but don't think I'll send it. I'm better off just forgetting about her.

It snowed all morning and afternoon, a wet snow with very little wind, the ground slippery. The sky was a dirty gray, and the trees more black than usual, the houses more dreary. I'm starting to feel hateful again, or at any rate resume my old cynical and contemptuous attitude. I've been thinking of all the years I've been in this town and how much and for how long I've wanted to leave and I'll be twenty-three soon and I'm still here! And when I do go it will be to teach. I feel sometimes I've let myself get caught in a windowless room, and suffocation is close at hand. If the rest of the winter is anything like the past week, today in particular, it will be a slow torturous remainder.

One thing I'm discovering about myself is that I tend to follow the line of least resistance. I drink when I want to drink (if the money is available), I smoke when I want to smoke, I eat when I want to eat, I read when I want to read, I study when I *have* to study (which isn't often), I write when I want to write, I do nothing when I want to do nothing. Whatever I feel the most inclination to do, no matter if good sense tells me to do otherwise, I do. Only when there is an inescapable necessity will I set myself against the tide of preference. And what I prefer to do is often the least advisable of choices. Of discipline I have next to none. My will is like an elastic band, bending out of the way at the least pressure.

But speaking of studying: I try not to do too much for fear of catching *Studiation Madness* — or *Brain Fag,* as it's also called. According to researches I've done, Studiation Madness (or Brain Fag) is caused by scholars *studying more than is good for them.* It's usually contracted by college or high school students — predominantly male students — and the symptoms are difficulty sleeping, concentrating, remembering, and thinking. Further symptoms are fatigue, shaking hands, rapid heartbeat, pain and pressure around the head and neck, crawling sensations under the skin, feelings of weakness, and blurring of vision.

If you don't believe me look it up; it's a very real condition and only an idiot would risk coming down with it.

§

I find it difficult to mingle with people. I seem to be made up of many persons and never know which one will emerge and how he will act. If I could settle on the person that's ultimately me, containing all the others in some consistent way, then I could exhibit that person under all conditions, and knowing it was myself (for better or worse) not be so put out if my actions and words proved unacceptable to others. But I react in one way with one person, another with another, and I'm forever at pains to present the self that's best suited to the occasion.

It's not a desirable way to go about, but if I don't know who my true self is, I have to select a persona from within me to face the world outside, and being an indifferent actor it doesn't always come off successfully. Also, as much as I hate to admit it, I'm probably greatly concerned with pleasing, and want to be seen as others would most like to see me, each in his own way (girls above all). And with everyone having different expectations I'm under continual pressure to keep changing masks.

Mostly this all goes on inside me. I have no idea what I look like to others.

There's a strong northwest wind blowing this morning, carrying snow like desert dust in a sandstorm. The sky is blue and placid with a few smears of cloud, and the sun is its usual bright and sunny self — that's the sky, but down on earth there's a regular tempest going on. The light snow is picked up by the wind and tossed high into the air, thrown in every direction, then settles towards the ground only to be violently snatched up again and flung across fields and streets. The wind howls and the trees cringe and bow as it passes through them.

§

I thought I'd go for a check-up, since I hadn't had one for some time. The doctor invited me into his office, and after thoroughly examining me passed me a form and asked me to check off the places where I thought I was in sound condition. It seemed an unusual request, but I did as asked, and when I finished he ran his eyes down the page and laughed. "No, no, no!" he said. "You're far too optimistic. You think you're in perfect health, but in fact you aren't well at all in the last seven categories. You've got a bad heart, your teeth are inwardly decaying and will have to be pulled, your hearing is practically gone, you're going blind, your hair will soon fall out, you've got an advanced case of appendicitis, and I suspect you've got cancer."

"Is that all?" I said.

"I can give you some pills," he said, "to keep some of the problems in check, temporarily. But you won't be able to do any kind of strenuous exercises with that heart of yours."

"My heart's okay," I said. "I had it examined a few years ago and it was sound as a bell."

He smiled and said, "That was when you were playing hockey. You kept in shape. But once you quit the change was too much and you developed a heart condition."

"In that case," I said, "I'll take up hockey again."

"It's too late. If you went back at it now it would kill you."

"I don't believe you," I said. "I don't believe any of this. I'm going to see another doctor."

"Please do. He'll tell you the same thing. I suggest you start praying. If you're humble enough and pray hard enough you just might deserve to get into heaven."

"Hah!" I said. "Heaven."

He looked suddenly less sure of himself. "What do you mean? You'd better start praying while you still have time – if you know what's good for you."

"I don't believe that nonsense," I said. "Why should I pray? And who are you to advise me? I know more about God and afterlife, so-called, than you could ever hope to."

His diagnosis and condescending attitude angered me. I told him I was going to ignore his instructions and that I'd see him dead and long in his grave before my heart gave out – and I didn't believe the rest of his diagnosis either.

It was true, I either didn't believe him or didn't care. I went out the door thinking I might see another doctor, or I might not, maybe I wouldn't bother. I had the fullest confidence in my *self* – that my will was great enough to keep me alive as long as I wanted, regardless of what disease tried to kill me. And heaven? I'd rather surprised myself saying right out that I didn't believe it. But it felt good saying it. My concern was with life in the here and now, not some hypothetical place in outer space or wherever it was thought to be. To me the doctor was a small vindictive man, eating his insides out with envy and resentment. I knew something about him. His wife had died the year before, leaving him with half a dozen kids on his hands. He detested children – especially his own – but was stuck with raising them. It galled him seeing someone like myself, young and unburdened and, to his eyes, carefree; thinking he knew what my life was like. Turning his malice my way, wishing on me that great list of afflictions, like some heathen witch doctor.

§

Walking back after my coffee at the restaurant tonight the sky was like coal dust. With each step I could hear the scrunch of crystalized slush underfoot. From an upstairs apartment came the sound of a hockey game on the radio, the announcer French, his voice rapid and excited. A heavy transport truck roared by at the intersection of Victoria and King and the stoplight box gave a dull clunk as the light changed back to red. At our building the front steps creaked. When I opened the hall door I was met by a wave of heat that pulled me in and closed around me.

If I have something to say I'm too lazy to say it. I awoke this morning in good spirits and remained that way until mid-afternoon, but then lapsed into moroseness. Right now I'm depressed. I think of Barbara quite often and am calling her a bitch with increasing conviction as time goes on. I find no good to say about her, and yet I want her badly, though I think my desire is gradually waning.

She's probably not a bitch, but that doesn't stop me from calling her one for breaking up with me.

I wonder if there's anything about me or in me to hold a girl once I've attracted her. I have my doubts. I search and can find nothing particularly likeable or loveable, nothing to make a girl cling everlastingly to me. I attract women all right, but the distance it goes after that ranges from two minutes (unsuccessful attempt at conversation) to a year – after which, frustration, conflict, disenchantment, resentment . . .

Corinne, now, my girlfriend of almost three years ago . . . I was a nice guy with her in the beginning, but as time went on I became increasingly impatient and demanding. I'm at a loss to know why she took it for such a long time. I was her first real love and I guess she pinned a lot of hopes on it, wanted to be a successful girlfriend.

With Darlene in my last year of high school it was the same. She was naturally good-natured and compliant – except when it came to sex. They were all Catholic girls and drew the line where the Church and Ann Landers told them; a big part of the problem, in my opinion. The frustration of never getting what your basic nature so urgently desires, repeatedly having the door slammed in your face . . . I'm not trying to excuse myself too much, but I can understand why I became edgy and irritable. I think Darlene still thinks well of me though, despite the fact I did the leaving.

And Julie, from two years ago . . . This one ended more quickly since my impatience got particularly extreme with her. But she stuck it out a long while too, and would have longer had I been a little more sensible. Another lovely girl.

It's strange to think of them – of any girls – being involved with me, and putting an effort into staying that way. Maybe I was a different fellow when I met them. Every day I think I grow more out of the ordinary, which seems to eliminate more women as possibilities as I go. This may not be true, and I hope it isn't; I hope I'll gradually swing around to encompass *more* women as possible mates. Or perhaps I'll run into a different type in my future travels, an *extraordinary* woman, of a type not found in these parts, and then I'll come into my own. But maybe I'm whistling Dixie (I think that's the expression). The greener grass in other fields may be nothing more than the effect of the lighting – coming from my bright hopeful eyes.

§

I met Barbara this afternoon as I was on my way to the grocery store. It was gray and cold and windy and there was no one else on the street. You could cut the scene out and present it to a stranger and it would mean nothing at all; nothing in it, nothing before it, nothing beyond it, nothing to it – just two people passing on the street.

Walking towards each other, the girl looking at the ground as she comes nearer, raising her eyes rather sullenly, her mouth moving to form the word "hello". Uncertain and assertive at the same time, a soundless word I read on her lips; and I, through the cigar in my mouth, returning an audible "Hi" in a voice devoid of expression; wondering as we pass if the wind is blowing my hair into a ridiculous state and making a mockery of my pose of steely indifference.

§

It's five-fifteen now and the sun has gone down, the horizon burnished a copper red. Higher up the sky softens into cloudy white and above that melts into blue. It's a luminous blue, still part of the afternoon, but dusk is setting in and street lamps and lights in houses are on. With each minute the horizon intensifies, the sun's aftermath tans to a heavy reddishness, like red-tanned skin. A raw wind is blowing from the east.

The streets are icy from the freeze that followed a few days of melting weather, but the sidewalks are walkable. They're sanded with a chocolate-coloured gravel to keep people from slipping and falling. The snow crust is studded with ice.

The wind blows huskily in the trees. They creak loudly as if their great branches are splitting and about to fall.

§

I notice I've been avoiding possessions since returning from Montreal. The thought of buying some day (supposing I have the money) more clothes than I need and can carry with me, or items like a radio or tape recorder – things I've thought in the past would be nice to own – repels me now. And the books I have on my shelves, my extra clothes, my record player, I see them as burdens, and wonder what I'm to do with them. I don't want to part with them, but they've become like vines holding me in a suffocating garden. My goal is to be like a bird who carries no luggage and whose home is wherever he wishes to make it and for as long as he wants to keep it – and who heads south when it gets cold. I dread confinement and immobility. I plan on buying one cheap suit in which to teach, and which I can afford to throw away when I want; and a corduroy sports jacket and sturdy corduroy pants which I'll keep with me, wearing wherever I go.

TWO

Every night the little boy prayed, down on his knees at the foot of his mother and father's bed, where his own small bed was, prayed more than an hour every night till his parents had to tell him to stop. He prayed above all that his mother wouldn't die. She wasn't sick but she might get sick, and if she got sick she might die. He promised God he'd be a priest when he grew up if only God let his mother live.

He wouldn't be a priest right away, he'd start out by being a profesional hockey player, and then at the peak of his career announce publicly he was retiring to be a priest. That would be okay, wouldn't it, God?

I don't know how old I was, I didn't then and I don't now, but I'd never been separated from my mother; she was at home most of the time taking care of the house and sewing to earn extra money and caring for me while my two sisters who were older were at school or out playing. If she went to the store or to church I went with her, and when she and my father fought and she took the bus to Port Morian to stay with her mother for a while I went with her too. We were always together. Then one evening she went down the street to call on neighbours, leaving me in the care of an aunt who was visiting us at the time.

I didn't understand my mother going away. It had never happened before. I thought she'd left for good, that I'd never see her again. I got into an awful state and started bawling and howling, in a real panic. "I want my mother! Waaa!" I tried to get out the door so I could run after her. My poor aunt did all she could to comfort me, assuring me my mother was only two houses from here, and would be back in a little while. But I was inconsolable. Wherever she was something might happen to her, I didn't know what, but the sense of impending loss was indescribable. We lived in a double house and the family on the other side must have thought I was being tortured, the way I went on, crying at the top of my lungs. My aunt finally had to give in and take me to the house where my mother was. When we got there I ran to her, and she set me on her knee, wiping away my tears, and everything was all right. I didn't care if I'd been a baby. I was with her again and safe.

I don't remember when she next went somewhere without me, but it must have been a good while later, when I was older and able to be a man better; the fact I don't remember indicates this. As I said she didn't often go out on her own, and my father never took her anywhere, he was too tired after work to do anything but rock in his rocking chair and smoke and go to bed early.

§

When I was in grade school at St Cecilia's we sometimes had movies after school on Friday. They were shown in the auditorium and it cost a dime to get in (the money going to the missions in Africa) and Sister Flanagan would operate the projector with one of the girl students assisting. Several girls walked up and down the aisles selling homemade fudge in little brown bags for a nickel (also for the missions). The films were shown on a small screen above the stage that could be pulled down and rolled back again like a window blind. While the nun was setting the projector up, clicking switches, turning wheels, whirring the film tape off one reel and onto another, the auditorium was like a muted version of the weekly Saturday matinee at the Empire Theatre downtown. It wasn't total bedlam, but there were chairs scraping and muffled laughter and a growing buzz of impatient anticipation, like a room full of bees. Suddenly at a signal from the sister a girl flicked the light switch and the auditorium was thrown into darkness. There followed a hush, or something like a hush, the noise tailing off to a chorus of shhhs! Sometimes the shhhing worked, at other times the shhhers were shhhed by other shhhers and there was a battle of one group to silence the other till the lights had to be turned on again and order restored.

The tall windows were covered with long green blinds through which pinprick sparks of light showed from outside. As the projector whirred static roared back from the amplifier on the stage. The picture (though it wasn't a picture yet, just a yellow square of light on the screen) was invariably off-centre and flicked up and down and sideways as the nun adjusted it, and then numbers flashed on from ten to one. The students took up a chant of backward counting, eight-seven-six-five-four and so on until the numbers were gone. And then – more times than not – there would be a flippering sound and the projector would shut off and the lights come on again. False start! A chorus of groans and boos until the lights went out, and this time the picture would begin. The music and dialogue were loud and raucous and it was minutes before anyone could adjust to it and understand the words. And if it was a British film you might never understand the words.

There were movies with Spencer Tracy and Bing Crosby playing priests and James Cagney as a boy gone bad and Mickey Rooney as a boy who didn't – movies about Boys Town and the Bells of St Mary's and other Catholic subjects – and one, I can't remember which, that was heartbreaking and hauntingly sad about a boy too wilful to reform who ended up killing a policeman and going to the electric chair with the priest comforting him. And every Lent we'd see a film about the life of Jesus with Pontius Pilate appealing to the crowd and the crowd crying "Crucify him! Crucify him!" and Pontius washing his hands and the crowning of thorns and Jesus carrying the cross through the streets and people spitting on him and the Roman soldiers nailing him to the cross and the sky darkening and the wind blowing up to a fierce gale and thunder and lightning and all the Jews and Romans terrified and Judas hanging himself and the lightning ripping the door of the Hebrew temple in two. We're all glad how scared the Romans and the Jews were, seeing what a mistake they made and what a power they were up against! But then Jesus died. It was awful, almost unbearable; the whole ordeal, the agony, the suffering, the dying. Kids sniffling, everybody sad and gloomy. But! Suddenly the scene changes! It's Easter Sunday now. And on this bright and sunny day Jesus rises from the dead! And we all cheer, happy again.

We all liked Easter Sunday, not just because Jesus came back from the dead and rose into heaven three days later, but it meant Lent was at an end and we could eat candy again after forty days and forty nights of giving it up.

The comedies were our favourites. Buster Keaton, Harold Lloyd, the Keystone Cops, Laurel & Hardy, The Three Stooges, The Marx Brothers, Ben Turpin, Charlie Chaplin — old films from the twenties and thirties, some of them silent.

When the show was over and the lights brilliantly on we'd get up and stretch, feeling (at least I did) empty and out of place. The sense of being dropped off in a lonely foreign land was increased when I stepped outside because by now, more times than not during the school year, it was dusk or even dark and the pale street lamps were on. But then I'd remember it was Friday — and there was no school till Monday! and I could stay out later than weeknights and sleep in tomorrow and read funny-books in bed — and the world all became bright again.

§

During my adolescent years we lived upstairs in a two-family apartment house. One summer afternoon, when I was thirteen, I went out to our back porch and lay on an old leather-covered sofa to read a book. Before long I heard two female voices, one sounding quite near, the other less distinct, coming from the flat downstairs. There was a small bathroom window down there that faced an enclosed back porch identical to ours. The two porches were joined by a rough stairway which continued down to the basement and a door leading outside.

I strained my ears.

"Don't come in now!" a girl's giggling voice screamed. "I'm in my striptease!"

Even at thirteen that struck me as a ridiculous description. But it was enough to get me peeking down the stairs.

There was a screen over the window and while I could see the girl in the bathroom it was like looking through a haze. I knew who she was however. An Air Force couple, the Scammels, lived in the apartment, and that summer they had two relatives staying with them: Mrs Scammel's pretty younger sister Aileen, and Mr Scammel's older sister Gertie, a mannish-looking woman in her thirties. The girl in the bathroom was Aileen.

"I'm taking a bath! You can't come in!"

The voice outside the door laughed. "Why not? We're both women. I've let you see me naked. Open up!"

Holding a towel around her Aileen got out of the tub and opened the door and Gertie stepped inside.

"Don't be afraid," she said. She locked the door and with a quick motion pulled the towel off the girl.

"Give me it!" the girl said.

"See, there's nothing to being naked."

She held the towel behind her back, and when Aileen reached for it she found herself suddenly encircled by the other woman's arms. "Now, now, Aileen," she said, running a hand down the girl's back and over her behind. "Aileen, darling, don't be like that. You know what we both want . . ."

They stood that way talking low so that I couldn't make out the rest of what they said, and then the woman reached up and swung the little window shut. The window had plastic curtains attached to it so I was cut off from seeing as well as hearing anything further.

I was thirteen and if all that wouldn't excite a thirteen-year-old boy I don't know what would.

§

Nonchalantly raising his tail the horse dropped a series of steaming balls of horseshit onto the road (of course it's *horseshit* but "shit" by itself doesn't sound quite right). A sweetish, not unpleasant smell carried back to us where we sat on the wagon. The performance seemed quite sanitary and not in the least embarrassing. The horse hadn't the concern even to break his hip-swaying stride, huge muscular rump rising and falling, and the harness creaking with his movements.

I write the above in memory of my younger days, when there were still horses on the streets, mostly country folk coming to town to shop or go to church. Our milkman delivered his milk and butter and eggs with a horse and cart. And there was the pony express, as we called it – a little pony an older boy next door, Pat Flynn, hitched to a dogcart each summer morning to cart the mail from the train to the Post Office – a job I'd have given anything to have myself. Only once did he give into my pestering and let me ride with him, more to show off than anything. Or maybe that's not fair; he was actually the kindest of the older guys in the neighbourhood. All the others ever gave us if we bothered them was a boot in the arse. And we got lots of those.

Some townspeople had horses too, keeping them in barns or sheds left over from pre-car days. In the winter they'd harness them to sledges and go into the woods for firewood or Christmas trees. We'd hear the jingling of one coming and as it slid by jump on for a free ride. Old Bill Pratt, who looked like a pirate with a patch over his eye, had a stable of horses he rented out for fifty cents an hour, either with a saddle or pulling a buggy. It was too expensive for my friends and me to get saddle horses, so what we did one day, three of us, Pat

Flynn's younger brother Arnie, Buck Connors and myself, was pool our money and hire a buggy and take turns at the reins.

It wasn't how we imagined it would be, which was along the lines of a stage coach with one of us at the reins and the other two riding shotgun, each taking turns. We hadn't anticipated how conspicuous we'd be. Every street we went up people turned and looked at us and laughed, and it was embarrassing. We should have known only eastern dudes and school marms rode in buggies! No cowboy worth his salt would be caught dead in one.

It wasn't really the reason, of course. People were simply amused to see three kids trotting up the street in a horse and buggy. But it's what we thought at the time.

Now the horses are all gone. There are still a couple of free-stands, as they're called, open sheds with hay bins where half a dozen horses could tie up. There's one behind Jackson's Barber Shop on the front street, and another back of St Cecilia's Church. But they haven't seen a horse in years.

§

That ride around town reminds me of Merlin Morgan, the local Protestant undertaker. He hired the same three of us, Arnie, Buck and myself, to work for him one summer day digging up and raking and seeding the scrubby weed-ridden yard in front of the building where he kept his coffins stored and did his embalming. We worked all morning and afternoon and for payment he let us go in the building and look at the coffins and his collection of antique flintlock muskets and pistols. We liked the second part, but not so much the first, and were thankful it wasn't a stormy night and we were locked in. There was no telling what corpses were in that spooky place, and when one would rise up out of a coffin.

That wasn't all — he wasn't finished paying us. Next he bundled us into the back of his long black hearse and drove us all over town with us looking out the windows and waving at people like the dead come to life! And then he bought us each a cone of ice cream.

He drove us back and when we asked for our wages he said wages? We'd had our wages. How many kids get to hold pirate guns as we'd done and then drive around town in a hearse? And have a cone of ice cream thrown in as a bonus?

Being young kids there wasn't much we could do about it. Later, when we thought of it, we could see he did have a point. Money comes and goes, but coffins and corpses and real pirate guns, well, those things don't come along every day. And neither does a hearse ride. Not everyone gets to ride in the back of a hearse, not more than once anyway.

§

You know how you can see a face in a cloud, or in a pattern on your wall paper, or in the water stains on your ceiling? I saw one today in the folds of my coat as it hung behind my bedroom door, and drew it exactly as it looked:

Maybe it's someone on the other side trying to get in touch with me.

§

An advertisement I'm thinking of running in the local weekly paper:

Young man requires position as tutor. Has bachelor of arts degree, specializing in History and Literature. Would prefer a position on a yacht sailing the Mediterranean while instructing the beautiful teenage daughter of a generous and liberal-minded tycoon, but will consider something better if offered.

A storm started early yesterday morning, just before daybreak, and raged on through the day. By evening ten inches of snow had fallen and the town plows were able to keep only the main roads cleared by going over them again and again; they were no sooner cleared than the driving wind was at work filling them back in. On every street there were cars spinning their wheels, and some were abandoned where they'd slid into the ditch by the road and sunk. It was impossible to turn your face more than a second into the wind. Buildings were obscured, the sidewalks were buried and impassable, people plodded along on the roads with collars high, glancing back every few seconds to watch for cars. All the schools and government offices were closed and most of the stores.

§

It's Wednesday now, two nights after the storm. The streets are plowed and the snow packed down hard from car tires. Most of the sidewalks are cleared, some still being plowed by small bulldozers. Everywhere the banks are high, six feet in places, looking like great mountain ranges seen from a distance.

Night and day there's the sound of tractors and bulldozers pushing and piling the snow and loading it onto trucks and trucks driving to and from the river dumping their loads over the Station Wharf onto the river's ice.

§

I've been summing up in my mind my situation here in Bannonbridge. I have one close friend, Harold Healey, who I see about twice a week. No money, other than the bit I skim off the grocery money. Local activities available: drinking, which I do too much of already and can't afford more or I'd do more. Dancing – only on weekends, and there's the expenses of a bottle to take along and paying your way in (if you can't find a way to sneak in), besides which the girls know me too well as a wild-man and I don't have a car in case there's a girl from out in the country somewhere who doesn't. Bowling – too expensive and I'm not interested anyway. Skating? Don't want to, I've spent about one-sixth of my life on skates and that's enough.

And there it is, the local activities. I have no girlfriend. I'm supersaturated with reading. I'm too restless most of the time for writing. Walking – I walk a lot. What it boils down to is: I'm bored. And maybe it's my own fault, I don't deny it. It's possible I'm not going about things in the right way. But that doesn't change the fact. You may be to blame for cutting your leg off, but you still have only one leg to hobble around on. Accepting the blame doesn't help you grow a new one.

§

February 26. We're over the worst of winter. Not so long ago it was dark coming out of church after Sunday's 4:30 mass, that is, about twenty after five. Today after mass it was more like afternoon than evening.

The church sits atop a hill and from the steps you can see well across the valley. The scene on the other side of the river is uniform and bleak. Black and gray masses of trees, snow-filled fields, a few farm houses and barns with snow-covered roofs. Beyond the fields the forest reaches back to the sky with the occasional tall pine jagging up from the even horizon line. At this distance the evergreens aren't green but black, and the leafless deciduous trees and bushes are different shades of gray, in some places with a dark purplish cast. If they've collected snow on their branches they have a gauzy out-of-focus appearance.

A drear picture altogether, and even more so when the sky is overcast, as it is today.

§

I should write a book and call it *A Kick in the Arse*. Then when someone goes into a bookstore to ask for it and they don't have it he can come back later and say, "Did you get *A Kick in the Arse* yet?" Some bookstores are run by prim old spinsters and it would work really well with them.

And if you got the book for a gift you could say to your sweet old mother, "Guess what my friend Charlie gave me for Christmas, Mother. *A Kick in the Arse!*"

Or a young lady in college sociology class could say bitterly: "All Daddy gave me for Christmas was *A Kick in the Arse!*"

"Oh, you poor thing. Did you call the police?"

§

I shouldn't leave writing these notes till late at night. I'm often drained of energy by that time and don't feel like it, as has been the case for much of this month. Yesterday for instance I had two tests to prepare for, and spent a few hours typing a story I'm working on, and then there was the Cassius Clay/Sonny Liston fight to listen to on the radio. Other nights I'm either drinking or I get reading and don't want to stop or I expend my dubious powers on composing poetry or a half-assed story of some kind. I was right in predicting this wouldn't be a legitimate diurnal journal.

THREE

March 1. I awoke to a clear sky, the sun beaming down on yesterday's snowfall. It was painfully bright to the eyes. I was late and ran much of the way to class, feeling light and vigorous on my feet. After class the sun showed through a screen of rising cloud like a glowing moon, the circumference clear as a silver pencil line. The snow was the lightest I've seen all winter; I think if a wind came up it would scatter to the air like smoke and vanish. The closest likeness I can think of is dandelion down, those white fluffy gossamer globes you see in early summer before the tiny particles get blown away by the wind.

It's midday now and snow has been falling off and on for the last hour. My window is mostly covered in frost, only a jagged crescent still unfrosted. Looking through it I can see a telephone pole and some branches of a tree against a backdrop of gray sky.

After mass Sunday afternoon I went with Harold Healey to Grogan's Grill. I had a coffee and Harold ordered a couple of slices of toast and a milkshake. He said he hadn't eaten anything all day.

"I felt this queer feeling in my stomach and wondered if it was something I ate. I thought, what did I have for dinner? Then it came to me that I'd had nothing for dinner — and no breakfast either. So that was the root of the problem."

"I saw you at communion," I said. "So you got a bit of bread into your stomach. While you were up there you should have said, 'Give me a couple of more of those, Father, I've had nothing to eat since yesterday.'"

Harold shrank back. "Get away from me!"

"Why? Look out the window — the sky's clear, no lightning bolts; the earth isn't opening up beneath my feet."

"No, you won't get it now. But on the day of reckoning the good Lord'll let you have it, with both barrels. When it's too late for you to repent."

"What? No forgiveness? No second chance? That wouldn't be Christian of him."

The waitress brought our bill and he asked her to bring him another order of toast and a glass of milk. She gave him a surly look and took the bill back.

"I don't think she's happy in her vocation," Harold said. "Speaking of vocations, did you get a letter from the Bishop?"

"Yes. A funny letter, made me laugh. Did you get one?"

"Not yet, but some other guys did. What was funny about it?"

"He wants me to be a priest."

"Is that funny?"

"I'd say so. He couldn't have checked me out very carefully."

We left the restaurant and crossed the street and I said, "See, I didn't get run over. God didn't send a truck to run me down."

"Not yet. You were watching. But don't worry, he'll get you. He'll catch you when your guard's down."

Harold's an odd bird. He's good company at times, but he's very religious. He told me one day that he wants to live a virtuous life, but was having difficulty with it, because the path to virtue is a long and narrow one and is strewn with snares. He had many faults in himself to correct, he said. When I asked him to name his biggest fault he went into a lament about the way he wastes his time when he should be studying. He said the good marks he made at Christmas were the work of God, and that he deserves no credit himself. God stepped in and guided him to study exactly what he should study and that was why he did so well.

It seems he's on that kind of footing with God. I won't go into what I think his real faults are, only to say they have nothing to do with studying.

Not to change the subject (if this isn't changing the subject I don't know what is, but that's what people say when they want to change the subject) I was sledding with Brigitte Bardot last night. She and I were racing down a steep bobsled run and halfway to the bottom missed a turn and went flying through the air. We might have been killed, but by pure luck we landed upright on the other side of the bend and continued down the course. When we got off the sled Brigitte yawned as though nothing had happened.

This took place at the old Grotto, by St Cecilia's Convent, where a movie was being shot. I was hanging about the site watching the proceedings, and during a break struck up a conversation with Miss Bardot. We seemed to hit it off and that's why I invited her to go bobsledding with me. When we were at the top of the Grotto hill on the bobsled I put my arms around and and held her close. And when we got to our feet after our mishap she left to do another scene, and . . . that was it. It's hardly worth passing this on to my reader, but people who meet famous people can't resist telling everyone, and I guess I'm no different, especially not when it's Brigitte Bardot!

Speaking of girls, I was in Grogan's Grill this evening, and two girls – two real girls – getting back to reality – came along and talked to four young fellows wearing black leather jackets who were sitting in the booth across from mine. I'd never seen the boys before, they were probably from Clifton. One of the girls wanted to keep going and get a booth of their own, but the other – I saw her glancing my way – said no let's sit here, and she squeezed in beside the two boys facing my way. She was about fifteen and I could see she had a nice figure, and would have been quite pretty but for the moist bright-red lipstick she had plastered all over her mouth. I pictured myself kissing those lips and thought I'd have to be drunk first. I'd come out of it looking like a circus clown.

I noticed she was looking over at me and smiling. I lowered my eyes to my coffee cup, not sure what to make of it. Then one of the boys called out, "Hey!"

I glanced up and the girl said, "Where's your — " The restaurant was noisy and I didn't catch the last word.

"Eh?"

"Where's your — " Again I couldn't make out the word.

"Where's my what?"

She made as if holding something in her hand. "Your pipe! Where's your pipe?" She drew the shape of my bent pipe in the air.

Where had she seen me with that?

"Oh. My pipe. It's, ah . . . it's in retirement."

"What?"

"I retired it."

She didn't understand, but before I could add that I was sticking to cigars and cigarettes these days the boy beside her said, "Do you want to trade places?"

"No, I'm fine here," I said.

"He means with me!" the girl said. "He wants you to sit beside *him*!" And with a laugh she jumped up and skipped down the aisle with her girlfriend running after her.

§

Certain people there are who, when times get tough, can count on something turning up, but I'm not one of them. With me, nothing ever turns up. Anything I do in the line of the adventurous and unusual is something I go out and make happen by myself. It's true I end up back where I started from, but I think I deserve praise for my efforts. These valiant efforts however appear only after long intervals, and with the catalyst of trying circumstances (boredom, self-dissatisfaction, perceived or imagined oppression) to get me stirred up and moving.

I know now not to expect a chariot from the sky, swooping down and whisking me away to a magical odyssey of life.

I'm not complaining; I like to see myself as the architect of my own fortune. Even if I appear a little lax these days in architecting something interesting, it doesn't mean I won't when I feel prepared. I assume I will *one day* feel prepared.

In short, I am where I am now, here in Bannonbridge, wondering about my future, and nobody is going to sail up the river in a three-master and call out, "You there, Macbride! I need a crewman to sail the world with me – will you come?"

Nor am I going to – at any rate I think not, though I don't know for sure – going to apply to teach school in Paraguay, Tibet, or North Borneo. A foreign land, a foreign language, doing a job that's foreign to me – that would be too much to take on.

What I'll probably end up doing is teaching in the depths of the New Brunswick backwoods, some place like Sheephouse Falls or Lower Gulguac River.

But really, a year teaching might not be all that bad; it depends how you look at it. It would give me experience at the trade, something to fall back on should I need it. And I'll get my debts paid. If my present state of mind continues it won't really matter where I am, just so I have a stock of books, a pen and some paper to write on, and a restaurant to go out to for a cup of coffee nightly.

While on the subject of coffee, there's a girl I see sometimes in Grogan's Grill who I'm sure nobody but myself finds attractive. I like her mouth. Her upper lip protrudes slightly above the lower, but she's not "buck-toothed", and her lip doesn't *hang* over her lower lip, it's firm. It's one of those mouths people have that seem to be never entirely shut. She has the look of a girl who knows she's not pretty but who says "what the hell" with a shrug and doesn't try to be, flouncing around in a most natural way. She keeps herself well looked after, and beneath her floppy coat and the long scarf she drags behind her she'll wear nicely-fitted slacks and a bright wool sweater. Being natural as she is she's welcome with any number of girls, and on the other side the boys feel comfortable with her, so she has plenty of friends. I suppose she cultivates, or finds herself drawn into, a quietly ironical approach to life.

Besides her mouth I like her eyes, which are warm and kind and trusting.

She seems the kind of girl to be a friend's sister, a girl to be friendly with, to take for a stroll, joke with, and not get tired of. And not have to endure in her company the discomfort of a futile sexual obsession.

Not that she has no physical attractions − she's slim and nicely proportioned and isn't outrightly ugly-looking, not by any means, not to my discriminating eye.

And why don't I try to get to know her? Because my appraisal of her is hypothetical: I've only *seen* her, never talked to her or heard her speak. It's extremely unlikely, perhaps even impossible, that she'd fit my analysis. As it is I can look at her and imagine she does, and never be disappointed.

§

This morning a mild west wind is blowing and the puddles of yesterday that froze in the night are opened up again. Birds are singing − I don't know what kind, but I'll say sparrows since that's what all little gray birds look like to me. A roaring Voodoo fighter jet passes overhead and in the stillness that follows I hear the dripping of water off a roof. When you're facing the sun it casts a blinding sheen on the wet roads.

It was recess time when I walked by St Cecilia's High on my way to class and the third-floor windows were filled with green-and-gold garbed high school girls. A number of them shouted, "Hi Walt!" I looked up and waved and the girls who shouted jumped back from the windows with girlish squeals. They were being audacious, up there on the top floor with the sun shining, feeling high-spirited. Girls, girls in St Cecilia's green and gold on a glittering spring-like morning – bright little things laughing and chattering as girls have done since the beginning of time. My heart went up to them, rejoicing at the wonder of it all.

§

A little verse I wrote last night:

SOMEDAY

In my mind I see myself
a wandering soul
without a name
a man in his thirties
who carries a cane
carefree capricious
and slightly insane

a cynical man
but not malicious
kindly at heart
and self-contained
with watchful eyes
and no ambition
who's fine with himself
and that's sufficient.

§

Our sociology professor, Father Clark, is quite comical, though not intentionally. He was in especially good form this morning, taking the effort to explain every third sentence he read from a magazine article on unemployment in the United

States. The last words of a sentence would go like this: " . . . and they were afraid they would have to shut down the coal mines altogether." A pause, then looking up from the book to give this explanation: "See, they said, *'We're afraid we'll have to shut down the coal mines altogether.'*" Then resuming reading.

He also read us something on the problem of population explosion. One of the lines was: "Regulation of population is becoming imperative", which he explained in this way: "That is, you see, that it's becoming imperative."

And this about ethnic groups: "'Within such ethnic groups there can be two states, each independent of the other' — That is, within such ethnic groups there can be . . . two states, each state independent of the other. See?"

He always starts the class off with the Lord's Prayer, standing facing us, a bespectacled square-built man with a square face and a flat bald head, hands clasped tightly in front of him, legs solidly apart.

When reading from the text he often stops and talks about something quite unrelated. Today it was General Franco of Spain.

"Did any of you see the television show they did about General Franco last night? It was somewhat against him, saying that he is where he is because of a will to power and so on, and that he hasn't helped his country very much. But still, there is a little idea running through the program that seemed to say he was helpful. He's been in power a long time — it's really marvelous. So he can't be too bad. He seems to be a good leader. And you can't really believe the press or TV programs and so on. He seems to have helped Spain quite a bit. Franco's a good Catholic, he's worked with the Church . . ."

Speaking of the Church he said, "The Catholic Church is changing. Before we used to look at Protestants and call them 'those black Protestants', but now we're supposed to be friendly with them, be brotherly and so on."

He's gossipy, never tires of telling us of someone in town who got married, or moved out of town, or is building a new house, or died. He has no trouble finding jumping-off places in the text — "Now, talking of interdependence, I'm always reminded of the people down the East End, how everyone knew everyone else and always helped them — see, that was interdependence — I don't know if it's still like that. I don't think so. But you never can tell. Take the O'Leary family . . . I remember they lived on the same street as the Camerons . . . Paul Cameron married Mary Murphy — her father was Peter Murphy who worked at the mill . . . "

He's in his mid-fifties but looks ten years older if not more. He comes from a small village downriver and graduated from St Timothy's before becoming a priest. After his ordination he attended Catholic University of America for a year or two and often reminds us of "when I was down at Catholic U". And we know quite a bit about trips he's made to Boston to visit his married brother and his family. We know such things as how old the kids are and the dates of their birthdays and what his brother works at and where his sister-in-law's family lives and what her father did before he got his present job.

While we were on the interdependence thing, he said, "My brother in Boston used to live on Jamaica Plains and didn't know his next-door neighbour. He moved to Quincy, a better neighbourhood, and he still doesn't know his next-door neighbour."

He's addicted, incidentally, to the phrase "and so on." He normally ends sentences with it, such as when he was talking about the birth control problem: "Husbands like to consort with their wives and so on."

I've heard him say "three thousand or so on years."

There are four girls in our senior sociology class, and the four best marks on the Christmas exams went to them, and no doubt will again on the finals.

He has some trouble pronouncing words. This morning he came to "administrative" and called it "administratative". He also referred to the French-English situation in Canada as "bio-culturism".

For three days running, at the beginning of the year, when he was doing roll call, he hesitated over the name of Ulysse Legere, before calling out "Eloise Legere." By the third day Legere had had enough. He banged his desk. "No, not again! It's Ulysse! Ulysse!"

I thought he might say, "It's Ulysse, Coll*iss!*" that being how the French swear word "Chalice" is pronounced. It would have made a nice rhyme.

I have to say, though, that for all his peculiarities he's a good-natured, kindly, always-smiling man. Prematurely senile perhaps, but you don't want to hold that against a man.

§

I just cut my finger putting a blade into my razor to shave. It's leaking through the band-aid which means there's now a sample of my blood on this notepad, should criminologists ever be looking for one. I'm also smoking a blood-soaked cigarette, one I just rolled.

I've been thinking I should be more grateful for Harold's friendship, whatever his faults. He's intelligent and witty and quite generous, lending me books and records and on occasion buying a bottle of wine to share. I find him stimulating to talk to. Hardly a sentence passes between us that hasn't got some element of humour in it, or what seems like humour at the time.

When I saw him a few days ago he told me he'd been talking to Hubert Ross — "You know, the guy who's always fishing off the Station Wharf? He asked me if my brother Donnie enjoyed the shad he gave him. I said, 'Yes, very much — he ate it with obvious relish.' Hubert seemed quite interested in that. He wasn't too crazy about shad himself, and so — "

Me: "So next day he went to the grocery store and asked for a bottle of Obvious Relish."

Harold: "Yes. He thought it might give the shad a better flavour."

Last weekend he came over and I put on a record of flamenco guitar music that he lent me. There was a part where the rhythm gradually accelerated from slow to fast, and I said, "It reminds me of a train pulling out of the station."

"Yes," he said, "with a fellow in the baggage car playing a guitar."

At the risk of sounding like a tiresome stand-up comedian, there was this other time we were strolling around downtown and came across a sign in a store window advertising a church-sponsored "Brown Supper". I suppose it meant they'd be serving beans and brown bread.

Harold said: "Hah! A Brown Supper. Hah! We've just cleaned out the latrines — come to our Brown Supper!"

A few days before this he'd run into the expression "shit-heads" in the novel *One Day in the Life of Ivan Denisovitch,* and it struck him as amusing. He said, "That word hasn't been sufficiently explored in literature. *'Yet once more, O ye shit-heads, and once more!* You bunch of shits — Scrape yourselves together!" When we got to my room he grabbed a pen and paper and composed some new opening lines to Milton's *Lycidas,* a poem we'd learned back in high school.

> *Yet once more, O ye shits, and once more,*
> *Ye composites of french fries and old beer!*
> *I come to have this moment on the stool*
> *And with stained shorts pulled down*
> *Spatter the bowl and leave you here*
> *Amid fumes most fetid and most drear . . .*

§

The air has a strange brightness to it. There's a veil of cloud across the sky, the blue background showing faintly through, and the ground is heaped with snow. The house across the street is painted white, and the maple in front of it has silver-gray bark, and there's a white fence along one side of the house and behind it, and in the yard there's a clothesline holding white sheets and supported up by a pole of white birch. Everything is white or gray, and the air outside, the brightness, is like the colour of water. It all makes for an unusual brightness, a rather dull and subdued brightness. Which sounds contradictory but isn't.

A girl I know slightly was sitting in front of me at mass this afternoon. I danced with her one night after having a jug of Hermit and told her she was the prettiest girl in town (and that I was the smartest guy, or some such horseshit). It was the night Barbara was there with her boyfriend.

There's no doubt the compliment I paid her is true. Her features are delicate, her skin clear and pale, her hair a fine silken blonde, like a little child's. Her nose, her ears, her mouth, all are perfect. Her mouth is shaped naturally in a faint dreamy smile, turned up ever so slightly in the corners; and she has a very attractive figure, slight but shapely – definitely shapely. Her name is Elena and she's about sixteen years old.

Perhaps we'll meet at a better time, after the passage of a few years.

I like such fantasies. They're more suited to me in my reflective moments than an actual romance. Judging from experience, the beginning of my association with a girl marks the beginning of its end; and once these things deteriorate there's no resurrecting them. So far as I know, Elena – to use her as an example – has nothing substantial against me, otherwise she wouldn't have danced with me more than once as she did, or smiled at me today; and so all sorts of wonderful possibilities exist. They might be not realistic ones, but they're possibilities nonetheless.

I know what it's like when it's the other way around, when there's no chance in the world of getting a particular girl. The finality of it is maddening and demoralizing. You can run this way, run that, speak or hold your tongue, stand on your head, roll over and play dead, but it's all futile. You're like a fly buzzing around her, something annoying to be shooed away. You could commit suicide in front of her and she'd be unmoved. Would she care that you did it because of her? Not in the least. "So inconsiderate!" she'd exclaim. "What did I ever do to him? I was going shopping but how can I now, after that? It's ruined my whole day!"

Now this is not all girls – or I hope it's not, since I'd like to keep some scrap of romantic illusion alive in me.

You hear it's a woman's right to change her mind, but in my experience the opposite is true. Once an idea is fixed in their heads they cling to it like bulldogs.

All this is merely my biased opinion, inspired by the specific example of having a desirable girl desire me, getting this girl, then bringing about the destruction of our alliance while still wanting to keep her, and her subsequent attitude towards me. I'm talking of course about Corinne. Corinne who held on as long as she thought what we had was salvageable and then reached the conclusion it wasn't. And who has been cold as ice towards me ever since, the fire permanently extinguished. Nothing I say or do has the least effect, doesn't shake even a little bit her conviction.

Which is not to say she isn't right. In fact, since it's me involved, there's a better than even chance she is. But that doesn't lessen my feeling of hopeless futility when I see her or call her up and get the same chilly reception.

But what I started out saying is, in such a case as this it's all hardship and pain. Whereas with a girl like Elena it's as glorious as my imagination wants to make it. Theoretically I could find heaven on earth with her, one fine day. And that beats the agony I've gone through with Corinne. It may not be real, but what's so great about reality?

§

I was living in residence up at the university when the fire broke out. We were between classes in the afternoon and some other students and myself were milling about outside, when suddenly an airplane came flying towards us, approaching from the direction of the river and no more than thirty yards off the ground. Everyone ducked as it swooped over, and in climbing to clear the residence building its tail clipped the roof. The impact didn't stop the plane, but the section of roof where it hit caught fire. And my room was on the top floor, right there beneath it!

My first thought was, my manuscripts! I dashed into the building and up the stairs.

The flames hadn't yet reached my room but the plaster on the ceiling was glowing red and cracking. People shouted for me to get out. I opened my trunk and was rummaging for the papers when a great flash burst from above, hurling me to the floor. The fire had broken through and a beam come crashing down on my head. As the room filled with smoke I struggled to my feet, dazed, unable to see, my head throbbing. I felt my way through the smoke, knowing full well the danger I was in, but trying to get to my trunk again. One of my classmates rushed in and yelled for me to leave before it was too late. When I told him my manuscripts were here he dived into the smoke and flames and emerged dragging the trunk after him. Together we got it out to the hall. There was a great deal of coming and going in the hall, students dashing this way and that, many of them in a panic.

I was in bad shape. My head was ringing, my eyes swollen, my lungs burning. Two of the students tried to get me away to a doctor, but I wouldn't leave without my manuscripts. "In there – in my trunk," I gasped.

"I'll get them," Herman said. He began rooting around in the trunk, throwing clothes and books and records over his shoulder until he unearthed the stack of papers.

After that my memory fails me. I have a vague feeling tragedy befell my rescuer. Perhaps he ran back into the fire to try and help others like myself and the flames got him. I think a number of students lost their lives. I know for a fact that the rest of us, those who got out safely, were taken prisoner by a group of armed political fanatics and flown to a slave labour camp somewhere in the far north.

These days you never know where you're going to end up.

§

It's Student Union election time up at the university. The hall walls are papered with campaign posters. There was one promoting David Feinberg, a Jew from Saint John (there are a few non-Catholics at St Tim's), which displayed a cartoon of Hitler saying, "Feinberg for vice-president? Well, why not?" In another a magazine picture of the boxer Sonny Liston declares: "Next to Cassius Clay I think David Feinberg is the greatest!" And there's one with just a statement beneath the candidate's photo: "Vote for Paul Elkin and he'll reveal where the FLQ arms are hidden!"

The most common practice is to cut photos of well-known figures from magazines and add a caption.

It's not the highest degree of wit, but I didn't think my fellow scholars had even that much in them. If the posters are still there tomorrow I should note down more of the captions. Some use cartoon drawings which are particularly good, whoever did them.

This morning I had an Ethics class on the second floor followed by a History class on the first floor. I was late arriving as I often am and classes had already started. As I strolled along the first floor hall I glanced at the afore-mentioned posters, stopping to have a better look at several, and then opened the classroom door — and walked into a room full of sophomores. I stepped back out quickly, confused. Wasn't this the room where History 400 was always held? (I'm telling this exactly as I perceived it at the time.) Obviously not — it must be the one further down. I continued on, still glancing at posters, and opened the door to the next room and seeing familiar faces from my History class walked in and took a seat. I noticed I was getting some strange looks, as if there was something unusual about my showing up late, which there wasn't, and then I glanced at the front of the room and to my amazement saw it wasn't Professor Murray behind the lectern but the language teacher, Professor Marchant! It completely threw me. Everything was cock-eyed. There were some History classmates of mine there, yes, but they were talking Spanish — and I didn't take Spanish — I had no languages among my courses. Students were waving at me to leave, shaking their heads and grinning.

It was like being in a dream. I got up and hurried out, bewildered, and stood in the hall trying to find some logical explanation for it all. And then it came to me. My History class wasn't till next period! I'd got things ass-backwards — I should be upstairs now in Ethics.

It was a relief to be back in the world of reality. I can see now there's something to be said for reality. Sometimes it's actually less disturbing than the world of unreality.

§

Nothing much to say tonight. It was a bright fairly warm day and quite a bit of snow and ice melted. But it's starting to snow now.

I've been thinking a great deal about what I'll do next year, and today wrote up a few general applications. So far I've seen no advertisements that suit me. I'm a little frightened about getting into teaching, but it appears teaching is where I'm headed. I'm not sure what I'm capable of putting up with. I don't want to find myself stuck for a year doing what I'd rather not be doing, in a place where I'd rather not be.

But this is drivel. I don't have the energy to go into anything. I've been feeling sluggish the past few days.

§

It's after midnight now and the old man is coughing. He does it every night about this time, and for some reason it irritates the hell out of me. Each cough makes me want to shout at him to shut up. If he did anything else but cough I wouldn't feel this way — but it sounds as if he's saying, "Listen! You hear that? I'm an old man now . . . I'm going to die before long . . ."

Of course he's been chain smoking hand-rolled cigarettes since he was a boy so it's not surprising he coughs. I can't remember a time when he didn't cough. But these post-midnight bouts are new, and I always think everything is directed at me in one way or another.

There he goes again.

I was thinking, if I could go to bed and stay there a month I could probably write several large volumes. The minute I lie down I start musing and feel an urge to reach for my pen and notepad. I don't always obey the urge, but then I didn't say I *would* write several large volumes, I said I probably *could*, theoretically.

§

The days are beginning to look pretty much the same to me, despite spring coming on. I'm not paying attention of late, not loafing my way home from class or on my night walk, taking in what's around me. I've been reading considerably, and when not reading thinking about next year and the teaching I'll most likely have to do. The thought bothered me as far back as last fall, but I was able to put it in hibernation for the winter; but now with spring approaching it's raised its unsightly head again. Knowing this is the time for sending out applications weighs on my mind. I wonder where to apply, and conjure up pictures of me in a classroom, trying to envision how I'll handle the job. I ought to know something about it after sixteen years of sitting observing it. Although that's rather like not being able to swim but thinking you can because you watched others do it. And then jumping in over your head.

I'm constantly debating with myself whether to try for more money in a city, where I'd prefer to be but where more would be expected of me, or to take a rural position at a lower wage in duller surroundings and get some experience. For all I know I might respond better where the standards are higher and the students more worldly. I might rise to the challenge rather than just hope to get by.

I have little confidence in myself most of the time, and at other times I feel no test could be too great for a man of my exceptional parts.

What I need is a carefree attitude, condition myself to believe that whatever comes up will be fine and dandy. See if I can't find some value in it, instead of always expecting the worst.

§

My father has the radio on in his room listening to a hockey game. Besides eating and sleeping, listening to hockey games seems to be his sole enjoyment in life. It's not much of a life as lives go. Occasionally he expresses an opinion, about twice a year at the dinner table, but it's usually a commonplace one, something about politics or young people today. When he does this I being the all-wise creature that I am have to set out the opposing view and elaborate on why both opinions are held and what's sound and unsound about them and then present my own assessment of the situation, which needless to say is the correct one. At which he growls in his throat and goes back to his eating, leaving me feeling like a jerk and wanting to kick myself.

Why can't I keep my mouth shut? Maybe because it's so rare I get a chance to actually discuss something besides hockey with him that I get carried away and overdo it. And because I'm incapable for the sake of harmony or anything else of agreeing with a remark I disagree with. Whatever it is, it never works out right. I think he sees my mother in me. She was a talker, intelligent and capable, and made him feel inferior, I'm sure, never living up to what she expected of him.

She did remind him he was the man of the house from time to time, when she needed something manly to be done, like sawing and splitting the wood for the winter. And I heard her say different times to her sisters that Joe — my father's name – was a hard worker and always brought home his pay, not like many other husbands who drank it away. Her sisters' husbands were all far more prosperous than my father, so she had to come up with something in his favour.

It comes back to me now that the old man would sometimes relate incidents from work at dinner, and my mother would laugh – and the rest of us, my sisters and me, seeing her laugh would laugh too. They talked some back then, but there were periods of weeks and months when he wouldn't utter a word, after they'd had a dispute of some kind. I don't remember now what they talked amiably about, I just remember the disagreements, which became fairly frequent.

And now I wonder, with my mother dead for some time and nothing for him to look forward to, is there any point in his life? Well, aside from the point that there's perhaps no point in any man's life (and one could argue that quite convincingly), I can see one important thing he's doing: he's supporting me. But what hope, if any, he has for me, I don't know.

He strikes me as a good man, there's nothing mean or nasty about him. He's not a successful man by society's standards, but that's nothing against him. I don't know that he ever had a cause to believe in or a mission to pursue. The majority of men don't. Procreating, breadwinning, surviving – that about covers it. Although, now I think of it, breadwinning for a wife and children is a service to others, and service to others is the basis of all worthy causes and missions. As the nobler of Romans used to say, *Nomo sibi vivat*... "Let no man live for himself".

§

The sky cleared this afternoon, after leaving us with a foot of snow. This morning it was still snowing and banks were piled up where the plow passed and where people had shoveled their cars out. It was still mild and wet snow clung to the sides of trees and lampposts and sheds, anything it could get a grip on. The town looked upholstered in white. By dinner hour only a few light flakes were dancing in the air, and these soon stopped. Snowfalls in spring (today apparently is the first day of spring) are usually intrusive unwanted events, and tend to settle a general depression over town. Everyone thinking, just when the snow gets melting and winter appears beaten a storm comes and we have to start over again — that sort of feeling. But I didn't mind this one myself; it left the town looking pristine and picturesque. As dulled as one gets by this time of year to the attractions of snow I could still look around me with fascination. Probably because I'm not going anywhere, and am in no hurry to get there.

I'm a loafer by nature, a born idler. By loafing I mean avoiding any activity that is materially useful. A loafer is free to stay in one spot for hours, musing, whistling, whittling, listening, watching; free to read and write what he wants, and when he wants; or to walk idly around town with his hands in his pockets.

He's obviously a useless being, by no means a good citizen putting his shoulder to wheel and doing his bit. He doesn't pitch in, he simply stands back and watches.

He's what you might call a connoisseur of life. Others are busy striving to reach the end of their span, sweeping their days behind them in pursuit of one myth or another, while he dallies and examines each precious moment.

Life is always here and now. There's no such thing as the future, of course, it's an abstraction, an imaginary place. The dreams you have when asleep are more real. To pursue the future is to chase shadows in hopes of grasping them. People who do it are pursuing death really, if they only knew it. Death is the complete negation of the present, of their existence; it's what they'll have when they finally stop running. When they *get there*.

I should know all this stuff, because I'm not only a loafer but a great dreamer of other times and other places. A mixed loafer, you could say, with a foot in both camps, one day one way, one day the other. I do my best loafing and staying in the present when the future looks grim, holding nothing but a job I'll probably hate.

The sky is clear tonight. Bits of cloud-wraiths trail here and there under the stars and across a new crescent moon.

§

If I ever did anything so foolish as to put my poems together in a volume there could be only one title for it: *Crisis*. But let's hope I don't make such a foolish attempt.

But if I did, I'd give the book this Foreword:

"You think there's no theme to these poems? There's a theme all right. A young man in the midst of crisis — all his inherited beliefs gone or going, and none in sight to replace them — only an intuitive feeling that real beliefs and values are to be had if they could be but found or created. The young man who wrote these poems over a two or three year period cared very little whether he lived or died, and was alarmingly close to choosing the latter. He dwelt in anger, hatred, contempt, seclusion — he claimed but one right, the right to be himself, to go his own way — and found just how difficult this right is to acquire and retain. I'm not that young man any longer. I believe the crisis has passed and the process of resolution is in the making. But I know him, I understand that young man, and appreciate the value of what he went through. Because he was what he was, I am becoming what I am to be."

§

A beautiful morning. This time of year can be the brightest of any. In summer the sun is higher, but it doesn't have the snow-covered earth to reflect it. I took my time walking home from an early class. As I cut across the hill by the church the scene before me was the same as I see every day: the farm houses and barns and fields of snow and purple trees across the river, the streets and houses in town. But like the sun itself everything comes up new and fresh on such a morning. It might be different in the heart of Africa but in this country you don't get tired of the sun. It's a renewing sight, when it rises — not that you look straight into it; but it's there, you feel its comforting touch.

As I strolled along I heard pigeons in the church bell-tower coodling (a word I made up, it's closer to the *tremolo* sound they make than cooing). And on top of Victoria Street a sleek boxer dog ran out in front of a car, the car slammed on its brakes, and at the same time the dog about-faced and ran back. If the driver hadn't been alert he would have hit it.

Bannonbridge is rife with dogs, especially Victoria Street. One little fellow caught my attention yesterday as I was coming back from the post office — a reddish long-bodied mutt with stubby legs and a head as alert as a bird's. He was out on the road with his back turned when a Volkswagen drove out of a yard. To get his tail out of the way he pivoted around on his front paws and faced the car, only his hind paws moving. He was like one of those fire trucks whose front and rear wheels operate independently.

The other afternoon a German Shepherd with a lame hind leg followed me downtown from school. I made a move to pat his head and slipped on the ice and almost fell on him. It gave him a start, but I guess he saw it was an accident, because he continued to follow me. He stopped to sniff at the base of every lamppost, quite intent about it, so I thought his leg couldn't be paining him too greatly. But it looked twisted, as though broken. He may have been sniffing posts to get his mind off it. It was another of many situations where I would like to have been of help — in this case, take him to a vet — but I hadn't the money. I often think money in my hands would be of great benefit to dogs and men, and to other creatures, such as myself, primarily.

§

There are few things I detest more than a "responsible teenager". I see their upstanding, youthfully self-righteous letters to the editor in the Moncton Times every few days.

The one today says she's a teenager herself and likes the Beatles, but "the Beatles are not going to pay for your education, or help you with your future. Stop idealizing the Beatles and start concentrating on your school books. You hold the key to your future. Please don't throw it away. Act like the fine respectable girls you are."

She spoke out against those kids who wrote letters protesting their parents' condemnation of the Beatles. "In our house we don't overdo the Beatles craze and so don't have that problem."

I can picture the family sitting smiling around the living room, the father engrossed in the newspaper's financial section, the mother in her copy of Good Housekeeping, the dog asleep, little brother in the corner with his stamp collection, and the daughter studying the newsletter she brought home from school. Suddenly from a transistor radio out on the street comes a song by the Beatles. The parents look apprehensive, but aware of their daughter's level-headed sense of proportion they say nothing, and their trust is rewarded by her reaction. She taps her foot softly on the carpet's nap, twice snaps her fingers (but not audibly), and hums only at decent intervals. Then when the transistor leaves and the music fades out she discusses the relative merits of the Beatles, as compared with the Drifters or the Beach Boys, and then the subject is put away, everyone at ease and taking comfort in the family's moderation, refinement and good sense.

Meanwhile, the daughter resumes her reading of *Today's Keen Teen* newsletter on "Responsibility and Ambition, Good Marks, Morals, Security, and The Path To Becoming Class Valedictorian".

§

Harold used to talk about a young school teacher he knew from downriver named Susan. He spoke with great enthusiasm about her and told me many times she was the ultimate in female desirability, on all counts. Well, one weekend night I was having a few and saw this girl sitting by herself in Grogan's Grill. I went over and sat with her and we talked — about what I don't know now, and didn't know the morning after. But it must have been quite a conversation because we left the restaurant and went to the bootlegger's for a bottle (her treat) and brought it to my room and drank quite a lot of it and then slept together. That's right, we *slept* together. Period. We spent the night lying on my bed and I pawed and groped her a bit but that was it. She wouldn't even let me remove her garments. It was a strange night. I was certainly drunk, and during our amourous activities, such as they were, I believe I fell asleep and woke up several times. I recall staring hard at her in the dusky light from the street-lamp outside my window, trying to make out her face, and suddenly thinking she looked like a man. I shuddered and stared harder. She wasn't asleep herself. When she saw me stir she kissed me and I almost spit. I knew somewhere in my mind who she was and that she was supposed to be a girl, but I couldn't make myself believe it. The next thing I remember it was morning.

When I woke she was sitting on the side of the bed straightening herself out. It was eight-thirty and I could hear my father moving around in the kitchen. I was still fully dressed myself and feeling none too spry. We said a few words before she left, actually very sane and friendly words, and I gave her a manuscript of mine to read, and followed her in my sock feet to the head of the stairs. I felt obligated to suggest we get together again tonight, but to my relief she replied she had to go back downriver. She looked up at me from one step down on the stairs, I suppose expecting a kiss, but I was in anything but a romantic mood. I said I'd see her around. She left and I returned to my bed and slept the remainder of the morning.

Harold came by about a week later, and at first I didn't say anything about the girl. I had no interest in her − she really wasn't my type in the way of looks, being pasty-faced and dark-haired with sideburns growing halfway down her cheeks. There was something out of whack about her as well − you might almost say there had to be, coming home as she did with the likes of me. I'd have let the matter pass, but then I thought she might mention it to Harold herself, so I thought I'd better get in there first.

He looked shocked. "Go on!" he said.

"Oh, yes, it's true."

"Go on! You don't mean it! She stayed the night?"

Making light of it, I said, "Well, you couldn't blame her, a man with a beard like mine. I had my sunglasses on too. She obviously went for the bohemian look."

"You wore sunglasses at night?"

"Why not?"

My room's not very roomy and as I usually did when I had a visitor I sat on my bed propped up by a couple of pillows. Harold was on the chair by my card-table desk. My sunglasses were on the desk, and he began playing with them as we talked. And that's the last I ever saw of them.

I asked him several days later if he'd put them in his pocket by mistake. He said he didn't think so, but he might have, he was always doing things like that. I pressed him to look for them. He didn't say he would or he wouldn't, changing the subject.

After that, one night, we got drunk together. I brought the subject up and said wasn't it possible his unconscious mind had associated my getting the girl with the sunglasses, and he'd reacted in the only way available at the time − to take them?

He said it was possible.

I still never got them back.

I'd better say that she really *was* a girl. I'd given her a reasonable feeling up, and she'd make a most unusual man with the parts she had. It was just the drunken semi-comatose state I was in, distorting my perceptions.

Harold and I sometimes lend each other books. He lends me more than I lend him, because I have the devil of a time getting mine back. He'll give them to other people, or lose them — so he says — and when he does return one after considerable badgering on my part, it's always in a sad state. I ask him why he treats my books the way he does, and he says it's just not natural for him to bother himself about material things. When he reads a book, for instance, that's the end of it; he's not interested in the physical book and never knows what becomes of it after.

Well and fine. But when I borrow books from him he wants to know what I think of them, and those I dislike or appear indifferent to he lets me keep (for, after all, what are books to him?), but when I praise one he can hardly wait till I'm finished to grab it back. The logical question is, what for, since he's read it and it's now just a material object? Because — if you want to know the answer — it's because I like it and not letting me keep it gives him some sort of weird satisfaction.

I never seem to learn. At times my forgiving nature astonishes me. For instance, several months ago I let myself accept another of his lame explanations, and putting that behind me, agreed to his request to write a review of a student drama production of "The Caucasian Chalk Circle" for him. He was at the time editor of St Tim's monthly newspaper *The Timothean* (till he got tired of the job and quit). I didn't go see the play, or bother to read it, but I talked to someone who'd been there and then wrote a lively review and gave it to him. I thought it was quite the ingenious piece of literary invention, and certainly not something I'd throw away; but innocent that I was I didn't make a copy. And not only did Harold not publish it after reading it and saying it was great and that he'd use it — he "lost it". He said his younger brothers must have got it and made paper airplanes out of it or something.

I get fed up with him sometimes, trying to follow the way his mind works. He was here last night, very peevish about something. Rather than try to fathom what was eating him — it would be anything but what he said it was — I decided to lie back on my bed and say nothing other than "yes" or "no". This went on for a while, until finally — after testing my resolve by sitting on my shaky card table which I've told him before not to do — he got up to leave. Standing by the door he said, "I'm not very good company these days. Now that I've got no vices there's nothing interesting to talk about."

By vices he means smoking and drinking. The week before this, as I reclined on my bed smoking, he told me it was five weeks since his last cigarette, and how good he'd been feeling since giving up the habit.

I countered by saying I'd started on a new diet, only nutritious foods prepared in the healthiest way, and that because of it I've been feeling wonderfully well myself the past few weeks.

He said he'd been doing yoga exercises, and it was amazing how fit and energetic he felt after.

Well now, I said, I'd read from an authentic source that diet is responsible for at least seventy per cent of a person's well-being. Exercise contributes only a small part to the body's basic needs, and it can be managed by several brisk walks a day, which I take.

Drinking he didn't touch on, because he's aware that of late I've cut my drinking down to a minimum.

§

Sometimes I think I'm the only person I know who's not entirely out of his mind.

I'm not boasting about it. It's a lonely feeling being sane.

§

The weather is turning colder, the wind sharp and piercing. Tonight all the stars are out, with Venus by far the most brilliant, like a far-off torch above the trees and roofs. When it's cold like this I hasten home, whether from school, the grocery store or Grogan's Grill, eager to get indoors and stretch out in front of my glowing fireplace.

I don't have a fireplace, that's a figure of speech, but there is a stovepipe in the hallway outside my room.

While I was having my coffee at Grogan's tonight a boy who's the younger brother of a fellow I used to hang around with came and sat with me. He's in his second year of Grade 9 at St Timothy's High, a big burly fellow. He's a few inches under average height but is large-boned and muscular. His head is solid, his hair black and curly, his skin tanned and smooth. You could easily imagine him on a pirate ship with a ring in his ear.

I describe him in such detail because . . . Well, for no reason. Just practicing my descriptions.

He told me a couple of his teachers are having a difficult time keeping their students in line. The main reason: the classes are dull, and being bored some of the boys act up and the teachers can't maintain order. When the boys see this they become scornful. Students might not like discipline, but they respect a man who can keep it.

The trouble with dull teachers, in my opinion, is the students feel they're wasting their time listening to them; their attention wanders, they don't hear what's being said, and they learn nothing. And strange as it may sound, even to my own ears, cynic that I am, most students do want to learn – not all, but most. Or perhaps not exactly learn, but pick up enough information so as to pass their exams and ultimately graduate. I know this because when I was in Grade 10 we had a teacher who gave us such an easy time that halfway through the year the class got up a petition with everyone signing it and gave it to the principal. The teacher in question, Mr Dower, was our homeroom teacher, and in an effort to cut costs he was assigned to teach us everything except Religion. In Grade 9 we'd had half a dozen teachers, now we had two. The Religion teacher, Father McDonough, was worthless too, but he didn't matter because next year's matriculation exams were non-sectarian so Religion wasn't among them. We wanted Mr Dower replaced in the subjects which he told us quite frankly he had never liked and still didn't like and knew nothing about.

Our petition didn't work, but we tried.

At the first of the year it had been great, no homework in these courses, and the periods meant for them given over to extra time on English, History, and Algebra, the subjects he favoured. Some days he'd set up a projector and screen and instead of studying French, Geometry or Latin, we'd watch films on the Queen's Coronation or the building of the Canadian Pacific Railroad or some other quasi-educational event. Other times he'd designate them "study periods" and we'd put the time in gazing out the window and daydreaming.

It might not have been such a bad way to teach if it was at the university level and we were left free to educate ourselves by reading books that interested us, those of us who could read. But we were learning absolutely no French, Geometry, or Latin, which would make Grade 11's work on those subjects all the harder, and for some could result in failing the year. And we had to write matriculation exams then, and if you didn't get your matrics you could forget about going to university, as quite a few in the class hoped to do. As it turned out when matriculation time rolled around I barely passed French and Geometry. Latin I skipped since it was optional and didn't matter.

Mr Dower was a slender man, six feet in height, blond hair, with traces of acne on his face, and false teeth that had an unbrushed, greenish look. He wasn't too fond of washing, either himself or his clothes, and there was a decayed smell about him. He used to come down to a student's desk, if the student needed help, and lean closely over him, face sometimes touching the boy's, body pressed in close to him.

It wasn't long before the boys decided they could manage without this kind of individual help.

One day he stood in front of his desk, half-sitting against the edge of it, with a great bulge in his pants where he had an erection, as obvious as anything. The boys all grinning and whispering, passing the word around — "Look, look — Dower's got a hard-on!"

He had a few favourites, helpless favourites they were for a time, not sure what to do about him. He was particularly attentive to them, stopping by their desks to lean over and see how they were making out with this or that problem in Algebra or English. A friend of mine, Tom Sheehan, sat in the desk behind me, the last one in the row by the windows, and being a handsome young fellow was the favourite of favourites. It became such an aggravation for Tom that finally one morning, as Dower was leaning over him and pressing his crotch against him, he snapped at him: "Lean on your own breakfast, will you!" Dower straightened up, said nothing, and walked back to his desk, and that was the end of his little visits. Tom remained his favourite nonetheless, and at year's end Dower awarded him the English Literature prize, worth ten dollars. All I ever got from the man was a strapping — the only student in Grade 10 to get one — for being a wise guy and asking him questions I knew the answers to but he didn't.

I was in the Air Cadets in Grades 9 and 10. Dower was the teacher in charge and during the summer he went with us to a two-week camp at Greenwood Air Force Base in Nova Scotia, wearing his Squadron Leader's uniform. I don't recall anything out of the way the first summer, but on the train down the second summer he found a friend among the Bathurst cadets who were travelling with us. This cadet was a putrid-looking individual with a pouting mouth and heavy eyelids and a worse case of acne scars than Dower's. As the train rattled along the two fell asleep — or so it appeared — in one of the seats with their heads together and Dower's arm around the younger man's shoulder. They looked like a pair of sweethearts cuddled up, with all the cadets crowding up the aisle to have a view and pointing and sniggering.

We saw another instance of homosexuals in public display two weeks later, this time on the bus driving us from Greenwood Air Force Base to the railway station for the return trip home. Several rough-looking youths from Moncton had sprawled themselves on a pile of kitbags stacked in the bus's wide middle aisle, and one fellow had his face buried between another's open legs, burrowing into his crotch. He did a great deal of vigourous rooting around, coming up for air every minute or so and extracting loud encouraging comments from his partner.

The cadets on the bus were smiling and laughing very urbanely (so they hoped) at the performance, as though it was a great joke, and I was too, but it was a strain to do so, because I'd never seen the likes of this before. I felt very young and out of place in what I saw as a mob of hoodlums and degenerates. There were bullying youths on the bus, not just from Moncton but from Newcastle, moving along the aisle over the kitbags, swearing loudly and bumping into those in the seats, insulting the cadets who had higher rank and smaller size, humiliating them.

Nobody bothered me, but it was a long trip to the station, and one I was thankful to have over.

§

I went to the tavern last night and drank till it closed. I didn't get drunk, but today my kidney muscles and right leg are tired, a dead aching sort of tiredness. My leg from ankle to hip aches clear to the bone, and continues on up to my right kidney.

I can feel a cold coming on. The roof of my mouth where it meets my inner nostrils is sore, and so is my throat.

If it is a cold it at least had the decency to wait for the Easter holidays, which begin tomorrow.

Quite a few people are getting colds. Through my wall I heard the little girl in the next apartment say to her mother, "I'm chock full of the cold, Mummy."

"Where did you get the cold, darling?"

"*I* don't know where I got the cold. Where do I ever get colds?"

§

When I awoke this morning my throat was so sore I could barely swallow. And it's moved up into my nose and head. I have about a dozen huge kleenexes on my bedside table and blow my nose about every three minutes but it stays congested. The outsides of my nostrils are chafed and the rim of my upper lip is dry and red, just waiting to break into a cold sore.

The wind is howling, drifting the snow, blowing it in sheets beneath the street lamps.

§

The colde (by which I mean my ailment — I've decided to spell it with an "e" to distinguish it from the weather) has made my legs weak, and it has a deadening grip on the back of my neck, under the skull. It's night now, and outside the wind continues to blow hard. The snow is crusted and shines in the moonlight.

I watched a dog this afternoon walk delicately over the crust in the yard across the street and disappear behind the house. Later I saw it again more closely and it wasn't a dog but a huge cat covered with bushy gray hair.

I saw another cat following a boy along the sidewalk, and every driveway or walk it came to it would run ahead and dart in expectantly, hoping the boy would follow and take it inside for a bite to eat.

A cat once followed me home doing the same thing. It would run ahead and dash up the steps of every house and pause in every driveway, looking over its shoulder and whining for me to take it in out of the cold and feed it. When I continued past it would return to the sidewalk and scamper by me, keeping a small distance ahead till the next house. I told him he wasn't my cat and there was nothing I could do for him, but he didn't want to hear that and kept after me until I got home and went in without him.

The crust really is hard. When I was out for my coffee I walked on top of it across the field by George Street, from one corner to the other, taking a shortcut, and my foot went through just once and then only partially. The field had a natural sheen under the moon-lit sky, with shimmery lines of yellow from street lamps and lighted house windows reflected on it.

My right ear exploded a few times this evening from all the nose-blowing, and stayed that way the last time for two or three hours. For all I know it might still be blanked out; I think it is and I'm so used to it now it seems normal. When I swallow I hear a few waves beat against my *left* ear, but the right one is a vacuum. It doesn't bother me that much now, but at first it was extremely unpleasant. I tried swallowing, and twisting my jaw, and gaping, but it wouldn't snap back into shape. I almost gave my left ear an ache trying to resurrect the right one.

When I was at the restaurant tonight I felt as if there was an invisible fog around me. I wasn't hearing too clearly, even my own voice. My head in general feels a few pounds overweight. I'm constantly sniffling, blowing my nose, sighing thickly with a moan . . . "Ah boy . . ." and sneezing for periods at ten minute intervals, which calls for a thorough blowing-of-the-nose to clear out my loosened-up skull.

My colde defences seem to have been wiped out entirely. I need a recruiting program; arm and train an able-bodied body of antibodies and lay on a full-scale counter-offensive. When I get up in the morning and clean out the casualties (my morning coughing-up and nose-blowing) it would be nice to see some enemy dead for a change.

§

I must be getting really bookish. I was washing the dishes and suddenly thought of a new History of the French Revolution I was going to read when I finished, and I got a horny sensation in the end of my cock. You can't love your books much more than that!

A part of a book's charm is physical, the way it looks and feels and smells. I know some books might take offense at that, thinking I'm only interested in their externals; but they shouldn't worry. I'm quite aware what counts is their inner beauty: their character, intelligence and sense of humour.

This reminds me of the books Professor Murray brings to class and passes around for his students' admiration. They're expensive, immaculate-looking volumes, printed on high-quality paper and finely bound. When you open them the first thing you notice is the underlining he's done with a ruler and different coloured inks. There are plain blue lines for significant passages, red for those exceptionally important, and a double line of red and blue for places that are simply the last word. And sometimes there's a note, for instance a cross-reference of some kind, in the margin in his neat precise hand.

You can tell each book is like a treasure to him. The type of underlining he does suggests long and lovingly laborious perusals, like the performance of a sacred rite. He must require a great deal of time to read a book. His adulatory approach is consistent with his lectures. They never contain a new idea, or even an idea new to himself, as I know from having taken courses from him the past four years. He goes on underlining, reinforcing his long-standing beliefs, revering and remarking on the words of others, and repeating himself year after year.

However, I can't deny there's an attractiveness about his books, with their neat and colourful markings. It's because of them I feel a bit guilty about marking a pertinent passage in my own new books with a careless ink scratch down the margin.

His American History students this year are a selfish bunch. When he passes around a book he starts at one side of the room and the student who gets it is supposed to look at the pertinent place and then pass it along until everyone has a chance. But it never gets beyond three or four students. What happens is, he's given them an alternative to listening to his babbling at the front of the room, and they hold onto the book as long as they can, especially if there are pictures. It's become so bad that yesterday the book didn't reach even the second student until minutes before the bell rang for the class to be over.

Once a thing like this starts it can only get worse, because whoever gets the book reasons, "I didn't see the last five so I'm going to get my share of this one!" And Murray does nothing about it. He's flattered that the student with the book is so interested he can't bear to give it up. And the student knows this.

§

I got the afore-mentioned history of the French Revolution from the college library. They're doing a "weeding", getting rid of tattered books and books no one has taken out for years, and trucking them to the dump. It's crazy, but I had to argue with the bone-headed student librarian to let me have it. He said giving them away wasn't in his instructions.

"But they're going to the dump!" I protested.

"I know, but – "

"Give it to me!"

"Oh, all right. Don't tell anyone."

§

The sun was out all day, there were no clouds, and a fresh spring wind was blowing.

My friend Roland Iverson is in town for the weekend, home from McGill University where he's doing post-graduate work in Theoretical Physics. When we were in high school he was the only one besides myself who wrote poetry, and he still writes it. Poetry-writing theoretical physicists must be quite rare these days.

He came down from Montreal by train, and said a woman and her little boy were sitting in the seat behind him. The woman kept telling her son to sit still and be quiet and stop being such a bother. She wouldn't let up until finally Roland looked over the back of his seat and said, "Will you leave the poor kid alone!"

The woman sort of smiled, not knowing how to take it.

"It's too bad little kids have to bring their mothers on the train," he added, and went back to the book he was reading.

Roland pointed out something that's obvious enough, but which I hadn't thought of before. We got onto the subject of debating societies — Harold being a star debater at St Timothy's — and Roland said "What debates are about is two people setting out to win an argument, never mind which side is right. Right is not important, it's about winning. The winner gets a medal and a write-up in the student paper. The teachers are proud of him, he's brought glory to the school. They say, 'Ah, he was brilliant! The way he twisted and distorted and dissimulated — took the truth and shook the hell out of it — stomped it into the ground!' They don't actually say that, but they might as well. It's a training ground for lawyers."

Roland said he doesn't remember much about high school. "There was one thing, in Grade 10 . . . I was late for Algebra class, Dower was already starting into the lesson, and as I was going up the aisle to my desk Gummer McCann sniffed and said, 'I think I smell horseshit . . .' Not loud, in an undertone, but loud enough for the guys around him to hear. I was beside him when he said it and pow! I hit him a great whack across the head and kept walking to my seat. Ha! Ha!" He demonstrated the backhander he gave him. "Dower was standing right there watching but he didn't say anything. Gummer wasn't one of his favourites, even though the guys said he had his front teeth pulled so he could suck cocks better – but he wasn't a fruit, I don't think . . . You remember my horse? The old man bought it to ride himself, but he called it mine so I'd have to take care of it . . . I'd ride it around sometimes and a lot of guys were jealous, that's why McCann said what he did."

Talking about most people, Roland said, "Most people don't listen when you talk to them. They just wait till you stop so they can talk themselves. They don't have a conversation, they alternate talking to nobody."

§

My condition hasn't improved any. My nose felt crusted this morning and seemed to crack around the nostrils when I blew it.

While I was having dinner I bit my underlip on the inside quite badly. I spat a mouthful of blood in the toilet bowl and soaked up quite a bit more with kleenexes before it stopped. There's an ugly inch-wide purple and red mark inside my lip now.

That kind of thing infuriates me. It's bad enough to suffer from external circumstances, but to have your own body attack itself! It's as if there's a devil inside you, a malignant spirit after your blood.

Then later this afternoon I was eating peanuts, reading on my bed – and I bit my lip again! And in the same place. I jumped up and dashed for the bathroom, just to be moving, to protect myself from myself. I'd been injured, and twice in the same spot, and someone had to pay for it!

The anguish, the frustration! I could have knocked my teeth out. I stomped around trying to calm myself. Fortunately it didn't bleed as much this time.

But now I'm afraid to finish my peanuts. What if I should bite my lip a third time? In the same place? I might snap. I might have to do myself in, show that son of a bitch not to mess around with *me*.

§

Here's a cameo half-story I wrote in the Hemingway vein, called *After The Stick-up* or *On The Run*.

Sid and Molly drove into the muddy yard and got out of the car, their bodies stiff after the long drive.

"Well, you see what a dump it is," Molly said. "Any place would have been better than this."

Her father wasn't home but her young half-witted brother Willie let them in.

"When's Daddy coming back?" she asked.

"Dunno," Willie said.

They sat at the kitchen table and waited. It was evening by now and Sid took a bottle of whisky from his overcoat pocket and said, "Any glasses in this house?"

Molly opened the cupboard above the sink and set two empty jam bottles on the table.

"Your folks live in style," Sid said, pouring the drinks.

"I told you. You can take your coat off. It's not that cold in here."

Sid removed his coat and threw it over the back of a chair.

"If he makes a fuss we'll have to go. We'll have come all this way for nothing," she said.

"We had to go somewhere."

It was dark when they heard the old man coming in the back way through the shed. He was in his late fifties and small and hadn't shaved for several days and his eyes looked sharply at the two at the table. Without a word he continued through the kitchen to another part of the house.

"He don't seem too friendly," Sid said in a low voice.

"He's always queer like that. Daddy, that's a nice way you got of saying hello!"

The old man came back and stood in the doorway. "What are you doing here? Montreal get too much for you?"

"We came down for a visit."

"Who's that fellow?"

"This is Sid. He's my fiancé."

The old man grunted.

"What's he do for a living?"

"Drive truck," Sid said.

The old man squinted, chewing on his lip. "What's that you're drinking?"

Sid turned the bottle around by the neck, showing the label. "Rye. Seagram's. It's good stuff."

"I know what it is." He looked at the boy. "Willie, get me a glass."

§

Well, I said I was a half-story. I don't know any more than you do what happens next.

§

I saw a huge crow this afternoon. He was in a tree alone and singing "Caw! Caw! Caw!" I heard another that looked like him a few days ago, and his cry was "Farook! Farook! Farook!" Maybe that one was a raven — I can't distinguish between the two. I believe ravens are either larger or smaller or the same size.

There was one all-black fellow I used to see over the winter while walking through Memorial Park. He was a tremendous size, the largest bird I've seen alive (there are bigger stuffed specimens like owls and eagles in the natural history museum on Albert Street). The noise he made was like slowly rattling gourds — a hollow wooden type of warble with each warble distinct. Sometimes I'd see him circling lazily above the park, other times peering down from one of the elm trees.

My teenage neighbour is playing pop-song records. She and her little sister share the room on the other side of my bedroom wall. What she's playing isn't as bad as the things that come out of her radio. Nevertheless I'm going to get revenge this evening by playing my classical records. She's fourteen and quite cute but doesn't like me and never says hello, I suppose because I'm a disreputable person. The reason I'll be at home playing music is I'm thinking of getting a bottle of wine for tonight. I've only drunk a couple of nights this month and the month's almost over — easily my best record in two years. I haven't been using self-coercion either, I've just preferred not to. But maybe I deserve a reward for good behaviour anyway.

I say I'm thinking of it, but of course I'm going to do it. Whenever the decision to drink or not to drink comes up in my head, the decision is already made.

§

And there I was, helping Robert Kennedy in his campaign for President. Kennedy had for a reason I can't recall (if I ever knew) replaced Lyndon Johnson as the Democratic candidate and was running against the Republican Barry Goldwater. I knew quite a bit about Goldwater, being a big reader of liberal-minded newspapers and magazines, and was able to find weaknesses in his platform, and attack them in my speeches.

But even with my help, Robert Kennedy lost the election, though it was close.

Goldwater gave his first press conference as President the next day, and said now that he was President the country was going to be run differently. He was going to stress good sound American values, root out communist subversives, and promote free enterprise. Industry would be further automated for better efficiency and higher profits, thus producing more jobs for the working man.

One of the reporters, a man of Chinese extraction, cried out at this, "Ah so! But that is contradictory! You contradict yourself!" He laughed, like a Chinese character in a movie.

Goldwater didn't laugh. He turned red with anger, and said if another reporter acted like that he'd have no more press conferences. Moreover if newspapers didn't fall into line and write good positive American stories in their publications he'd establish a healthy censorship of the press.

He came over to the wings where Robert Kennedy and I were sitting among a group of observers, and with an air of satisfaction said: "Well, I fixed those jokers. This country will be run *my* way now." And looking directly at Kennedy, he added, "Because I'm *President!*" As if to say, "And you're not! Ha Ha!"

Next he lit into me for campaigning against him, saying I'd been even more against him than I'd been *for* Kennedy. I listened for a few minutes and then interrupted to say I thought the Chinese reporter was right and that his program *was* contradictory – and what did he really mean to do, what were his *hidden* plans?

But it was as far as I got. He threatened to throw me in jail for subversive activity.

"It's bastards like you that have kept this country from becoming really strong," he said.

That decided me. I left Washington in a hurry. I said goodbye to Kennedy and slipped out the back door and jumped on a plane for France.

That night I went to a play. Actually I was in the play. I was on stage lying on a bed, feeling rather tired after the hectic activities of the political world. There was a large cast around me, mostly sitting at tables. A pretty girl was on the bed beside me.

"So this is Marseilles," I said. "Ah oui, Marseilles!" I was quite proud of my French pronunciation.

The girl had a sour look on her face. She had only a minor role in the play, and was obviously none too happy about it.

"This is where they filmed the movie *Fanny*," I said.

"You don't say," she said.

"And they have an interesting waterfront."

"What's interesting about it?"

"I don't know. It's like your face!" I laughed. "I mean you have an interesting face, even with that disgruntled look on it. I wish I had some money, I could stay here a few days and get to know you better. But I have to take the train to Paris tonight."

She shrugged, as the French like to do.

"It's sad to think," I said, "that I might never see you again."

I felt at ease with her, despite her coldness towards me. Perhaps I was a little drunk. But I don't think so, since I hadn't had a thing to drink.

"You have good wine in this city," I said. "If I had some money I'd buy a bottle — several bottles. We could drink them together."

She was wearing tight-fitting pants and a striped seaman's sweater that seemed a few sizes too small. She wasn't just a pretty face, she had a very nice figure as well.

It's a shame I had to wake up then. I think she was starting to like me.

FOUR

There was frost on the windows this morning. The sun came out and melted it and towards afternoon the day got warmer – but grudgingly; by late afternoon it was cold again.

The sidewalks are covered with choppy ice. With my leather-soled boots I have to walk around like a tightrope walker, my arms butterflying every few steps to keep my balance.

I have nothing else to say.

I have a cold that clings stubbornly. I've had it a week now. Today is its hebdomadariversary (try fitting that one into your conversation).

I've been reading Norman Mailer's serialized novel *The American Dream* in Esquire Magazine and it's absolute rubbish. He's trying to do it like the old-time writers, Dickens, Dostoievsky, Dumas, those kind of lads – composing it against a monthly deadline so as to force himself to get a novel written. The difference is, they could do it and he can't (not that Dickens didn't compose some clunkers).

None of Mailer's installments are any good, and the further along he goes the worse it gets. At this stage, the fourth installment, he must be in a terrible state, sitting across the table from himself trying desperately to claw another chapter out of his guts. I can see the sweat all over the pages. Maybe he realizes it's a hopeless cause and is thinking, "Okay, okay, let's get this over with, for God's sake, so I can put my dark glasses on and slink the hell out of here."

According to Macbride's psychology of literature, he's a man with a divided "self", like two people in one. There's the writer doing the writing, and an invisible writer that hovers over him watching. The hovering one says, "Well, if we were a great author — as we hope to be — what would we write? Come now, you there, write something, and I'll see how it compares to our idol, Mr Hemingway. The question before us is, how to write so as to be like Hemingway and achieve his renown and riches and opportunities with women — his *success*, in other words? For that's what this is all about, isn't it? Well the first thing to do is put some words on the paper — come on, I'll guide you — I'll watch that it's done in the way the heir apparent to Hemingway would do it. I'll nudge and check and guide you along the path to literary fame and fortune!"

As though Mailer were a receptacle of words, and his other self, his invisible monitor, being equivalent to an editor with an eye for superior writing, has simply to extract and rearrange the words in the right combination to result in literary greatness.

It's impossible to do anything really good that way. You have to start with something to *say* — something you're *driven* to say. Otherwise it's all contrived and artificial.

§

I don't know if you'd call this coincidence or what, but I was in a corner of St Cecilia's auditorium washing dishes, and at the far end, on the stage, Norman Mailer (yes, the same gentleman) was at a lectern reading from a new novel he'd written. It was late afternoon and the room was dusky, almost dark. Between myself and the stage there were tables and chairs occupied by members of the Home & School Association. Norman was reading over a microphone, pausing for several seconds between sentences to let his words sink in. I hurried with my dishes, eager to go up on the stage and meet him. I thought he'd be pleased to see me, for I was sure no one besides myself had much idea who he was beyond being a Jewish writer of some kind from New York.

But the dishes held me back. There seemed no end to them, and the pots and pans wouldn't give up the bits of cooking stuck to their insides. I was worried Mailer would finish his reading and leave before I got to talk to him; each of his pauses after a sentence seemed like the end. Finally I could wait no longer – I threw down the dish rag and dried my hands and ran to the front of the auditorium and climbed onto the stage. Seeing me Mailer left the lectern and came over and shook my hand. It was as though he'd been waiting for me . . .

"I guess you know me, I'm Norman Mailer," he said.

I said I knew him, yes, and told him my name, but I could see that didn't interest him, as I wasn't a person of consequence. Now that we were face to face I felt self-conscious, and wished I'd had something to drink before introducing myself. Stammering a little I said there was a good view of the room from up here on the stage, better than down in the corner where I'd been. And that was all I could think to say. And he said he didn't believe me.

He led me to a large table, around which a number of young men were sprawled in chairs.

"Would you like a drink?" he asked me.

"A drink? Yes!" I exclaimed. "I mean, yes, I think I would."

At a nod from Mailer one of the young men rose from the table and walked over to a small makeshift bar at the back of the stage. There was a crowd at the bar, some twenty or so people standing in front of it three deep.

"What will you have?" the young man called over his shoulder.

"Scotch! A double scotch!"

Norman smiled approvingly. "Yes, scotch – a man's drink."

He was wearing a brown leather jacket with the collar turned up and looked a lot like the movie actor Steve McQueen.

While I was sitting at the table I accidentally knocked a bottle over, but to my relief it was only a pop bottle. Then my drink came – in a tall glass, and after a considerable wait – and I knocked that over too! I quickly righted it, but managed to save only a half inch of liquid. I was very annoyed by this. I could still think of nothing to say to Mailer, even though I knew there was a great deal we could talk about, and a drink would have loosened my tongue. I glanced over at the bar but it was hidden from view by the crowd. I'd be a long while getting another drink if I went over, and might lose my seat at the table. So I stayed where I was.

The young men at the table with us were wearing black leather jackets. They were a tough-looking crew. All of a sudden they began jostling Norman, a sort of playful pushing around – or so it appeared at first. Norman laughed and pushed back at them. He was quite drunk by this time. I guessed he'd got himself in with this gang of hoods in order to demonstrate what a tough guy he was himself, a real man's man, even if he was a writer – like his hero, Ernest Hemingway. So he pushed back, as if to show that what was play for them was play for him too. But of course he wasn't like the others at the table, and it showed. They smiled at him, but their eyes were cold and their smiles scornful. I saw they weren't playing at all, but were goading Norman. And I saw it was time for me to get myself out of there.

I was disappointed with Mailer for risking himself so foolishly, trying to prove what a manly fellow he was. Nobody was impressed; nobody thought he was any more manly than he ever was.

I jumped down from the stage and started to walk away. Hearing a noise I looked back and there was Norman coming behind me, tottering on drunken legs. His mouth was grinning, but behind the grin was fear. I turned to help him, but then two of his hoodlum friends caught up and pushed me out of the way. They took Norman's arms and half-led, half-dragged him down the centre aisle of the auditorium. The others left the stage and followed. I edged over to the row of windows and watched. I knew something horrible was going to happen but I was too concerned with my own life to try and help. There was nothing I could do anyway, one man against all of them.

Mailer protested as they dragged him along, but it wasn't until they had him almost to the rear of the room and threw him down on the floor and encircled him that he knew he was going to die. Then the most awful desperate shrieks came out of him, cries, sobs, wailings for deliverance. I felt sorry for him, as anyone would. But I knew I wouldn't move a finger to help. This wasn't a scene in a book of fiction. It was a man about to be killed before my eyes.

One of the young men — they were really not much older than boys — bent over Norman and placed a knife flat on his chest; like a sign, a ritual. Then he took it and drove it into Norman's stomach up to the hilt. Norman grunted, and the others moved in around him, and all of them stabbed him with their knives.

Women in the audience were screaming. During all of this no one had left their seats, but now they dropped to the floor, crouching behind chairs and tables, afraid of being noticed and getting murdered themselves. It was a thought that occurred to me as well and I instinctively shrank back against the wall. The youths had seen me with Norman, I'd sat right there at the table amongst them. I was the most likely next victim. I was by one of the tall windows along the wall but I didn't dare open it. It might be stuck and even if I got it up the drop to the ground was a good twenty feet. I could break a leg. They'd notice me in any case and come running after me. Then I saw them looking my way. They had already noticed me . . .

§

They didn't kill me I'm glad to say. If they had I wouldn't be here telling you this. I'd love to recount what happened next, how I got away and so forth, but I don't remember. Maybe I never knew.

§

Dogs have pride too. I met one on the sidewalk today coming towards me, and being wary of humans he stepped onto the snow-covered strip of ground dividing the sidewalk from the road. At no time did he look at me; he sniffed at the snow, and as I drew nearer glanced around then walked casually across the road, stopping along the way to sniff the pavement. When he was on the other side he resumed his course, passing me with a good safe distance between us.

His pride wouldn't let him show he was going out of his way because of me. He was just interested in sniffing what was across the street, that was all.

There's a little dog in the neighbourhood who likes to bark. I threw some snow at him a few times and he knows me now. If he's on his veranda, or if some of his household is around, he'll bark, but sometimes I come along when he's out on the sidewalk by himself. The minute he sees me he'll begin bustling around, as if he's got something on his mind, and go trotting with all the dignity he can muster into his yard. I can see it wounds his pride to have to do this, and I'm sure he knows I see through his act, but he keeps up appearances nonetheless. He won't run in, and once in the yard he won't bark at me, even though he's safe, but pretends he hasn't seen me. If he'd seen me he'd bark, certainly he would! And as for going in the yard, that's what he was going to do anyway. It had nothing to do with me.

He's more obvious than the average dog. If he's barking on his veranda and I reach down as though picking up something to throw at him he doesn't dash into the yard but quickly changes his demeanour. He stops barking and appears suddenly uninterested in me, and steps behind the veranda wall – there's something there he wants to investigate. Only he makes the transition with such rapidity, in case a missile is coming, that his act wouldn't fool a newborn babe.

§

It was during the time I was boarding at the university. I had a room to myself, and there was a girl student there who was very pretty, and very well constructed. Her name was Melinda and she was blonde and playful and tantalizingly elusive. Nobody could manage to get to first base with her, and most gave up trying. I didn't have to, because I didn't involve myself in the competition in the first place, reasoning she was out of my league anyway so why bother?

One night she came into my room as I was reading and said she was going to sleep with me. I set my book down and said okay, I can stand that. Then she said no, she didn't think she would after all. I said okay, that's fine with me too; and paid no further attention to her.

There was something about her face, the mischief in her eyes, her half-smiling mouth, that seemed to say, "I know what you're thinking. I know what you want." A suggestive teasing look, enjoying the effect she created.

She paused at the door and said, "You're the only one who doesn't pay attention to me." The truth was, I felt quite at ease with myself in those days, and well able to do without a girl I couldn't have. I told her if she wanted to stay with me I'd be happy to have her, but I had no intention of being toyed with. My advantage lay in my independence — my apparent lack of craving for her. I told her if I asked her to sleep with me she'd say no, and if I attempted to take her in my arms she'd run off. She agreed that was true. Then I told her she might as well be on her way since I had to get ready for bed. She seemed hesitant about leaving. She came over to me and said I was the kind of man she was looking for. She wanted to stay with me tonight, and every night.

Get into my bed then, I said. I have to go to the washroom and brush my teeth.

She was already in her nightie, had come to see me wearing it. Don't be long, she said. We kissed and she got into bed and I went down to the floor below where the lavatories were. It was eleven o'clock.

What with one thing and another I got held up. Talking with guys in the hallway and the washroom, having to wait until about thirty guys ahead of me used the sinks. When I finally got away it was to discover a large section of the stairway had been torn out in my absence.

By then I was getting a little concerned. Well, more than a little. What if I couldn't get back to my floor? If I should be kept away from my room now, of all times?

I hollered to whoever was on the floor above to throw me a rope. Several students came to the stair head and asked what the shouting was about. They said they had no rope. But then I saw that someone had improvised a ladder where the stairs were torn away, and I went up this.

It was midnight by the time I got to my room. The girl was steaming. A whole hour she'd waited!

Don't be mad, I said. I wasn't seeing another girl.

I bet you weren't.

Well, I wasn't. I didn't mean to take this long.

But she wouldn't listen. She got out of my bed and left. It bothered me, because by this time I'd lost my attitude of casual independence. I wanted to have her and no mistake. And she knew it, she'd seen it in my eyes, in my changed manner.

All the time downstairs I'd been thinking of her, imagining the night ahead. Word had already got around that I'd succeeded where everyone else had failed. One of the students had seen her go into my room in her nightie and not come out. Some of them took it well and congratulated me, but most didn't, being too filled with envy.

The walls in the residence were thin, and as I stood lamenting my bad luck I heard her voice. She was talking with the Assyrian student in the room next to mine. I could make out every word she said — as I was meant to, I'm sure — and heard her say *he* was the kind of man she was looking for!

I had to get away from there. I was restless, in no mood to go to bed now, the way things had turned out. I climbed down the makeshift ladder and left the residence. As

I was standing on the street three drunken sailors from a navy ship came along. They asked me for a match, and invited me to join them at a bar nearby, the drinks on them. I said why not, and set off with them, but almost at once had second thoughts. Shouldn't I go back and try to make up with Melinda? I looked over my shoulder, not sure what to do, and suddenly there she was, coming out the residence door and walking towards me. I stopped, and the sailors stopped with me. At that moment I noticed two young men across the street assaulting a Russian priest. One of the youths picked up a rock and threw it at him, knocking him to the ground. They then started cleaning out his pockets. We were standing together now, the three sailors and the girl and myself. The boys saw us watching them and they picked up the rock and threw it at *us*. As it rose in the air we tried to get out of the way but it was very large and hit the five of us at once, knocking us down. There was blood and crushed limbs all over the sidewalk. I crawled to the girl and took her in my arms and we held each other, kissing, dying together.

I thought briefly about an afterlife, but I was too bitter to seek comfort there. I was filled with the cruelness of fate, the awful tragedy of our dying just as we were being reconciled, and both of us so young. Our lives should have been ahead of us, not behind, like old people. I tried to draw up my body to press against her, but her look discouraged me. She saw the absurdity of it, our bodies pressing together with desire when we were near our last breath. So I didn't try anymore.

§

Such a sad story. But that's the kind of life I lead when there's no one around.

§

In spite of last night's snowstorm there's less snow on the ground than there was yesterday, as is only proper, this being the month of April. The roads didn't dry all day, and the air was damp, but by mid-afternoon the new snow was gone and the old sooty slow-melting stuff came to the surface again.

At places on the road where there were puddles there are now mires of slushy wheel ruts and sunken footmarks.

I'm getting impatient with winter. It's about time I put my will to work and rid the world of all this mess of ice and snow and mud and slush.

It might be a good night to go to the tavern. I've been irritable these past days — irritable and sluggish. Or the other way around. Like a lump of clay with an electric current running through it.

It's great to have money so I *can* go to the tavern if I choose. My income tax refund came in the mail today. After I pay for my Esquire Magazine subscription and contribute ten dollars to my clothing bill (seven suits, twenty-three pairs of shoes, twelve sports jackets, a hundred and fifty pairs of socks . . . no, that should be one suit and two pairs of socks) I'll have thirty dollars left. Since it only has to last me until September you might say I'm ludicrously lucritous — have money to burn.

The sun is setting, with clouds hanging above it, soft undefined clouds, scraped apart in places, lavender coloured. When I crane my neck towards my bedroom window — over my bedside table, which is in front of the window — I see the sky straight above is a blend of blue and white — a soft luminous white.

The old man said the scallops I cooked for dinner today gave him cramps and diarrhea. He doesn't like scallops (or anything else out of the ordinary) but I didn't think they'd affect him that badly. He only ate three of them, possibly two, and I had the rest, around fifteen, and I didn't get cramps and diarrhea.

His cramps might be psychosomatic, a reaction to an inner conflict; because it's impossible for him to tell me directly that he doesn't like scallops, and that we shouldn't have them again. "What are those?" he said, growling.

"Scallops."

"What are they made out of?"

"They're shellfish."

"Them's them waxy things. They're bad for your stomach."

"They're good for you! It's food that's cooked too much that's bad for you. Your stomach needs something it can work at." I got this information, unrelated as it might be, from a health periodical.

So I guess we don't have scallops anymore. But I don't — and can't — complain, because I don't pay for the food, or heat, or electricity, or my room, or anything else for that matter. I haven't even paid for my booze up to now, shaving a bit off the grocery money every day, as I've mentioned before.

§

Well, I went to the tavern, and talked a lot (as usual), and bummed a few drinks (as usual), and then went up the hill to the college dance for the last half hour but didn't participate.

Brenda Lee has a song I hear on the jukebox at Grogan's Grill occasionally. It's called *As Usual* and I think goes like this (the words aren't that easy to distinguish):

> *The sun comes up*
> *As usual,*
> *The sun goes down*
> *As usual,*
> *The moon comes up*
> *As usual,*
> *The moon goes down*
> *As usual,*
> *I'm singing a song*

As usual,
It's on the hit parade
As usual,
It's no fucking good
As usual,
But people buy it anyway
As usual,
And I get richer
As usual,
People are stupid
As usual.

There may be a few more lines, or maybe she just repeats the whole thing over, making it sound longer.

§

It snowed heavily again. It's still coming down. Everything is covered with it – ground, roofs, trees, lampposts, telephone wires; it clings to everything, even the smallest twig. The evergreen boughs droop with the weight of it. The outdoors has the bright white Christmas-card look of deepest winter.

§

I don't think I should ever consider myself superior to anyone. What have I done that others haven't? It's very well to say *I'm going to* do something remarkable but until I do I deserve no credit. It's time to stop talking about what I'm going to do – time to get out of an imaginary life, stop dreaming and start *doing*. Not for the purpose of *having done*, for that's more projecting into the unknown. Everything, everything has to be doing, every moment about living *now*. It's a sickness of the soul to ignore the present, losing oneself in achievements in the future in order to have them in one's past. It's artificial, self-destructive, and delusional.

There's been so much that's wrong in my way of life. Concerning myself not with what I've done but how I stood in relation to others and what they've achieved.

I began my writing, such as it is, with a good enough attitude. It went well until I got a typewriter and started getting a few poems published. Then the drive for success and approval reared its mangy head. And I began drifting into the future, drinking and dreaming dreams of glory, feeling I'd accomplished that which I hadn't even begun yet. Like someone lost in how he'd spend his Irish sweepstakes winnings before he'd so much as bought a ticket.

§

I suppose I could write of many things tonight, if I had the vitality. I was lying here smoking when the phone rang.

"Hello," I said.

"Hello."

Pause.

"How are you?"

"I'm fine."

"Did I get you out of bed?"

It was a male voice, a teenager by the sound of it.

"Yes, but I was just getting ready to read."

"I see."

Pause.

"Do you know who this is?"

"I don't think so."

"You don't recognize my voice?"

"I'm afraid not."

"Are you sure?"

"Yes. Who is it?"

"You're *sure* you don't know?"

By now I was sure, and getting suspicious.

"Take a guess," he said.

"I have no idea, so there's no point in guessing."

"Go ahead."

"No."

"Why not?"

"Why should I?"

I used to have giggly girls call and go on like that, back when I was in high school, but never a boy.

"Aren't you curious?"

"Not much." But I was.

"I'll bet you are."

"Why do you say that?"

"Just think, if you don't find out you'll have to go to bed without knowing."

"I would have gone to bed without knowing if you hadn't called."

Fallacious logic, I know. There's a muffled murmuring at the other end. Then silence.

"Guys generally call *girls* when — " But I stop. He might say something like he thought I was a girl, which would annoy me.

"What?"

"Nothing."

"What did you say?"

"Nothing. Why are you calling me? If you've got something to say get on with it."

"What?"

"What did you call for?"

"I wanted to talk with you."

"What about?"

"Oh . . . the weather."

I say nothing.

"It's nice out, isn't it?"

I'm standing in the kitchen with only a T-shirt on, and am fumbling with my pants which I brought out with me, trying to get my legs into them.

"Are you still there?"

"Yes."

"Do you know who this is?"

Another voice says something behind him. It sounds vaguely familiar.

"If you let that fellow you're with keep talking I might guess who it is."

"Yes, you might." His hand muffles the mouthpiece, and he says something to the other.

"Did you hear that?"

"No."

"You didn't? You should have."

"Why?"

"Then you might know who I am. Are you sure you can't guess?"

I decide to say nothing, see what happens. The phone becomes muffled again and there's more murmuring.

"Hello. Are you still there?"

Silence.

"Are you there?"

Silence.

"Hello? Hello?"

I wait. More talk at the other end, and I hear him say something off the phone which doesn't clarify itself till I'm back in my room thinking the call over.

He hung up when I didn't speak, but as he was putting the receiver down he said, "How many minutes?" It was distant and didn't come to me right away.

I was sorry I hadn't been a little sharper. For fun I could have said I recognize your voice, I've seen you around, I know who you are if not your name. Bluff my way through. Describe him, tell him he's fourteen or fifteen, or looks that age, and is from Clifton. There's no long-distance charge between Clifton and Bannonbridge, and if I'd been playing that simple-minded game of seeing who can keep a complete stranger on the phone longest I'd have called to the town I didn't live in. And I could tell him the girls think he's good-looking; he'd be sure to agree to that. He'd think I really did know him.

But I'm slow catching on (as usual). Always thinking later what I should have said or done.

§

When I was eleven years old the pregnant young wife of one of my uncles on my father's side came to visit my mother in the afternoon. I passed through the room where they were several times and when my aunt left I was on the verge of saying to my mother, "Aunt Lois is really fat now. She never used to have such a big belly." But I held my tongue. Something kept me from speaking, and I was glad it did when later I learned what pregnancy was.

I can't put my finger on what stopped me, the recollection is too elusive. Maybe it was because my mother said nothing, when surely she'd noticed the great size of the woman's stomach. Or was it some primeval instinctive recognition of the woman's condition — that she wasn't in fact fat, so why should I say she was? It was a strange fatness anyway, only her stomach; and even then it was like a great bone pushing out her belly.

At the time, at age eleven, I didn't know where babies came from, and indeed the question seems not to have occurred to me. People were simply "born" — some family or other "had a new baby". I wasn't the least curious about it. I didn't believe storks brought children, or fairies left them, though I might have had I been told so, for like children everywhere I believed what I was told. Children have to believe what they're told if they want to learn. I was told by my parents and other people about Santa Claus coming at Christmas, for instance, and I was able to learn other things from books and movies for the young. Then I got older and began finding out that one thing after another was not what I was told it was; and that what I'd believed life would be like was not really what life is like, when you get there.

§

Why does a man need God to exist? What does he want from God? Well, it's someone to protect him, to keep dangerous forces from hurting or destroying him. Man sees the world without God as largely a threatening wilderness, and on his own he doesn't like his chances.

But man values his free will, and wants no part of a God who makes his choices for him. However, once he makes his choices and is involved in the struggle of carrying them out, he's not against support from a superior power. He wants to have his cake and eat it too.

A painter might insist he paints his pictures wholly out of himself – he won't abide being a mere instrument. *He* is the creator. If he's following an intuitive flow it's *his* intuitive flow, *his* power of creation. He doesn't do a picture in the same capacity as a brush – what credit would there be in that? When he's away from his studio however, when he's shopping or at a movie or visiting friends, he would like God to keep an eye on his studio so it doesn't catch fire and his paintings burn up.

Man wants the world to be his world, to do and make with as he pleases. As for God, so long as he interferes discriminately – which is to say, in accord with man's wishes – all will be as it should. Man will choose, God will protect his choice, and if man changes his mind and chooses differently then God will change his course and give protection to this new choice.

The God of man's desire is like a doting father, who showers his child with gifts and lets it toddle where it will, but does not allow a car to come along and strike it down.

Further on the matter: assuming there is only one God, and that God has a favourite offspring, that would be me (since I'm the one writing this). If he has other offspring they're simply supporting actors in the stage show of life. That's what we'd all like to think.

What I'm talking about, as you may have guessed, is human egoism vs God. Man wanting to be God himself – or what amounts to the same thing, to have God do his bidding.

Or his ego might decide there is no God. In the land of the mediocre a mediocrity can be king; in the land of the Godless an atheist can be God. Or a sort of god. In his mind, at any rate.

§

I'm in my periodic state of low-level panic concerning next year's occupation. I keep checking the newspapers but still haven't seen a job I'd like. I think I'll try to stay in New Brunswick though. I don't know if it's fear of foreign parts, or a lack of confidence in taking a job where the standards might be higher than New Brunswick's. It *is* these things. But there's a positive side to it too. I've been in this province all my life and yet I've never paid adequate attention to it. Now that my eyes are beginning to open somewhat it wouldn't hurt to do some catching up.

A true sign of spring: hopscotch squares traced in the damp earth. Today is the fellow of yesterday, probably warmer still. There are vestiges of cloud, but so filmy they're like part of the sky's pale blue. When I step out into a morning like this morning I have no concern over my future (where to teach, will I teach); not for a few minutes anyway, till my thoughts catch up to me.

I'd like to know the names of the birds and trees I see around me, and the flowers, weeds and assorted plants I'll see when they come up. I did learn about many of them in grade school but the knowledge didn't stick.

I guess it's natural I feel some tension these days, what with exams at hand, and the openings for teachers running out — if they *are* running out. Maybe they're not, maybe it's the other way around and they haven't hit their peak yet.

It's unsettling being unsure even about this.

My exams shouldn't require too much exertion, just a matter of getting myself in gear. It's better when I'm in the midst of them than when I'm waiting for the contest to begin. I'm always afraid of starting my studying too soon, putting more effort into the task than is necessary. When I work I work hard but I'm jealous of my time and energy, and don't care to waste either. It's what's known as being efficient, or bone-lazy.

§

I get a kick out of the nicknames you hear in this town. There's no shortage of them. Some that come to mind are Bird, Wrinkles, Rab (Rabbit), Fuzzy, Nipper, Boney, Short, Jumbo, Magoo, Goof, Gooby, Pussie (derived from "pus" and pronounced like "fussy"), Crooner, Clipper, Freaky, Wiener, Ears, Mouse, Moose, Dog, Pig, Bear, Hog, Doot (pronounced like "foot"), Ditty, Sooty, Weasel, Duck, Crow, Sleeper, Asleep, Bub, Bubs, Bubby, Bubbles, Buts, Butsy, Swanny, Goose, Rat, Dink . . .

I wonder if attaching names like that isn't instinctive and primeval, going back to when people didn't have family names and needed some way of being identified.

Others I can think of: Bing, Bung, Bundles, Punk, Sappy, K-O, Dingy (hard "g"), Bimbo, Pounder, Pop, Hotdog, Feathers, Swish, Strangler, Tud, Toot, Squiss, Squirt, Folly-me, Chink, Coony, Smokey, Ming, Spider, Gunner, Cuffy, Egg, Yig, Iggy, Rubber, Dirty Louie, Manface, Half-a-man, Tanker, Bumpy, Bliss, Knobby, Bass, Lurky, Muff . . .

I could probably come up with dozens more, just in this little town, if I put my mind to it. Some are short-lived, not outlasting school days, but many become permanently fixed and are carried to the grave. In these cases few could tell you the owner's actual given name.

Nicknames for girls are more rare, and are usually put on by their families. Honey . . . Bunny . . . Mitsy . . . Tootsie . . . Lulu . . . Wee-Wee . . . Those are all I can think of at the moment.

§

The brook that passes under George Street broke away yesterday in the thaw, swelling to five times its width as it gushed out of the culvert. The snow in the field there is receding, sinking darkly into itself, moving off in a body. Anywhere there's an incline water is running. I saw my first robin — he landed quite close to me, posing with his proud orange chest, beak erect and high, as if waiting for his "first-robin-back" medal.

Where two days ago only the grass on the shoulders of the hills were showing, and one day ago the crowns of the hills were bare, now there are whole slopes and much of level fields free from snow. It was good to see the brown tussocks of grass standing up to face the sky again.

The other night the top sheet on my bed ripped slightly, and I didn't change it, and by several nights later it was rent from head to foot, presumably from my tossing about in my sleep. I took it off then, and now I have the next layer, a soft flannelette blanket (sheet?) against me. It's warmer than the cotton sheet, much cozier to get in under.

It reminds me of Julie, one of my former girlfriends, the time I slept in her bed while she slept in another with her younger sister. It was when I visited her three summers ago. When I told my friend Sully about it he said, "I bet you rubbed your cock all over the sheets." Her sheets were flannelette too, why I make the association. Sully quit school in Grade 9 but he wasn't stupid.

Julie and her family had a summer cottage by a small lake outside Saint John. She was my age and had a diploma from Teachers' College and had already taught her first year in a grade school.

It was in late August, the weekend I went down to see her. She met me at the bus station and we took another bus out of the city and walked a couple of miles on a dusty road to get to the lake. The day was warm and sunny, and as I walked beside her I remember thinking to myself, this is the girl I'd like to marry! Which, with my fear of confining attachments, was a very strange thought for me to have. Perhaps she reminded me of my mother.

The family had a rowboat, and she rowed me around the lake while I lay back in the stern like a lord. She was a pretty girl, petite, her hair black and cut short like Leslie Caron's. She had a natural unaffected way about her; she said what she felt, and if she felt like saying nothing she said nothing. She was very much her own person. When you talked to her she was so genuine and forthright you couldn't help checking your own remarks to see they weren't artificial in any way. She was a lovely girl, no two ways about it. The only thing I had to complain about was her unflappable demeanour. She was always calm under any circumstances, including when we were locked in what for my part was a passionate embrace.

She had a sense of humour, she could tell a joke remarkably well without cracking a smile; and yet I've seen the two of us laugh for ten minutes over a funny situation. She was near-sighted, and blinked a lot, but didn't wear glasses. That was her sole vanity.

I liked her family too. Her parents were quiet people, and they approved of me, I believe. When I first met them that weekend at their cottage there was scarcely any introduction, and no conversation. Her mother and father were quite old, in their late fifties if not older. The father was of Irish descent — their last name was Delaney — and the mother was French and spoke with a strong accent.

Julie's sister Louise was a talkative and likeable fifteen-year-old, and I got along well with her too.

And there was Timmy, the five-year-old son of Julie's divorced sister Marie — bright, inquisitive, full of all kinds of information — a little genius, I thought. He was staying with his grandparents for the summer. Marie lived and worked in the city. I never got to meet her.

It was my native idiocy that caused Julie and me to break up. The next time I saw her was New Year's, when I again hitchhiked to Saint John, this time staying with an aunt and uncle in the city. It was a cold journey, standing on the frozen roadside waiting for drives, and I guess I expected a warm welcome, but she showed no emotion at seeing me. As I said, except for a good laugh now and then she never showed emotion over anything; but it irritated me.

I had it in my mind at the time that a girl ought to hit the sack with a man she cared for, or at least come close to it, show some sign of physical interest. We did the usual couch-maneuvres but we might as well not have bothered. She sat with her hands folded in her lap, passively accepting my kisses, only stirring to stop me when I tried to touch her breasts or between her legs.

It may sound as if she didn't care for me, but she did. If she hadn't she would have told me so. We'd been writing regularly to each other, and she'd been up to Bannonbridge a few times in the fall to see me. Or mostly to see me. She'd stayed with a friend from Teachers' College, Darlene – this is a little complicated to explain in a few words. Darlene, if you remember, is one of the former girlfriends of mine that I mentioned earlier; she was at a dance with the fellow who's her boyfriend now and I was there too, and when Darlene saw me she suggested I ask her friend from Saint John to dance. And after the dance the four of us got some beer at the bootlegger's and went "parking". And that's how Julie and I got together.

And now it was the dead of winter and I was in Saint John, and on the second of the three nights I stayed we had an argument. She had her father's car, her own having broken down, and she wanted to go to a movie, but I said we had only this weekend together till probably Easter and should put it to better use. So we drove to a dark place to "park", even though she didn't want to. We'd spent the evening before parked in a graveyard, and I suppose she felt my insistence could only get stronger tonight.

She cut the motor and we sat in the semi-darkness, facing what looked like the back of a warehouse. "Okay," she said, "we're here. Satisfied?"

What can you say to that kind of question? I sat slumped in the seat, shoulder against the door, not answering.

"Well?" she said.

I still said nothing. She shrugged and stared over the wheel.

"What's wrong?" she said, demandingly. "You wanted to come here, didn't you?"

I finally said, in exasperation, "Look, if you don't like it, if you want to go to a movie then we'll go."

"It's too late now. It's already started."

"You act as if there was something sinister in parking here."

We sat half frozen and silent, the ignition turned off because we were low on gas. After a while I spoke up and imparted a few thoughts on her lack of passion. It made no impression that I could perceive, and we froze some more, until at last I got tired of it all and said, "Okay, forget it, never mind, it doesn't matter". We had a reconciliation of sorts and she drove me back to my uncle's house.

I didn't want to end things just like that. I liked her, and I thought she might change, with my help. So the next night – our last night – was one of good clean fun, a Jerry Lewis movie and hot chocolate at her house after.

When I got home to Bannonbridge we continued our correspondence. Meanwhile my sexual frustrations weren't lessening any, and in a moment of madness I wrote her a letter asking her to come up and stay with me for a night or two. If she didn't want to, well, maybe it meant we weren't suited for each other after all, one of us being a passionate individual and the other the cold type.

It took her a few weeks to reply, and in her letter she said she was sorry I felt as I did; she'd hoped things might work out with us, but obviously they weren't going to. She wished me well and closed by saying it would be better if we didn't see or write each other anymore . . .

I was a little upset with her anyway, even before sending my letter, because someone had told me she'd gone out with one Willard Moore on an earlier visit with Darlene, before I came along. Willard was a guy a year younger than me, a high school dropout who did odd jobs about town, painting, mowing lawns, that kind of thing. You'd see him walking around like he was half-asleep dragging his feet and yawning, and you think: that guy'll never get a girl. He's like a character out of a cartoon strip. No self-respecting girl would be seen with him. And she went out with him.

In reality he wasn't a bad guy; he had a nice dry wit, which I liked — but that didn't matter. He wasn't handsome, rich, well-educated, athletic and talented. I might have understood it if he were all those things, but he wasn't. He was just some local buffoon.

It ate away at me, picturing them together. I was disillusioned. In a previous letter I asked her what they did together. I said surely you didn't kiss him? Not a dopey guy like that? You wouldn't stoop that low, I hope? And so on.

It shows how crazy I was. And unless something has changed in me that I'm not aware of, probably still am. Where it all comes from I don't know.

I idealize the girls I fall for too much. They aren't supposed to be mortals, but beings from a higher plane, like angels. Angels (the female variety) would of course be happy to go to bed with a guy like me, but Willard, they wouldn't give him the time of day.

I wrote her a final letter, saying it had been unnecessary for her to formally end things, since for all intents and purposes it had been ended two months before, at New Year's, and we both knew it. Then I set forth a point-by-point analysis of her personality and mine, why we didn't jell — mostly in my favour, emphasizing my poetic emotional nature and her rational frigid one. At the time I considered it a fine letter, and took the trouble to make a copy, something I rarely did or do. But just recently I dug it up and it was a clumsy affected thing and I did with it what I should have done in the first place, tore it up and threw it in the trash. Unfortunately I mailed the original.

§

I suppose I'm saying that Julie was a great girl and I should have realized that sex isn't everything and that if I hadn't made such a difficult request maybe we'd still be together even if miles apart.

The trouble with that is, while it's true sex isn't everything it's still quite a lot, and it certainly isn't nothing. It's not like wishing you had a cone of ice cream, that sort of impulse; it's a powerful force. You can't just say, well, we'll go to movies and play checkers together, and as for sex, we'll pretend there's no such thing. Sooner or later a girl's got to come across.

§

Speaking of my friend Sully (the late Sully who was killed in a car accident a while back), I remember being in the tavern with him and another guy, Nick Doyle, and Sully trying to get me to go and see a couple of girls with them. The girls were sisters, daughters of one of the local bootleggers, and he said he and Nick had had great success with them last night and there was no reason I shouldn't get in on the action.

"You'll love their house," he said. "There's no bathroom, what they got instead, they keep this bucket full of shit under the bed – and the stink! . . . I hope my cold gets worse before we go down there. We have to go back and see them tonight. We pretty near had to sign a formal paper saying we would, eh Nick?"

"Jeezless right."

"You shoulda seen Nick, drunk as a skunk. Falling off the bed – he didn't know where in Christ he was. And her grabbing him like this – " Imitating the girl trying to lift Nick – "Nick trying to get away and her trying to haul him back on the bed – "

"Don't you talk, Sullivan. Little cocksucker walked right in past her mother sitting there –"

"Boots and all — "

"Mud all over his jeezless boots, walks past the mother and climbs right into bed with Janie. Drunker'n arse, mud all over his boots — "

"She had on a pair of panties, she must've been wearing them the last four years, they were all brown and yellow stained. I could feel this hard stuff on the back of them — it had to be hardened shit — and she takes them off real dainty and folds them up and sets them on the bureau. She had to have all the preliminaries too, no getting right to it. She grabbed me — you don't got to do nothing, her tongue all over my mouth and nose. She had it half stuck down my throat. And the breath — God! I can still smell it. Let me tell you, a lad has to be drunk, otherwise forget it. I washed my mouth out for an hour when I got home. And that shirt of mine, it's ruined now for good. If the old lady ever smells it . . ."

"You think that's bad," said Nick. "I had this one out, I don't know her name, from up Sillikers, when I had the old Pontiac. We got drinking beer — she bought it all, didn't cost me a dime — and about one o'clock I figured I better ride her and get it over with. It wasn't only her breath, she stunk all over. We got laying down on the seat and I couldn't take it any longer so I stuck my head out the window — it was like shit, that kind of smell. Heh! Heh! She must've wondered what was going on, me with my cock up between her tits trying to ride her with my head out the window. Christ she smelled rotten."

"So you coming with us?" Sully says to me.

"After what you just told me?"

"It's not bad if you're drunk."

"I don't think I could get that drunk. Thanks all the same."

"Ah, you don't know what you're missing."

"Drink your beer, Sullivan, and we'll haul arse," Nick said. "We don't want to keep the ladies waiting."

§

It's been raining all day, the weather still mild. The morning was foggy but cleared up towards afternoon. The snow is melted in Memorial Park but low mounds of condensed ice remain in many places, a milkish haze hanging above them.

I've gone and bought a bottle of wine. No more sociology classes for the year, or forever. That leaves me the morning off tomorrow to sleep in.

This afternoon I wrote one of Professor Murray's asinine history exams. He likes to get them over and so schedules his set before everyone else's. My memory was perfect – forty minutes of unbroken writing. I rushed through without missing a word and was the first to leave.

Murray's exams consist of writing a summary of one of the chapters in our text book. He tells us the chapter and everyone writes a summary at home beforehand and commits it to memory and then goes for the exam and vomits it onto paper – and that's it.

It doesn't matter what I write, I'll get the same middle-of-the-pack mark out of him that I always get. He considers me a pain in the arse because I ask him questions in class that he can't answer. He detests questions, all he wants is to read from the text and pontificate, deliver set speeches. Questions throw him off, he gets flustered and goes blank, and doesn't know what to reply. And he doesn't forget. So no matter how brilliant an exam I write I get the same mark of 80. That sounds like a good mark, except he never gives lower than 75, and marks of 95 are common (he always rounds off his marks to the nearest five).

This morning Father McGuire didn't show up for Theology class, and while we waited I sat listening to my classmates conversing. The girl who has the top marks in Murray's American History was there, throwing off from memory a number of acts legislated in President Wilson's administration. She was in high spirits, laughing with another girl and few boys. She said frankly that she didn't know what she was writing about on the history paper, it was all memorization.

"What's a 'trust', anyway?" she said.

"Yeah, what *is* a 'trust'?" said the other girl, who has the second highest marks.

I forgot to mention that Murray has a soft spot for the girls. They're sweet and smile at him and never ask questions, not even easy ones.

§

Mankind is forever oscillating between extremes. When restricted, men want freedom, and when free they want order and security. An unbalanced race trying to balance itself.

It's a race of beings that lives by distorted principles, wavering between greed and fear. Striving to satisfy its basic needs and when this is achieved clamouring for toys and trinkets. And the more it comes to possess materially, the poorer it becomes spiritually – the opposite of what's good for it.

§

When I send my graduation invitations out (and I expect I'll be sending a few out) I'm going to type on each card "No gift please". The practice of sending invitations which are nothing but invitations for the recipients to send gifts doesn't sit well with me. I'm sure most people receive them with a curse: "Thunder and lightning! If it's not a bill it's a goddamn graduation invitation!" And their reaction would be right, to my mind. It's an accepted form of begging, nothing else.

If there are people I really want to come to my graduation then it's their presence I want, not their gifts. Others shouldn't be invited at all, except it's standard not to leave out your relatives. If I don't want someone to come, or am indifferent about it, what right do I have to invite them so as to get a gift? I might as well ask a stranger for a handout on the front street.

It's the practice to send invitations to relatives so far away they couldn't possibly make the ceremony. Why? To show you would *like* to have them there? Ha!

If so, then each invitation should bear the note: "No gift please".

There is, I suppose, the rare bird who actually enjoys giving gifts — who wants to send a little something out of generosity or the appearance of generosity. But that person will probably send a gift regardless.

As a matter of fact, my "No gift please" may not deter too many, but my conscience will be clear. They'll have the invitation and so won't feel omitted — and they'll have an out where the gift is concerned, it they want to take it. It won't be my fault if they go ahead and cough up anyway.

§

I got a phone call today about a teaching job I applied for in Hartland. The man who called is secretary of the school board there, a grave man, very serious. He wanted to know when I could go over for an interview. Hartland is a long ways from here, more than two hundred miles. I said about the middle of next month. Oh no, that wouldn't do, he said. The job might be gone by then. However, if I wanted to wait that long and take my chances . . .

His tone of voice implied the job would certainly be taken by then. It also implied it was up to me to accommodate them, not the other way around.

Their advertisement in the newspaper said they required someone to teach high school History and English 1 & 2 (Composition and Literature). But now he said I would have to teach arithmetic as well. And I was to be teaching commercial classes, not academic.

I asked him how much the job paid. Apparently he wasn't expecting that question. He said, "Well, uh . . ." and asked me how much I was looking for. I said I wasn't an old hand at this and couldn't quote a figure, so would he quote me one.

Well, there'd be so much as basic salary, he said, and so much additional for high school subjects, and then there was the government supplement . . .

I did a rough calculation. About $4,300 for the year?

Let me see, he said, and added the figures together precisely. It came to $4,355.

That's not too bad, I said.

He asked me if I was going to go to summer school for my Certificate IV – he wanted to get the money issue straight. I told him yes, I'd be going to summer school. Then that was right, it was $4,355.

I said I didn't know when I could get over, since I'd be writing exams the next two weeks. I also mentioned I had several other applications out and would like to think the matter over for a few days. I would write him a letter in a day or two.

"Very well. As you wish. By the way, do you know Gerald Hanson? He goes to Saint Timothy's."

I asked him to repeat the name.

"Doesn't ring a bell. What year is he in?"

I thought he was warming a little, wanting to talk over mutual acquaintances. That the guy was a nephew or a neighbour's son or something.

"Oh! That's the wrong one," he said. "Just a minute."

I heard paper shuffling.

"I meant James Conroy."

Conroy was one of my graduating classmates.

"Has he got a job yet?" he asked.

"I couldn't tell you. I haven't been talking to him." I knew what he was doing now. "He's applied for the same position, has he?"

"Yes."

Hmm.

Anyway, I still didn't commit myself. I said again I'd write him a letter. When I do I should put in it: "I don't know if an interview would be of much benefit. I can give you a picture of myself right now. I'm of average height, average weight, my appearance – when I wear a suit and tie – is perfectly acceptable. I wear glasses, have little aptitude for arithmetic, and have no money and consequently would have to borrow some for a trip to Hartland with no guarantee I'd get hired. My interests are reading, writing, music, smoking, drinking, swearing, and loafing. I am greatly interested in sex and if there are any pretty girls in the classes I'm to teach please let me know. That would have a definite influence on my decision whether to come work for you or not."

§

My father is concerned about my future. This is understandable because he knows I owe the university seven hundred dollars. The subject came up at dinner today. We were having steak which I cooked as it should be cooked, broiled rare and without salt. He prefers it fried to a crisp and heavily salted. He looked at his plate and, shaking salt deliberately and liberally over his portion, ignored the meat and hacked at the fat part with his knife. He got a piece of it into his mouth and chewed at it with obvious disgruntlement, then with a growl in his throat reached for the salt again and began shaking it vigorously on the remaining fat. Then he said, with another growl, "Did you find a job yet?"

"No," I said, carving a piece off my lean rare serving, letting him see how it was done. "No."

He growled in his throat again. That was the extent of our dinner-hour conversation, one of the wordier ones we've had. I've probably mentioned this already, but we don't say a lot to each other and never have. It's a hard habit to break.

Our association is this: He works, I go to school. I do most of the shopping and cook the dinners all week and wash the dishes, and he immolates a roast on Sunday.

On these Sundays he walks heavily past my bedroom door at noon and I wake up and go to the kitchen. The potatoes and carrots by this time are cooked but still boiling in their pots, there's gravy in the roasting pan heating in the oven, and a black wizened lump – the roast – is sitting on a plate by the kettle keeping warm.

It's my duty to drain the potatoes and carrots, take the gravy from the oven, and see that all the burners on the gas stove are off. Then I must announce the meal, for my father is in his room by then, rocking in his rocking chair.

I feel a little guilty about calling "Dinner's ready!" on Sundays, as though I'd prepared it myself. So in a voice different from my week-day dinner call, in an abstract, objective, neutral voice, just loud enough to be heard, I announce from the kitchen door, "It's ready now," as though the meal had prepared itself.

§

Speaking of my father, he'll sit in his rocking chair with a cigarette in his mouth, legs crossed, hands clasped around his knee, back rounded, rocking methodically and humming to himself – and this has been his posture as long as I can remember. For a long time he's had an ashtray on a stand, but the tray part came apart at some point, and he replaced it on the post with a Player's tobacco can. This can always seems to be filled to overflowing. He never takes a cigarette from his mouth until it's a half-inch in length. He then rolls another, lights a match with his thumbnail, the loose tobacco at the end flares, and he resumes rocking, eyes squinting against the smoke. Rocking, smoking, humming a strange tune. You hear the sound clearly and in a pleasant enough baritone for a brief moment, and then it fades to nothing (though I think it's still going); and then the same routine repeated. He has different tones, but no melody. It's like a droning Indian chant, only without the chant, just the droning.

§

Several things bother me about going to a strange place to teach. What sort of lodgings will I find myself in? It's customary for teachers to board in a private home, but what sort of home will it be? An old Puritan couple who pray all evening and lock up and put the lights out at nine? A family with a dozen screaming kids? And what will I do with myself in the evenings and on weekends? I've only applied to village schools since they're the only ones I've seen advertised. The bigger schools, those in the cities and larger towns, don't need to advertise, they have a waiting list with the names of experienced teachers on it who are trying to get out of the type of place I'm trying to get into.

What will happen when I break out drunk in whatever village I end up in?

I'm not applying just here in New Brunswick, but to places like Slave Lake in northern Alberta and Hudson's Hope in northern British Columbia. When I picture teaching near home, Slave Lake seems less enslaving, and Hudson's Hope more hopeful. But when I shift my imagination to those cold isolated regions, New Brunswick suddenly seems the better prospect. Whichever I lean towards the other looks better. Not that either looks *good*, just better than the alternative, the lesser of two evils.

§

I received an answer by mail to another of my applications, this one from the Catholic School Board in St George, on the Bay of Fundy, with regard to teaching English at the junior high level. I'd really rather teach History, and at the high school level, but I put a feeler out there anyway, just in case.

In its favour, St George is a town of two thousand souls, probably as large a community as I can hope for. And it's by the sea. I've lived all my life near the estuary of a good-sized river and inland places tend to give me claustrophobia. I like to look at the open water and imagine that if worst came to worst I could build, buy or steal a boat and sail out on the tide, away to freedom.

Their letter wasn't a job offer. They wanted me to send them a character reference, preferably from my parish priest. So I went and saw Father O'Connell, the parish priest. He invited me into his office and we faced each other across his desk. He's a big bald unsmiling man with the habit of staring at people over the top of his wire-rimmed glasses. I explained about my teaching application and the request for a reference, and he said, "Going to teach, are you?"

"Yes, Father. If I can land a job."

He asked how my father was doing, and several questions about school, and why I wanted to teach. Then he paused.

"I haven't noticed you at communion lately," he said.

"You haven't?" I said.

"No."

I'd half-expected something of the kind, and wasn't entirely unprepared. It would have been strange indeed if he'd seen me at communion, since I hadn't been near that sacrament in two years. "I go now and then," I said. He had an assistant parish priest, Father Byrne, so he wasn't the only one who said mass. I might have been getting communion from Father Byrne, mightn't I?

He glared over his glasses. I looked straight at his tight lips, which was almost as good as looking him in the eye.

"I hear you drink quite a bit?"

"Oh no, Father. Not me, not anymore. I haven't had a drink in months, two months for sure. It's just a waste of money, drinking, you do stupid things, make a fool of yourself and feel sick in the morning. It's not worth it."

His gaze didn't waver, like a ray gun boring deep into my skull.

I lit a cigarette and looked around for an ashtray to drop my match in. He pushed one across the desk.

"You aren't having trouble with your religion, are you?" he asked.

I said not at all, what made him think that?

"Well," he said, "some people were saying . . ."

Some people. One of my pre-seminarian classmates no doubt, pissed off because I'd got a higher mark in theology at Christmas. Sneaking around spreading the news about what a heretic I am . . .

"They must have misunderstood, Father, whoever they are. I get into discussions now and then and play the devil's advocate, that's all. It's the kind of thing we learn in our theology and philosophy studies: know your enemy if you expect to defeat him. You can't refute atheists and agnostics and heretics if you don't know what they're saying, eh? But I suppose if people aren't paying attention they could mistake my hypothetical arguments for my own opinions. Perhaps I'm too subtle in how I go about it . . ." And so on.

It might not have convinced Aristotle, but it apparently satisfied him, because after staring me down a bit more he glanced at his watch and scribbled a reference.

It was just a standard reference — so-and-so comes from a good Catholic family, has done well in his studies, and can be expected to carry out whatever duties are given him in a capable and responsible manner — but to me it was a glowing recommendation, considering what it might have been.

§

The moment of decision draws closer. When they send my contract it's possible I won't sign it. I have such a dread of its coming you'd think it was a warrant for my execution. I've been searching for an escape route, a way out. I said I liked to live by the sea — one of my great-great-grandfathers was a ship's captain, and I've often dreamt of being a sailor; I feel the sea is in my blood. When I was in high school I even went aboard several ships down at the Station Wharf and asked if they'd take me on, but they wouldn't, they had all the hands they needed. They only hired union men anyway, they said.

So getting on a ship isn't the answer. In my desperation I think of building a raft, a very large raft with a small cabin built on it, a rudimentary sail, a steering oar, and two large oars, one on each side; and then finding a companion to join me. We could keep in sight of shore at all times and sail down the Atlantic Coast to Central America. It's a good plan, but we'd need charts for tides and some knowledge of sea navigation, and a two-way radio for sending out an SOS if we got in trouble. And we'd need money for provisions and other necessities. And I can't think of a companion to come along. But I like the idea. What I need is another like it that could actually work.

§

My contract came, or letter of intent, which I guess is somewhat the same. I'm to be given one class in high school in order to receive the extra money a high school teacher gets. I've been staring at it a full hour. Several times I reached for my pen, held it over the place for my signature, wavered, put it up again. I can't seem to think. An alternative, an alternative, I need an alternative! My brain is fogged in, I can't get things into proper relation with one another . . .

I finally come to a decision. I decide to procrastinate and go for a walk.

§

After two ill-advised nights at the tavern (I still have an exam to be written) I conclude there is no way out. My bills must be paid, my father placated. I'm too much of a coward to just run away penniless seeking my fortune. I tried that three times before. The first two I came home starved with the heels worn off my shoes, convinced I was born to be a gentleman, not a tramp. The nights on the road are too cold, the dew on the morning grass makes poor bedding, and I'm not very good at asking for things, such as food, shelter and work – unless I'm drinking; and to get something to drink I'd have to ask for money. On my third escape I succeeded in getting a job in Montreal and slaved all fall and winter for considerably less than a teacher makes. It was that experience that decided me I'd return to university and get a degree and try teaching.

I feel like a poor mean specimen of a human being. With hungover hand I sign a trembling signature.

I put the agreement in an envelope, carry it to the post office, drop it in the slot – and no, I don't suddenly want it back again. I'm too far gone for that. The die is cast. My spirit is – if not broken, badly bent.

On the way home I drop into the tavern. The old man won't mind what I take out of the grocery money, when he hears I've got my job.

I look at my situation from the standpoint of a duty, an onerous burden I'm shouldering like a man. Then I say it's only temporary, I'll break free when my year's servitude is up. I consider that it's the lot of man to labour in one way or another. Walt Whitman taught school, Samuel Johnson did it for a spell, and D.H. Lawrence. The experience will strengthen my character.

Condolences like this bolster me until the beer takes up the slack. Waiter, a couple more! Pretty soon I'm the best teacher in the country, too smart to have any trouble, loved, respected and obeyed by my students, everything under control.

§

Words (I think they're the words, what they sound like to me) from a song I keep hearing on the jukebox at Grogan's Grill:

Don, get the fuck out of here, you prick!
Don, get the fuck out, Don, you're sick!

Bang her!
Bang her!
Bang her while you've got the chance!

The last three lines are, I take it, the voice of his bad angel. The first three lines would be from his good angel.

§

Another phone call, this one from a pleasant-sounding man regarding a job teaching high school English in Barker's Ridge, a small rural community somewhere between Moncton and Saint John.

I've asked around and it seems a Letter of Intent is not a contract, which means I'm still a free agent, able to entertain other offers.

This man said his name was Somers. We discussed the courses and classes I'd teach and the wages I'd get and where I'd live and so on. When we were finished I said I'd write him a letter and let him know if I was interested.

Which I did, as follows:

Dear Mr Somers,
"I'm inclined to accept your offer. I've received another one, but it involves teaching Arithmetic along with History and English — and I could teach arithmetic about as well as I could Latin, French, Geometry or Physics." [*This is a lightly disguised warning that they shouldn't try to stick me with any of those courses, something I'd cornered him into admitting might be possible.*] "My high school arithmetic matriculation mark was 86, it's true, but I still don't know how I did it. I must have learned something at the time, but whatever it was I haven't retained it. At present I have a faint idea how to add and subtract but it goes little further.

"The position you offer: does it entail teaching English Composition as well as English Literature? I don't think that was made clear in our telephone conversation. As far as grammatical construction goes, I know what I'm doing, but I've never seen the point in systematizing my usage. I believe rather in developing an inner ear for correct phraseology from reading good authors. Experience shows me one person in a hundred – at the most – remembers grammatical categories. I am among the other ninety-nine.

"On the positive side, I am very much at home with Literature and History.

Yours sincerely,
Walt Macbride"

Perhaps a little strong and not too subtle, but with two phone calls for jobs in two days I'm suddenly filled with confidence. Everyone wants me now – I'm in demand, so why shouldn't I dictate terms, play one against the other?

Besides it would be detrimental not just to myself but to the students if I tried to teach things I know nothing about.

§

I wrote another History exam so that's History out of the way. It leaves me with three more, only one of which, Ethics, requires any amount of application. And I have five nights to study for that.

§

I had a bottle of Hermit Wednesday night, and Thursday night I went to the tavern and had six beers. Last night, Friday, I was down for seven beers. But I've been getting some studying done – not much but some. For the time being I'm doing no reading of my own. I have this idea that if I read anything before exams other than the material required I'll crowd out examination knowledge. My conscience says, "If you're going to read, read your course books. Don't drain off valuable mental energy." It tells me I'm in a period of emergency where all must defer to my studies.

It's a kind of self-deception, because if studying is all I'm allowed to do, it gives me freedom to laze around, since I can probably pass my exams with almost no study at all. I can drink and watch hockey games in the tavern, and still have a satisfied conscience concerning time-usefully-spent.

§

I come home half-drunk, or half-sober, whichever way you want to look at it, and feel like continuing on and staying drunk the rest of my life — or stopping completely. That is, going to sleep and not waking up.

I've been out drinking many nights this past year, and while drinking I've insulted people and in general acted like a lunatic — and yet there are people, some of them, who still take the trouble to stick their heads out of a window and call, "Hi, Walt!" as though they're happy to know me. I'm a walking aggravation when drinking, and when not drinking I don't talk to anyone, hardly, so you'd think all I'd get would be frowns of disapproval.

When I drink I couldn't care less what people think of me. It's one reason I like it so much, because when sober I'm exactly the opposite. It matters too much to me. If I recollect the slightest incident which has a bare possibility of discrediting me I cringe and castigate myself as if I'd been out beating up cripples.

§

Ah me. I smoked two pipes in a row and I'm woozing around like I drank a gallon of wine. I'm not used to a pipe. I feel like I'm going to throw up. I had four beers this afternoon, then home for supper and slept till nine. Down to the tavern for six more beers.

I feel sick. My stomach bothers me.

I felt sick last night too, when I only had about a dozen beers. I knelt before the toilet bowl but the nausea passed and nothing came up. I feel like that again tonight.

Dear God, let me go to sleep and stay there for a few centuries.

No more drinking.

Writing about it only heightens the discomfort.

People are fighting lately. A minor battle broke out in Grogan's Grill last night, one booth got knocked over in the fray. The place was overcrowded and a mad herd chased around the aisles following the two young guys who were fighting, not wanting to miss any of it.

One of the young men got picked up by the police after.

Tonight outside the tavern there were a few more fights. Two more got arrested.

I bought a new suit on credit. I cut quite the distinguished figure in it. And two pairs of socks. And a can of shoe polish for when I get some new shoes.

I think I'll try summoning up erotic images in my head to take my mind off my condition.

§

I woke this morning around six, waking slowly out of a dream, and then drifting back into it. I was only partially conscious, just enough to open my eyes, but not enough to lose the dream. I even reviewed it before going back to sleep. It was very long and very interesting, and as coherent as a series of events in conscious life. I thought, this would make an excellent novel. It was dreamt in words too, like reading a book, so in a way it was already written. But I was too sleepy to get up and copy the words. I did dream I wrote them down a bit later but I awakened again and knew I hadn't. The dream was still there before me, all clear in my head, but just to be sure I went over it again.

When twelve noon rolled around and it was time to get up I'd forgotten the whole thing. I remembered some dreams I'd had since that one, but not the dream that was to be the germ of one of the greatest novels ever written.

Not that I'd have gotten around to writing it. I hardly had the energy to get out of bed.

§

Two places habitually turn up in my dreams: the church and the movie theatre. Most often it's the church, but lately it's been the theatre. For example I was watching a movie, and as might be expected I became a character in it. It was a strange movie. I was on a tropical island inhabited by all sorts of monsters. There were huge serpents and half-human ape-like creatures and a great fire-breathing dragon. They were all pursuing me but I had magic powers. I ran like the wind and when the dragon still came after me I dipped my hand in the sea and placed myself in the care of a sea god of some kind or another. And as a result the dragon was paralysed.

I dream quite often about my mother. She died when I was seventeen but in my dreams she's always alive, even if the time of the dream is the present. Sometimes I have a half-notion she's dead, or will be — but it's never strong, and usually comes to me only when I'm nearing consciousness.

I dreamt of her last night. She told me she was going to Moncton for a visit. For what reason, I asked? No particular reason. I told her I couldn't go with her because I had exams to write this week. She understood, and smiling, in a light mood, left.

I feel refreshed when I wake out of a dream. Nothing much may take place in my waking hours, but my dreams are a kind of compensation, invariably full of incident and interest. If I remember them I take them as experiences. They've happened to me, and provide a curious and colourful background to my life. This struck me quite strongly this morning when I awoke.

Not that the dream of my mother was any of that, but many others are.

There's still snow in the ditches and gullies and at places on the roadside where it was pushed back into piles by the plows. And there are still shrinking patches (I almost said shrinking piles) in fields where the drifts were high in the winter. It's April 24.

I wrote another exam this morning.

I feel fatigued – not physically, but mentally, morally, spiritually. I think of my future and there's no magic left. Only a gloomy road to nowhere.

§

I was rather taken by the hair of a girl who cashiers at the grocery store. It was so attractively styled I felt a sudden impulse to remark on it – and perhaps might have if she'd been closer to me when I noticed. Sometimes I can do that; not often, but every now and then. I've known the girl a good many years, she wouldn't have minded. But the slight delay between thought and action undid me . . . I lost the spontaneity. I thought of what I'd say and how she might reply and my attention went from her hair to my performance and I became self-conscious. And I knew then that I wouldn't say anything for fear of flubbing my lines.

I'm not an actor, I'm not good enough at it to act my way though life. And I'm too conscious of myself to function naturally. What I'd like to be able to do is talk to others as though I were by myself, as I might speak to a lamppost. Never mind the effect my words have, or what the other person might expect or prefer me to say. Just be what I am and say what I feel like saying. If I could do that my life would be a lot easier.

I remember a thought I had in a twilight period this morning, between sleeping and waking – that I wasn't one person but a great many. There was in me a saint, a sinner, a miser, a spendthrift, a healer, a murderer, a philosopher, a soldier, a priest, a poet . . .

I thought that a man is composed of different lives, and that perhaps the theory of reincarnation is valid, and many previous lives are summed up in me now, which would account for the complexity of my present nature.

I think the notion came out of some thoughts I had before falling asleep the night before, about the soul living on through reincarnation. I thought the concept was self-defeating, because it's very well to imagine yourself living on and taking a new body and identity, but what does this benefit you if the new identity, the new life on earth, has no recollection of the former lives? They might just as well have never been.

But you can push the theory a little further, and say that you do recall these former lives, but vaguely, as in dreams, and in the phenomenon of *deja vu*.

There was a dream leading to my twilight insight. It took place in a former age. I was conscious of the murderer in me, and frightened of him, that he'd get the upper hand and be my undoing (not to mention that of his victim or victims). But there were opposing beings within me, and I believed they were stronger and would suppress the murderer; and the strongest, the most dominant among them, was the poet.

§

Enough of this worry about where I'm going to work next year. I know I'm going to be bothered enough around graduation time, when others are all at the graduates' dance and I'm sitting home alone drinking wine, or in the tavern, or at the Legion. I need to get something settled, take a few days to think. But it's hard to do when I have to keep my exams in mind.

Once things are settled, once I get a job or go off on the bum, or some other definite choice − then I can locate myself and erect a world around that choice that can hold me with *some* comfort and consolation.

It's becoming evident to me how much I magnify troubles. Here I am now, a young man in good health graduating with a bachelor of arts degree. The possibilities ahead of me are endless. I'm not like guys my age with Grade 9 and 10 education, the limited opportunities they have before them, having to settle for menial work that pays hardly anything. They'd love to have my problems – I know it. I'm smart and capable and officially educated and will have no trouble (or not a whole lot) with whatever occupation I tackle. I'm one of the fortunate ones in life. And yet I go about fretting like an old woman.

So stop it! Take a deep breath, and look around you – give a *little* thought to the morrow, but none to the day after. Look around you instead of inside your own head all the time, and consider how black the situation really *could* be. And let life take its course.

Every so often I need to give myself a pep talk like this.

§

It's warm and bright tonight, not a cloud in the sky. Sometimes when walking at night I run into warm currents of air that have a sweet milky smell, like cigarette smoke sometimes smells.

Last night I could smell the river when I reached Church Street, which is three blocks from the river.

Some people are burning grass. Quite a large grass fire was going in the field behind our house, with a good-sized crowd around it, watching it didn't get out of control.

You could almost call that the smell of spring around here, grass burning.

There are still squat mounds of ice in places. Memorial Park is ringed round with them, miniature mountains topped with sand and soot. Where there's melting at their base the water is grayish, a sickly-gray colour like dishwater.

There's ice in sunless corners and alleys as well, and the river has a broken fringe of ice along its shores. The river was perfectly calm and silvery this afternoon. A few small floes were drifting on the outgoing tide.

The ferry has started running for the season. I just heard its horn sound. You hear that all summer, every night until midnight, every fifteen minutes or so. A dull ship's horn, not a disagreeable sound.

A bridge is to be built across the river, and after next summer we won't hear the ferry's horn any longer.

I'd rather stop "progress" and people's hurrying in their cars. It's much better for the soul to sail leisurely across the river on a ferry than it will be to race across in a car.

§

Too much studying, it's giving me a headache. The Ethics exam requires more work than I thought. I must have put nine hours on it in the past three days.

What would suit me is a cabin on a lake, with hills around, and no other cabins in sight, and a rowboat. I could live by myself there from May to October, and spend the colder months in Spain or Italy or Greece.

If there is a God, and I'm sure there is, might he not see to it that I came into a pile of money — I, who could use it so well?

We're on daylight saving time now.

Today was a cold raw day, heavy with cloud and wind until supper hour. The sky began to clear then, and the wind let up.

It appears I'll be teaching in Barker's Ridge, at a non-sectarian regional high school. I've checked the map and while it's not on the ocean, which I'd prefer, there's an inlet or narrow bay of sorts in the area, and a line that looks like a small river. Wherever it is, I'm grateful to get this job. Looking at the Help Wanted section in the Montreal Star I see I'm not qualified to do a single type of work advertised there besides teaching, and I have no experience in that.

I wrote St George to tell them I no longer have the intent I had when I signed the letter of intent. I said (not without a certain smugness) that I'd accepted a better position, one more suited to my qualifications – implying it was their loss and not mine; and that rather than treat me like a grovelling supplicant as they'd done, they should have pursued me with the zeal of a pirate chasing down a richly-laden Spanish galleon.

I didn't put it in those words. That's just how they were meant to understand it.

§

I wrote my Theology exam this afternoon. I knew all the answers and stated them with little elaboration – in fact, no elaboration. There were twelve questions and my answers altogether didn't fill two sheets.

I suppose I'll get an "honourable mention" in Theology. I should get the prize, since my mark at Christmas led the class and was about ten points higher than the next student's. But I'm not the sort of person who wins theology prizes.

Although you never know, stranger things have happened. I like Father McGuire who teaches the course. He's kindly and tolerant and views himself as a Catholic progressive. He might take a chance on me. He specifically told the class he wants succinct answers on exams (as opposed to bullshit), and answers don't get any succincter than the ones I gave.

FIVE

It's the merry month of May.

The tavern and its draft have seen the last of me. For the third straight night after being in that place I've been sick in the stomach. There must be something wrong with their beer. Last night I was *really* sick, throwing up all over the floor by my bed. Three mighty upheavals, like Vesuvius erupting.

I got up this morning, Sunday, while the old man was at mass and cleaned the mess up. It still smells vomity.

Vomit, puke . . . a couple of the more evocative words in the English language.

In addition to my stomach I contracted a sore right kidney last evening. I felt nothing till I took a leak, and immediately it was as if someone had kicked me in the kidney. An ache with a mild throb. It went away after some minutes but came back repeatedly, every time I pissed.

This afternoon I went over to the Grotto, where I used to play as a kid. They've built a high wire fence around it, barbed at the top, but the gate was open. These days the place has fallen into disrepair. The floor is littered with dead leaves, broken bottles, scraps of paper, cigarette packages, a Chiclet package, a match card, and of all things, three rusty bread pans. But no little blackened mounds of fecal matter with flies buzzing over them. So the fence has been effective to some extent.

The Grotto is in a field just below St Cecilia's Convent and belongs to the nuns. It's constructed of gray porous stone and mortar, and with its tiny passages and windows has the appearance of a church for little people. It's roughly made, stones hanging from the ceiling like stalactites, and sticking out at every angle in the crooked passageways. The main way in is through an open archway at the front. Inside there's a small altar with the tabernacle door half torn off, and a pulpit facing the outdoors that's reached by a winding stone stairway from within.

As kids we used to climb up on the roof, an easy thing to do, using the protruding stones as hand and footholds. There are stones like great jagged boulders jutting out of the roof, and two holes in the high facade to allow rain water to drain off. In the front of the facade there's a blue and white statue of the Virgin Mary with an electric halo above her head, with a pipe at the back carrying a wire through the facade and across the roof and over the edge to a padlocked switch box — a discordantly modern touch in that rugged medieval-looking chapel.

The high wire fence doesn't fit either, but it's necessary I suppose to keep kids from shitting on the floor. There were no old French safes lying around either, as there usually were before the fence.

If I owned the Grotto I'd grow a high hedge to hide the fence and keep the world out visually as well as bodily. Then I'd have a nice retreat — a place to wear my hair shirt in peace.

§

Professor Burns, in Ethics class: "Your questions are supposed to be constructive, not destructive. Don't be too critical of St Thomas's proofs for the existence of God. These are right. You should be a *little* critical, so you can see the proofs better. But not more than that."

§

I'll admit it − I sent my graduation invitations out without qualifications. There are some who would want an invitation (or rather, feel slighted if they didn't get one), even though they're not likely to come to the exercises, and if I were to ask them not to send a gift what would they think, getting such an invitation? That I mean "come or nothing"? Wouldn't I sound presumptuous? And who said they intended to send a gift anyway? There's nothing on the official printed invitation that says send a gift. It's optional, up to the recipient. It's not my place to make their minds up for them. And if I chose to put my proviso on some − the ones who live a long distance away − and let the others do as they wish, there's always the chance they'd get together someday and compare notes, with one party feeling they'd been slighted and the other that they'd been singled out for plundering.

So I said piss on it and sent them all conventional invitations, with no amendments.

For one thing − or one other thing − I've got an investment of three dollars in the invitation cards and envelopes. And for yet another, they can respond (if they want to respond at all, which I don't expect any of them to do anyway) for the sake of my parents. They're all brothers and sisters and in-laws of my parents.

I'll just be glad when the whole bloody thing is over.

§

On the subject of free will − which nobody has brought up, but that doesn't stop me − it's been said by some that an individual's environment, his past experiences, all his previous make-up − or existing make-up to the time of decision − decides which way a man will act, and therefore he has no free choice. But one could reply that this make-up which decides what he'll do, which dictates his choices, *is* the man. He is the composition of all his past existing in the present. It's what the man is.

I wrote Sociology yesterday afternoon, and marked the occasion by getting a bottle of Hermit after. In the evening I took what was left of it and went to call on Professor Marchant in his room in residence. Professor Marchant teaches languages and was something of a prodigy in his student days at St Timothy's, graduating with a BA when he was only nineteen. After graduation he went overseas on a scholarship to study for his Masters degree, and now, in the coming year, he was returning to Europe on a grant to work on his doctoral thesis. He's never been out of school since he started in Grade One.

I took a French course from him in my freshman year but didn't know him that well; he was very strict. He's short, slightly built, intense and defensive. With his cold eyes and hot temper he reminded me of a psychotic killer in a movie. He wasn't the sort of person I would normally go visit, but I was having a drink or two, and at those times I tend to get sociable and consider myself welcome anywhere.

The reason I went was I happened to be looking through some old St Timothy's year books in the library and saw his graduation picture with a blurb under it saying he was the class poet. That immediately altered my view of him. A fellow bard, right there all the time, and I hadn't known it! So I went to see him. I knocked on his door and he let me in and I asked him about his poetry, if he was still writing it.

Oh, he said, the poems he did in college were Latin poems, and he never writes any of any kind now.

He looked uncomfortable having me there. We ended up arguing for an hour till he said he had to get back to correcting exams. He has a sharp mind – and mine would have been a lot sharper were it not wine-sogged – but I think I came out ahead on points.

He's a bitter little chap. He does things like give students a mark of 49-point-something when the pass mark is 50. It seems to give him some kind of satisfaction.

We argued about writers and writing mainly. As soon as he told me he admired T.S. Eliot and Ezra Pound I was able to predict the rest.

Thoreau, he said, was "a fairly good essayist" – that was all. Mark Twain wrote some entertaining stories. Walt Whitman was not much of a poet. Jean-Jacques Rousseau and Friedrich Nietzsche were both insane, all their lives. *The Catcher in the Rye* was a light book, of no significance, a bit of entertainment in it but nothing of lasting value. And so on . . . Everything I thought worth reading he didn't and vice-versa.

I probably became more belligerent with him than I should have, but literature is a subject I can get quite heated about. I told him his opinions weren't his own, that he didn't have any of his own but merely repeated those prevailing in academic circles. I said unlike myself who was gifted with an intuitively flawless comprehension he had no *feel* for literature. An appreciation of literature can't be taught, you either have it in you naturally or you don't, and all the intellectualizing and analyzing and systematizing in the world won't help you. If your feelings are dead or locked away you won't get anything from a book other than dry information. What the scholarly approach does for the most part, I said, is turn students off reading who might like it if left alone.

He asked me what I was going to teach when I started in the fall and I said English and History.

He said with my outlook I shouldn't teach school at all, and I replied that the students would be fortunate to have someone with my outlook and not his, and would benefit greatly from it.

And on that note we parted.

§

It's windy today, a warm westerly wind. This afternoon I sat at the open back porch window watching a robin and another bird that had blue tail feathers and a white band across them. I don't know the other bird's name. He sat on a tree branch a while and then flew away.

The robin was on the ground pecking. He wasn't after a worm, just a peck here and there in the earth, eating gravel maybe and looking very displeased about it. I think birds need gravel for their gizzards, and have to spend time taking some aboard, even though they'd rather be munching on a worm.

He's a fine slender bird. There's something friendly and comforting about robins. I'm sure most people feel that way about them. Other birds come back with spring but it's the robins who are celebrated.

I like the proud way they stand, as though aware of being admired, chests out, showing their best side in profile.

I threw him some scraps of bread but it only startled him and he flew away.

§

To drink or not to drink, that is the question. Whether 'tis nobler in the mind to stay sober or better for the soul to get drunk.

Seeing as the soul takes precedence over the mind, as we've learned in theology, I think I'll get drunk.

§

I'm slow to learn the art of living, but I'm getting there, gradually.

When you wake in the morning and think what an ass you made of yourself while drunk last night – when you think of the enemies you made, and how people despise you – and you moan and berate yourself – then consider for a moment: if everyone else is against you, why join them? Give yourself one friend at least. The others have enough strength on their side without you chiming in to support them.

I have to remember I'm a solitary individual, a separate entity, a me-myself-and-I in a single package, a subjective being facing the outer world. I'm not in the crowd that's observing me. I'm not watching me and at the same time having the feelings of the one being watched. If I do that I suffer without the satisfaction experienced in inflicting the suffering.

I'm learning. I mean to be more on my side and less on the crowd's from now on, and accept what I do simply because I'm the one who does it. Maybe make a note not to do that same thing again if possible, but stow the hair shirt and whip and move along to the next humiliating performance.

§

I vow here and now that from this time hence I'll get up in the morning before ten o'clock and go for a walk. I've been robbing myself of the day's choicest portion, and giving myself too much of its least salutary part, night. Morning is the springtime of day, full of awakening life and optimism. Night is the closing of day, its death.

Just witness my trouble getting out of bed in the morning. It's not easy rising from the dead.

§

A cold dark windy day, heavy clouds overhead. It rained last night around 3 AM. Heat lightning and distant thunder. I lay with my eyes closed and the lightning flashed and quivered through my lids. Then a long wait, followed by the thunder rumbling in the distance like artillery.

I got up at ten and went downtown and bought a pair of shoes. Or I should say, charged a pair of shoes. I didn't pay for my suit either, which I got last month. Everything is on credit.

My stomach is uneasy with anxiety – I suppose for a lot of reasons. The same feeling I get when thinking of approaching a pretty girl. But there is no girl.

I need to get away from this town for a while. If my invitations bring in any money maybe I'll go up to Montreal for a week or so.

Still no contract from Barker's Ridge Regional High, nothing since a letter saying they'd send one.

The grass is quite green now.

My spirit is flagging. Sagging, dragging. In spite of the cold weather I might get a bottle of wine and go across the river on the ferry and sit on the shore.

Speaking of robins, my friend Harold and I were speculating about a really fat one we saw on a lawn the other day, how he came to arrive from the south looking so well fed and prosperous. He should have been all feathers and bones after such a long flight. I said he looked to me like a businessbird, perhaps owned a tourist hotel in Florida popular with feathered Canadians and got so fat from the profits he couldn't fly on his own and had to take an airplane back. Harold said the bird hadn't gone south at all, but had burrowed a hole in the back of Lane's Bakery and spent the winter gorging on cake crumbs and day-old bread. It's impossible to know which of us is right.

We spent the early evening listening to records in my room. It's good that I've got one companion of like mind, or of somewhat like mind, even if we don't get together now as much as we used to.

I often feel quite isolated. It is not good for man to be alone. God had something there; it's all right much of the time but not all of the time.

§

Tonight was good. There are still some fine fellows alive in the world.

I wonder why I have so many friends, so many who wish me well even though when drinking I can be such an egoistic son of a whore. I'm just back from the tavern and too tired to write much . . . The warmest day of the year so far. I sat on the wharf this afternoon and watched the river run by. Tree stumps and bushes and clumps of ice drifting leisurely out to sea . . .

§

I hear crickets at night now. A light rain-mist is in the air. At the edge of the black sky there are trails of yellow cloud haze.

As I was going by Grogan's Grill four girls straggled out single file. I noticed one of them was Corinne. She smiled at me and then was gone. The smile she gave me, it was as though we had a joke between us. I guess we have — given enough time, any relationship I have with a girl appears in the light of a joke.

I'm worrying again about next year's employment. Still no sign of the contract. I think I'm the only student left in my class without one. We're all going to be teachers, except for a few off to the seminary to be priests.

This afternoon I met a German Shepherd padding along on the street. He barked at me as we got closer. It was a bit unnerving, for he weighed as much as I do, if not more. I kept walking and whistled to him, and he stopped barking. When I came up to him I clicked my tongue and said, "Here, boy," and patted him on the head. I've seen him before, and he carries his tail low, a very large dog but nervous and apprehensive. His spirit must have been whipped out of him as a pup. I could see that but I still wasn't comfortable approaching him as he barked, and when I left him I half-expected a rear assault.

I think I'll go fishing this week. A day in the woods might settle my anxieties. I'll buy a line and some hooks tomorrow, or look in the old man's trunk — he probably has some gear there.

If I were braver I'd get my hands on a sleeping bag and spend some nights in the wilderness, by a lake or a river.

I'm okay when it's daylight, as could be expected; but I know my imagination and how it reacts with nightfall. I'd be hearing bears and coyotes moving around in the dark . . . axe-murderers . . . zombies . . . vampires . . . they'd all be out there.

It's unfortunate because if I don't feel at home in the wilderness I've become too far removed from nature. Too civilized for my own good.

§

I'm in the back shed with a quart of beer, sitting at the open window. Being on the second floor I can survey the world below as from a godly position; not that there's a lot to see from here. It's been raining lightly off and on. There's a huge gray and white cloud overhead with the sky around it clear and blue. I hear birds chirping, whistling, singing. The neighbour's little pug-nosed dog is lying in the sun, on a small patch of green grass. A breeze fans the pages of my notepad as I write this. There are puddles on the unpaved driveway in the neighbour's yard. The neighbour is a car dealer and has a nice house next to our not-so-nice apartment building. He has a wife and two kids, a boy and a girl.

A black shiny bird with a yellow beak flapped across my window and settled in the maple tree a few yards away.

I found some ugly black bugs in the garbage bag earlier, and every time I feel an itch I think it's one of them on me.

The bird that did the fly-past has a fan-shaped tail that opens as he lands.

A jet plane roars somewhere in the distance.

I'm still feeling low, the longest and deepest stretch of depression I've known since last summer.

The black bird has some grass in his beak. He comes and goes. He flies to a limb close to me and when I look at him he turns his head uneasily and flutters to a branch further away. Another black bird shows up, this one with a white plume on his head, like a helmet. I haven't seen that fellow before. The first black one saw him land and flew over and chased him away.

I notice the original black bird has a bronze chest. I should know what kind he is. A green-bronze chest. No, he changes colours, his back feathers look bronze also. I used to know his name, his family name, I learned it in grade school . . . I remember now, a starling.

One tankard's worth of my quart of beer is gone. Tankard, stein, flagon. A half-quart clear glass mug with a handle on it.

Undoubtedly I'll buy some more, or some wine. I'm too uneasy today to stay sober. Perhaps after the graduation exercises I'll settle down . . .

I throw the empty bottle to the ground. The dog gets up and is out at the end of his leash now, wondering what caused the clinking sound. It landed in a heap of rubbish — torn cardboard boxes, a bent-up TV aerial, a dented garbage can set a few feet to one side, three fir trees left over from Christmas (two still green, one a rusty orange), and a beer bottle — my contribution. The bottle hit a rock but didn't break.

Most of the massive rain cloud has passed. The last shower stopped five minutes ago. Off to my left is a wide expanse of blue with a peninsula of cloud moving into it. The sun is shining again.

Here's the funny thing: I'm worried about not having a job — and yet I don't want a job. Did I say that before? I thought I had the one at Barker's Ridge but they haven't sent the contract, so maybe they changed their mind.

My starling is back, shining ebony in the sunlight. He flew within a few yards of me and circled to a near branch. His throat gleams green in the sun . . . He flew again, this time within a few feet of me. Maybe he's looking for a handout.

A tree is an especially beautiful sight when waving in the wind, with the blue sky behind it. There are yellow flowery buds on it.

Two little boys are in the yard now, playing with the dog.

"Does he bite?" one of them says.

"I don't know. He's small, isn't he?"

The dog bounces about joyfully, nodding his head, pawing the air with his forefeet. A little girl with a scarlet coat and tam joins them and says they aren't allowed to play with him – the woman said so – he always gets loose.

Now there are three little boys in the yard, all with bicycles. I suppose they're about eight or nine years old, wearing dungarees and little jackets. One fellow has sneakers on, the others shoes. The little girl in red tries to attract their attention but they ignore her. They move away and go up the street, the dog looking round the corner of the house at them.

I don't see the point in writing this. It seems useless, like everything else. While I'm writing I feel good, but depression lies in wait for the drop of my pen. And when I stop I say to myself, "Why should I bother, no one will see it. I'm not writing a book. I'd like to, but I can't get the freedom and time I'd need for it." But if I had the time and freedom, I wouldn't write a book either.

My starling hasn't returned. He left when I went to the kitchen to get some bread crumbs for him.

The little kids are up the street a piece. I can just see them from my window. There are two boys now and four girls. Another dog over that way barks, and the little one who's leashed ran to the corner of the house and barked back. The other dog leaves, but the dog on the leash continues barking.

He's stopped now and stares at the kids who continue on out of sight. He gives a final little bark after them.

My pages are flapping.

The dog whines, barks again.

The sun is behind a cloud.

My bread crumbs are being blown off the window ledge.

In the next apartment two women are talking. The back door must be open since their voices seem near, though I can't make out what it is they're saying.

§

"Anyway, how did things go in Toronto? Do you like the city?"

Etc. Talking on the phone to Corinne.

She's home from the Ryerson Institute of Technology where she's studying fashion design or interior decorating or some such thing; I'm not precisely sure what. When I talk to her my concentration is affected and I miss details.

During the conversation I could hear her old man trying to get her off the phone. At length she said, "I have to go, my father needs to make a call."

I said it was nice to talk to her and maybe we'd talk again. When I said goodbye she said "Bye-bye," in what I would describe as a sweet voice (certainly not the cold and disapproving one I know so well!).

Bye-bye . . .

And therein lies the dream, the hope. Did she read the Weekend Magazine article two weeks ago that said when a girl says "bye-bye" over the phone it means she has a special interest in the guy calling and would like to hear from him again? . . . And if she hadn't read it, doesn't the psychology of the article still hold true?

I think it does, because I'd drawn the same conclusion *before* reading the article – and my brilliant mind and a scientific study could hardly both be wrong.

But that aside, she really did sound pleased to hear from me, because when I called she was bright and bubbling with her, "How are you?"

I'm afraid I still have strong feelings for that girl.

Maybe I'll never rid myself of them.

§

My graduation came and went. I won the Theology Prize after all, and looked very handsome in my new suit. Some relatives from out of town actually showed up, laden with bottles of scotch and rye, and took me to dinner at a licensed restaurant where we continued the celebration. But before we left, while we were sitting in the living room, the doorbell rang. I thought it was Harold who had promised me a bottle of wine (which I never got), but to my total and utter astonishment it was Corinne with a gift for me, a set of mother-of-pearl cufflinks and matching tie clip. I invited her in and she sat a while but said she couldn't join us for dinner, she had to get home and mind house.

I looked highly respectable for a change, clean-shaven and in my suit. While she was there I don't think I could have been happier: a drink in hand, a beautiful girl at my side on the sofa, relatives showering me with praise, and (though this was the least of all, believe me) my pockets full of prize and invitation money. I could scarcely believe it was me in the middle of it.

Unfortunately I made the mistake of calling Corinne after the relatives left, when I was drunk as a nit. She's dead against drinking, her old man being an alkie and all. So the good will I'd built up is now gone again.

§

Sober at last — and about time. But I feel lousy. Absolutely rotten.

The loneliness of a man. He's born into love, and bred in it; he has his mother and he has God, and trusts and relies on both without question. Then both depart and unless he finds a wife or a communal belief or cause he becomes isolated. And supposing he finds a woman to love him, would that really do it? Would he escape being a separate and lonely individual? I don't know much about this. But there are degrees of loneliness, and a woman would certainly make up for a lot.

And God? I'm looking. He slipped out of sight – or I did at some point. I hope I find him soon.

You walk down a hill in the twilight and see the lights of cars across the river following a thin thread of highway. This is my hometown, I've lived all my life here, and I might as well be stranded in Vladivostok. Those strange cars driving into the deepening gloom . . . are there people in them – are they empty?

I talk to a few people and I forget my isolation for a minute, but they go and I remember again.

Tomorrow should be less of a burden. The day following heavy drinking is always depressing.

§

My contract came and is signed and in the mail, my fate sealed. I'm subdued tonight, fatigued. I don't care – let the world tumble down around me, I'll accept it.

Once Tuesday is gone by, one weight should be off my mind. I may have to appear in court as a witness in an accident case. I don't like the whole affair. When two sides are both wrong, but neither altogether wrong – and the one most wrong is the one I sympathize with and would appear for – then there are bound to be complications.

Yet if I don't appear – and I can manage that – I might be letting people down. I'd also feel like a coward, never mind what others think – afraid of involvement and responsibility and – as much as anything else – of law courts. And I'd miss out on the experience.

The case is this: on one side a carload of young men driving from the tavern to a dance, and the man driving has neither a license nor insurance; on the other side, a boy and girl parking on the side of a dark road with their tail lights off and where there's a No Parking sign, and this fellow has no insurance either. Result: the first car (in which I'm a passenger) slams into the back of the second, sending it flying off the road and into the ditch.

In the headlights we could see the the driver and his girlfriend crawl out and stagger up onto the road, holding their necks. They both suffered whiplash. Being drunk some of us thought that was comical, picturing the couple cuddling and smooching in the peacefulness of the night when suddenly WHAM!!!

The mood-altering shock of it all. One of the guys said: "That was some kiss, honey!"

The guy driving our car, Robbie Kelly, wasn't amused. When the Mounties came they took him to the station and charged him with impaired driving and driving without a license (which he didn't have because of another drunk-driving incident). And the guy in the front seat with him, Crooner Cripps, couldn't work up a laugh either having given himself a concussion when his head smacked against the windshield. But the three of us who were in the back seat enjoyed it all, being unscathed and uncharged and under the influence as we were.

The trial is to settle who pays the damage to the cars — and, I suppose, whether Robbie was actually impaired or just shaken up and appeared that way.

Now, I can testify that the car we hit had no tail lights on. The condition of the driver of ours is the question . . . I'd rather shy away from that one. Who can say when a man is "impaired" or not? But do I want to put my word against three or four Mounties?

I thought I'd got out of being a witness, though. I told Robbie's lawyer I'd do it if it was absolutely necessary, but I didn't feel comfortable with it. He started asking me questions I'd get asked on the witness stand but stopped when I got into how much Robbie had put away in the tavern. No doubt he deemed that information irrelevant and immaterial, as Perry Mason would say. It was at that point he said he could probably manage without me.

But then Robbie's father, whose car it was, came by the house and pleaded with me to help his son, almost getting down on his knees. He couldn't understand why I wouldn't do that for my friend.

I don't know what to do. He's not a friend, just a fellow I know from the tavern crowd, and from earlier days when we were in the Boy Scouts together.

I told his father I'd probably see the lawyer again tomorrow and discuss it with him. I didn't say for certain, but I did give the impression I'd help out.

The whole case comes down to whether Robbie was impaired. If he was, something of a stalemate is reached, with both parties being at fault and maybe having to share the cost of the damage. Or Robbie's culpability might be seen as greater, and his old man get stuck with the bill, since Robbie isn't employed and in fact hasn't been for several years, if he's ever been.

If he's deemed to have been sober then the guy with the whiplash, being illegally parked and without lights, would have to foot the bill.

That's the crux of it. And they want an upstanding university student like myself to perjure on the Bible that the drunken guy was sober and that the Mounties are all liars . . . a situation that would make me very uneasy, to say the least.

So what I'm thinking is this: me alone against the Mounties wouldn't convince anyone; the lawyer is going to have to sell the judge by other means. And if he's able to do that, why would he need my paltry testimony which I'd likely give in a shifty-eyed guilty-looking manner anyway, since I'm not a good liar?

Why I even bother myself over this is, of course, I don't like disappointing people. I was with the accused and should be supporting him, not siding with a gang of Mounties who come from God knows what parts of the country – outsiders every one of them.

The lawyer and Robbie's old man don't want the other guys in the car to testify because they're a bunch of low-life drop-outs and street-loafers. I'm the only one with some vague shred of respectability, superficial as it is.

§

Well, I went to see the lawyer, and he was definite that he didn't need a half-assed witness like myself. So I'm off the hook, praise the Lord.

§

My eyes are sore, like I've been in a smokey room. I probably have been in a smokey room, smokey because I smoke so much.

I got up at ten this morning, a lovely morning, the sun out, the birds singing. The grass is fully green now, and leaves are beginning to show on the trees. Dandelions, my favourite flowers, are out with their bright yellow heads.

And I still have a lurking fear it will snow! I can't imagine summer being long enough to get over memories of the past winter. I know from experience I'll be ready for the snow of next year by the time it comes, but I can't imagine it now. The months of summer ahead look all too short.

No pressing engagements this evening — as if there ever are — so I'm free to drink if I wish, and probably will. I'm a useless bastard if ever there was one. What brought the thought to mind was the fishing trip I considered. I bought a line and some hooks this morning, without the least intention of drinking. Then I said to myself, if I'm going out fishing I ought to have a companion. Meaning a bottle. It would make a nice outing even nicer. But then I lost interest — I'd have to dig worms, gather various items together (frying pan, potatoes, grease, knife, etc.), walk all the way out to the lake and back — as I said, a useless bastard — so the fishing idea left me, but the wine idea stayed behind, sole survivor. And once brought up it's hard to put down.

Well, I'll get the bottle anyway. It's still early afternoon and I might as well do something.

§

This morning Harold and I hiked out to Beaver Lake and spent most of the day there. I actually got my fishing expedition in. There were little swallows swarming over the lake like mosquitoes, wheeling and interweaving, their wings patting the water surface as they shot along.

It's a nasty business, catching fish. I hooked four little ones — actually six, but I threw one back, the hook having caught in his lip, not injuring him too much; and another one, the largest of them all (of course), fell off the hook an inch from shore and swam away. We didn't have proper angling gear, just lines and hooks and a couple of saplings we cut down for rods.

Taking the hooks out of the little creatures' panic-wide mouths, hooks that were swallowed whole and imbedded in their innards, wasn't particularly pleasant. But bad as I felt for them I still slid on another worm and threw my line in again. I guess the savage inside me isn't entirely gone. I had no difficulty threading the worms on either, something that used to bother me as a little kid.

A wind blew in the trees all afternoon, providing soothing background music.

Harold caught one large trout, a foot long, which was about equal in weight to my four small ones. While I cleaned them he built a fire and we had a small feast. We'd forgot to bring a frying pan, so we cooked them on the end of sharpened alder twigs and they couldn't have been more delicious.

I think it's good for the soul, being out in the wilderness like that. Everything is peaceful with the wind sighing in the trees, the occasional piping of a bird, the sun dazzling on the water.

There were fiddleheads around the lake, and logs and dead stumps in the water.

I returned with a sense of time well-spent, thinking I must go out again one day, but alone. Not to fish but simply to gaze and wonder and absorb it all the more deeply.

§

Harold has come up with a catchy singing commercial he says Dow Breweries in Quebec would love, and pay good money for. A sample verse and the chorus go like this:

When through the woods and forest glades I wander
And hear the birds sing sweetly in the trees;
When I look down from lofty mountain grandeur
And hear the brook and feel the gentle breeze . . .

Then sings my soul, my favourite beer to thee —
How great Dow art, how great Dow art!
Then sings my soul, my favourite beer, to thee —
How great Dow art, how great Dow art!

§

I bought (charged) a new corduroy jacket, a piece of clothing I've wanted for some years. Another pair of shoes towards the end of summer and my wardrobe is set for life. I'm still wearing my old army boots for day-to-day getting about and saving my graduation shoes for teaching.

It's raining hard. Far away there is thunder rumbling, like a growling in the throat of the sky. The rain beats and splashes on the veranda roof outside my window. I have the window open with the screen on to keep out mosquitoes.

It's a relentless driving rain. I like rain, the single-minded way it goes about its business. It doesn't care whether it nourishes your crops or soaks your shoes or drowns you. It's quite indifferent, hasn't the slightest interest in what you think of it. I respect that.

§

Robbie Kelly had his trial, and got off with a fine for driving without a license. They dropped the impaired charge. The other guy was fined for parking where he shouldn't have been. I don't know who's paying what for damage to the cars.

§

A cold damp morning. Last night I got drunk and had a fine time. By having a fine time I mean not having a bad time, mainly. I usually have a bad time. Last night I went to a dance at the university and danced several times with Elena, the pretty sixteen-year-old girl I mentioned earlier.

That was it – my good time.

It's not much, I grant you, but I'm used to much less. She's blonde, very sweet, and very nicely built. It's strange nobody's warned her about me. Or maybe they did . . . Maybe she just has an adventurous spirit . . .

I think I'll get another bottle tonight. All my classmates are going to the May Ball, and I can't just sit home alone feeling left out of things. I have to do something with myself.

§

Ah, notebook, as could be expected tonight was not good. No dancing, no women, just drinking and hanging around downtown. I almost got in a fight and that's never nice. It was my fault. I was in Grogan's Grill and the jukebox was playing Dean Martin singing "Everybody Loves Somebody", a song I really don't care for, and so I reached behind the jukebox and pressed the shut-off button there and stopped it. The guy who'd played the song, an airman from the base, came running up to where I was sitting at the counter and said, "Did you shut that off?"

"Me? No."

"I think you did."

"Uh-uh. It must have been someone else."

"I saw you over by the jukebox."

"Really? Well, there's no law against that."

He was fuming. He went back to the booth where he was sitting with a local girl and glared at me. I thought the matter over, and went down to talk to him.

I said, "I did it. I shut your record off."

"I thought you said you didn't," he said.

"Well, I did. I might have said that, but it was only to keep the peace. But I did it. Okay?"

"What did you do it for?"

"Never mind. I did it. It was a lousy song."

A friend of mine, big Jumbo Flaherty, was watching from the counter and came over, and the girl said to him, "Take that away — We don't want a fight."

"Eh?" said Jumbo.

She pointed to me. "Take that away."

"Don't be fucking stupid," said Jumbo. "You want to take *that* guy there away" — pointing at the airman. "He's getting smart. We don't like smart guys around here."

Airmen, or pigeons as we call them, aren't popular in town, especially when they're picking up local girls. This one could see he was in trouble and backed off, wheedling his way out of the situation, so there was no fight. But I hate it when I do that. I get crazy when drinking, sometimes. It's no wonder I have the reputation I have.

But what the hell. Why should I care what people think of me, a man with such a slight grip on life as I have? I can give it up any day and perhaps will. I'm drunk but I understand my feelings now.

§

From my window I see two cats sitting on a lawn in the dark, like stone statues.

The red traffic light at the corner casts a dull blush on the maples across the street. In the distance I hear the hard whistle of a jet fighter plane warming up.

The sky is clouded and there are streaks of black ribbed clouds against the gray.

It begins to rain lightly, single drops pecking at the veranda roof.

§

I was dreaming of a young lady who loved me. I'd just met her, but felt I knew her quite well. We were in the back seat of a car, and we came very close to kissing, but at the last instant she wouldn't. "Oh, I can't! I have two children." Her brother was driving the car and we drove around for a while. Her brother took my part, encouraging his sister to give in to me. I thought she would if I persisted, and would have telephoned her, but I was sitting on a rock in a neighbour's yard and of course there was no telephone there.

§

I was sitting on a rock in this neighbour's yard, and on a nearby rock was a man I recognized as Jack Kerouac. He noticed me looking at him and with a friendly smile said, "I know you'd like to ask me about my books . . ." I saw he was holding a copy of his latest in his hand.

"You could see I recognized you by the intelligent glint in my eye — that was it, wasn't it?" I said, thinking that a brilliant thing to say.

We walked down to the brook in the field below, and as we strolled he began talking. He talked at a terrific rate! I wanted to tell him I'd read his story *October in the Railroad Earth* but couldn't find an opening. The words poured from him like a gushing water main, in one long seemingly endless punctuationless sentence. I reached for my tobacco but it wasn't in any of my pockets. "We can't talk without smoking," I thought. "Maybe he can but I certainly don't feel up to it."

I said "Excuse me" (I know he didn't hear me, being still busy with his sentence) and went back and found my package by the rock. But then I discovered I had no matches and would have to run home for a card. It was such a long distance that my meeting with Mr Kerouac was bound to be frustrated. He'd be long gone by the time I returned, if I ever did return. So I woke up.

I've noticed almost all of my dreams end in frustration of one kind or another.

§

Saw some little kids in a yard playing an old game, one of those games that have been passed down through the ages from one generation of kids to another . . .

"Cathy, take one scissor step . Yes, you may."

"*You* don't say 'yes, you may'!"

She's right! As I remember the game it goes like this:

"Cathy, take one scissor step." (Or giant step, or baby step).

"May I?"

"Yes you may!"

If you don't say "May I?" then you have to stay where you are — or take the same step backwards — or go back to the start line — well, I don't remember *exactly* how it goes.

The trouble is, in this game the caller pretty much chooses the winner by deciding who gets the "giant" (standing broad jump) steps and who the very short ones (baby steps), the winner being the kid to touch the side of the house first.

But fundamental flaw aside, it teaches the kids to be polite and ask permission. It might also teach them to say "May I?" instead of "Can I?", except it doesn't. The only time they ever say it is during the game.

A similar game we played was for the child at the front — say it's Cathy — to turn facing the side of the house, and when she's not looking everyone tries to get closer and whoever gets to the wall first wins. But if she turns quickly and sees you moving you're "out".

This was a better game, a fairer game, requiring alert senses and cunning anticipation.

There were a lot of games we played as kids. Hide and Seek, Hoist Your Sails (or Oyster Sales, as I thought it was), Red Rover, Kick the Can, Inny-Eye-Over (Pig's tail!) . . . The boys on their own played war and cowboys, with lots of shooting ("Ka-Pow! You're dead!") . . . and the girls skipped with their skipping ropes and played hopscotch and bouncy-bouncy-bally . . .

We were in a world of our own, without adults, and we couldn't have been happier. There were never adults around when we played, they were glad to be free of us for a while, and we of them.

As the philosophers of old liked to say, life is for the young. Now that I'm a philosopher myself I can see that. And the younger you are the more life was designed for you. Which isn't a promising thought to have in your early twenties.

§

I woke this morning at six, and found the sun already up. The grass and trees were vividly green, and the sky bluer than I'd ever seen it, and the air resplendent and flashing – I was awed by the sight, like waking into a world of make-believe, or the Garden of Eden.

I thought it would be dark out at six o'clock and looked around for my watch to see if the clock wasn't mistaken.

I woke up again at ten and the outside was to all appearances the same as earlier, but the sparkle was missing. It was like a reproduction of the six o'clock original.

§

It's not raining today, but the sky is a dirty gray. The streets are drying off from yesterday's rain. A fresh wind is blowing. The leaves on the trees across the street are growing – though still undersized, and the trees have a bare look, the boughs swaying.

I accidently have a rhyming poem here:

It's not raining today
but the sky's a dirty gray –
The streets are drying off,
A fresh wind is blowing,
The leaves across the way
are young but busy growing . . .

I used to have the rationalization for my drinking that I did it to put the time in, since I wouldn't begin to actually live until I was out of Bannonbridge. My time here was like a prison sentence and every day spent drinking ate up a portion of it, to my benefit. But I know today that's not true, and that no matter where I was I'd still look for a reason to drink, since it's my nature. The cause is within me, and that's where the issue must be settled, within me. When I was in Montreal I drank. Toronto, Quebec, New York — all interesting places, where I had money and time and could do what I willed – and I drank. If I went to heaven the first thing I'd say was, "Where's the liquor store?"

The fact is, unless I stop it here in Bannonbridge I'll continue elsewhere.

There's an expression about violent family feuds which goes like this:

Blood cries for blood!

And you know, after a night of sound and solid boozing and waking up the next morning still partially intoxicated, you learn that alcohol cries for alcohol. For you — or I at any rate — have a strong inclination to pick up the thread of the previous night and keep it going.

And to apply it another way, the more you drink, once you start, the more you want to drink. *Wine cries for wine!* Or beer, rum, gin, etc.

And again: after a night of heavy imbibing and general carousing, with the morning's sobriety comes a cloak of depression. And you know how to fix that. All you have to do is resume drinking. Of course the following day the depression will be even deeper and heavier on the spirit, since you're not only physically more worn down but have additional recollections of bad behaviour — those you can remember (and there are always enough). So what's the answer? It's have another drink! *Wine cries for wine* . . . And on you go, postponing the reckoning, keeping one step ahead of it, until your constitution can take no more and you collapse in despair, with no alternative but to suffer for your sins . . .

It's a bitter aftermath, a period of total desolation, when all brightness and hope is gone from your life, forever – or so you feel.

And another thing. As others have done, I've said to myself that one of man's greatest gifts is the ability to forget, so as not to carry painful experiences around permanently. It enables a person to get back on his feet and resume living with fresh optimism. Get over the agony of lost love and such things. But it's a two-edged sword. For the torment that turns you against drinking, causing you to swear you'll never do it again, also passes. Once a few days go by, or in extreme cases, a week or two, your misery becomes a faded memory, and then no memory at all, or even something to joke about. And you go get another bottle. And it starts all over.

§

Saw my starling today flying about making little squeaks. He landed on a nearby limb with his feathers ruffled, looking like a fluffy ball. Then he shook himself – gave a sort of shudder – and his feathers smoothed down perfectly, and he was a slim shiny bird again.

Sometimes in my dreams I notice myself standing with one leg straight and the other bent. When I try to straighten my bent leg the other comes off the floor by a good three or four inches – in other words, I have one leg three or four inches longer than the other. It's my right leg that's always longest. I find it uncomfortable to stand with one bent leg, and when I straighten it I feel much taller, naturally, and it's a good feeling, except for the fact the other foot is entirely off the ground.

§

I wake with a start – my alarm is ringing. I shut it off with a semi-conscious reach of my arm. And a revelating sense of wonder comes over me, as it has on several other mornings. The sun is shining, bathing the earth in gold, the sky is a vast and glorious blue, the birds are singing merrily. And my wonder is – *what for*? Why do I wake up? Why do I get out of bed every morning and move about and think and do this and that, and in fact – live? Unless there's a reason for it. And if there's not – and my realization of this is overwhelming – what an empty meaningless thing a human life is. No human being deep down in his being could accept this, no matter what he tells himself.

This feeling lasts but a few seconds, but is absolute and overpowering, and is followed at once by a full, direct, and comforting sense of God's reality – a certainty that it's God's show that's playing out here, and that the universe and all it contains has *not* been wandering around on its own all these eons like some ultra-complex mechanical toy that somehow and for no rhyme or reason created itself out of nothing and continues to exist with the same absence of purpose.

This insight passes in an instant too. Once it's gone I can't revive the sensation, but I have the memory of having had it; I can say what I've said above, but not relive or communicate the actual experience. Spiritual experiences (I presume that's the heading it comes under) obviously are felt in a place beyond emotion and intellect. And when you have one you *know*, even if you forget all too soon how well you knew.

§

I've been watching a black bird on the ground. I don't know if he's a blackbird or just a black bird. He doesn't seem to be a starling.

He moves around in a different fashion from the sparrows and robins I've seen on the ground. A sparrow bobs on quick little legs, and a robin is similar, though he covers more ground with each bound. The robin takes three or four bounces and stands erect, as though posing for photographers. He's still as a statue but his careful eye is taking everything in, for he'll suddenly dart his beak and begin tugging at a worm.

The robin plays with the worm like a cat with a mouse. He gives it a few tugs, then lets go his hold, pausing to pose a while. You might think he's forgotten about it, but this carelessness is only an act; he knows what he's doing, and soon has the worm out and shaking it about in his beak. After it's had a good shake he sets it down and holds himself erect again for the cameras. And when the pictures are all taken he swallows the worm and stands again as though nothing has happened. All in a day's work.

I wish birds were vegetarians though. I wouldn't mind coming back as one in my next life (if such there is) if I didn't have to eats worms and maggots and such delicacies.

But getting back to the black bird — with his shining black coat and long tail. He doesn't bob on the ground but plods flat-footed, one foot after the other, bent forward like a man trudging with his hands in his pockets. Maybe he's a small crow — I don't know. Whatever he is he looks made for walking. I watched him hike through a stretch of long grass and tangled vegetation and up a sharp rise — terrain that any sensible bird would have flown over. But the black bird strode on through, looking very serious and self-preoccupied.

The robin doesn't always bob and bounce, he sometimes just lowers his head and runs.

But the black bird walks. He walks, plods, trudges, methodically and unconcerned.

§

There was a tunnel of mirrors, an immense tunnel, with numerous passages running off it. I knew this without going inside.

The tunnel was the object of a game. Men entered it with guns, and there were other men inside with guns, and the idea once in there was to kill or be killed.

I was standing to one side of the cave's mouth with some friends of mine. We all had guns, but mine was only a toy, a water pistol, although it looked like the real thing. With a water pistol for a weapon I had no intention of entering the cave, and when the others went in I stayed behind.

As I stood at the entrance waiting several dead bodies were dragged out and thrown at my feet. Some had their heads half-blown off. Among those I could recognize were two of the friends I'd been talking to only minutes before.

A most voluptuous-looking girl was sitting nearby with her back to me, and to take my mind off the horrors I'd witnessed I went over and put my arms around her.

Alas! I woke clutching my ribs with one hand, holding them when I thought I was holding a girl.

Perhaps there's something after all to the Old Testament tale of Adam and his missing rib.

As I thought over my dream I slipped back into sleep and resumed it. I can do that sometimes.

There was a great oaken beam above the tunnel entrance and Harold was sitting on it with his legs dangling and a machine gun across his knees. Below him the girl I'd tried to embrace was helping to drag a body out, bending over with her back to me, giving me a nice view from that angle.

A police car was parked not far away. I was glad my gun was just a water pistol because I didn't want to get arrested for carrying a deadly weapon.

You might think that doesn't make a lot of sense, since the game being played was illegal and there were men with deadly weapons killing each other all over the place and *they* weren't getting arrested. But they might have used me – an armed but peaceful non-combatant – for a scapegoat to give the appearance they were doing their duty.

Anyhow, I got tired of all that, and took a walk along Water Street, and there was an old woman there with an art studio, and she had a display of sculptures laid out in front of her store. There were bizarre abstracts scattered about, and several life-like nudes reclining across the sidewalk, but the work that most caught my attention was a bust of Nietzsche, with his big General Bullmoose mustache. As I stood before it the bust's mouth began moving – there were sounds coming from it! Soon it was chatting back and forth with the woman, like a thing alive. I heard the old woman ask it a question: "What was Jesus Christ?"

And Nietzsche replied – I don't know what he replied. His voice was muffled and I couldn't make out the words.

It probably wasn't very complimentary, Nietzsche being who he was.

When he stopped talking I complimented the woman on her work, and asked her if the bust was for sale.

No, she said, nothing of hers was for sale.

She didn't want to talk to me so I continued on. In front of the Five & Ten Store a burly rough-looking man staggered up and grabbed hold of me by the shirt-front. This sort of encounter was quite common on Water Street, drunks coming from the tavern looking for fights. I knew if he threw me down I'd be in trouble because he wouldn't scruple to put the big boots he had on to me. As I struggled with him I saw the sculptress approaching. I'd heard she was extremely strong for her age, or any age, and I convinced the drunken man to back off for a minute so we could watch her perform a few feats. She asked the drunk to lie on the sidewalk, and with the walking stick she carried she prodded him over several times, then gave him a series of sharp raps on the head and walked away laughing. I took off myself, running, and the drunken man followed for a while, but I was too fast for him and escaped.

§

The brook I pass every day is greatly diminished from its springtime spate. It runs quietly now in a thin line, and the shores it overflowed are already sprouting long blades of bright-green grass, like swamp grass.

The maple leaves are growing, and there are little sprigs of winged seeds on the branches around them.

The first lilacs are in flower, not burst fully out yet, but displaying their comely lilac colour. I enjoy eating them — a few of them anyway. Moderation in everything, that's my motto.

PART TWO

"Summer has set in with its usual severity."
Samuel Taylor Coleridge

SIX

We're into June now. It's been cloudy and rainy all day, even though early this morning the sun was out. I know it was, because at 5:30 in the morning I was walking around the empty streets drunk and singing.

I was with a couple of guys I met in the tavern, drinkers of my type who think the night should never end.

I'm going to have to mend my ways. I didn't get to bed until 9 A.M. and got up three and a half hours later at 11:30, still half-lit. This lingering intoxication ceased lingering by mid-afternoon and depression set in and I went back to bed after supper and slept for three-and-a-half more hours.

The apple blossoms are in full flower. I picked one and stuck it in my lapel this afternoon while still in my state of euphoria.

§

I caved in, without much of a fight, and went to the tavern again tonight. If I continue recording my daily struggles and capitulations this journal will sound like an alcoholic's diary.

But I'm home now, at one in the morning, and quite sober. Not sober, but quite sober.

The rain stopped and the sky cleared and the stars came out.

My evening was uneventful, but gratifying; uneventful in that I avoided jail or the favours of any maidens, fair, unfair or otherwise; but gratifying to see that among the young men in this town – at least the tavern habitués among them – I'm still in good standing as a citizen and human being.

I'm *quite* sober now, but not perfectly sober. I'll have to keep a bottle of ginger ale by my bed, for my throat and tongue are dry, and will get more so as the night moves along.

Tomorrow I'll be up for Sunday morning mass, dressed in my white shirt and tie and sports jacket. And after mass I'll stroll about the town in the sun. Or so I think now. Maybe I won't tomorrow.

§

Scientists are forever pursuing the "unknown" in the belief that all unknowns must be revealed to man. But they ought to consider there's an ultimate unknown which they can never get to – Death. Until a scientist can subject himself to a personal experiment of being thoroughly and unequivocally dead he should reconsider his belief that all unknowns must be sought out and revealed.

Science would like to blend man and machine together until one is indistinguishable from the other. You have a certain set of them bent on bringing man to a state of total predictability and determinability, and another set busy developing machines to duplicate all human faculties.

It's a sad prospect if the thinking of today extrapolates truly.

I read an article in Playboy Magazine by Frederik Pohl, the science fiction writer, about the possibility of immortality on earth. Pohl is convinced it will come about, and not that far in the future, and he's in favour of it.

A brave new world of beings like Dracula and his fellow bloodsuckers, destined never to die, at any rate not from old age . . .

Pohl obviously doesn't appreciate the implications, should it ever become possible. Who, for instance, among mankind, would be kept immortal? Since it couldn't happen at once and *en masse*, and could never include everyone, else the earth would become too crowded, it would be the wealthy and the powerful, the politicians, the industrialists, the financiers, the generals. These would be the first immortals, and the ones who decided who would join them, and in what capacity.

Anyone perceived to be a threat to their privileged positions would naturally be left out – including writers, traditionally a thorn in the side of authority. Maybe even science fiction writers, by association. They'd all have to kick the bucket as usual.

Of course the new immortals wouldn't be immortal for long. They'd soon be clashing and killing each other off as they've always done.

Pohl also made the statement that a human being could be successfully counterfeited by an electronic computer, simply by feeding it the books the man has read, his likes and dislikes, a record of his past, and so on.

This is so stupid it doesn't bear talking about. I'm doubtful now whether he was serious.

He's the sort who believes in man's progress through science, that a future instinctively hateful to most of humanity is the most desirable future.

I read a novel by him once, and it was bloody awful, the worst kind of escapism fiction. I'd have done better to read a Buck Rogers comic strip.

§

We did it up in fine style last night, or I did – five of us in my little room with a quart of whisky, a case of beer, a pint of lemon gin, a good edge from the tavern before coming up, and a *tape recorder* one of the boys had.

We sang all sorts of bawdy songs – *Roll Me Over in the Clover, the Ballad of the Halifax Whore, Red Wing, Sam*

Hall . . . I elevated the tone a bit by doing the old folk lament, *Peter Emberley*, and we ended with a reading of a couple of salacious stories I wrote. I say we ended, but it was the old man who did the ending, storming in and breaking up the party. "Reading your dirt in here! There's three other families in this house!"

So I'm up this morning with the *Theme From Exodus* on my record player and with nowhere to exodus to but the valley of the grape, which is where I'll be making for.

My voice I found interesting — not as I expected, of course, but quite a clear and melodious voice. It was the first time I heard it, having never been recorded before. I sounded somewhat Scottish, but talking I sounded like a local guy. All in all a fairly interesting voice and one I don't mind. With something like that you never know, you could discover you sound like Donald Duck.

We got fairly merrie at the tavern, as I said, and when we left, before going to my place, we stopped in at the bootlegger's and then drove out the dump road in Nick's car and began *dancing*. Four of us, while Ross Trowbridge played the mouth organ. Shuffling around doing an Indian war dance, and then pivoting like a chorus line, the inside man holding firm and whipping the others around him in a circle — a centrifugal force dance. As we swung round and round Jackie who was at the end of the line went flying off and landed in the waist-high grass by the roadside. We had to tramp about in the dark for a while before we found him curled up in a ball, half-asleep.

While we were in my room swapping those off-colour tales I mentioned, Nick said he had one he could tell but he'd only do it if I wrote it down and put his name on it so people would know it was his. He didn't want me selling it and getting the money for myself.

"I'll copy it in the morning," I said.

"With my name on it?"

"Right at the top."

"Don't forget."

"I won't."

"It would go good in a book. Anyway, here it is . . . Did you ever try to piss with a hard-on and grunt so hard you shit your pants?"

"No."

"Well, I had a girl out one night and I got her in the back seat of my car, and I had my fly open and her pants down, but I had to piss real bad and I wanted to get that off my mind before going any further. So I got out of the car and went back in the bushes, but I had a big hard-on, and you know how hard it is to piss like that? Eh?"

"Yeah. Go on."

"I grunted like a bastard, trying to force it — and shit myself!"

It's no wonder the old man came in. You could have heard Nick out on the street, and we were all laughing our heads off.

"What did you do then?"

"I scraped the shit off my shorts with a stick and climbed back in the car and fucked her. She never noticed nothing."

"Well, the girls you get after are pretty high-class there. Maybe she noticed but was too refined to say anything."

Nick cackled. "Maybe."

Jackie Hooper, the guy who landed in the bushes, was in the hospital to have his appendix out last month. The hospital is Catholic, the Hotel Dieu, and is run by nuns, the Religious Hospitallers of Saint Joseph. Nick went to visit him and told us about it later.

"Jackie was in bed and he pulled me close and said, who are those women running around with curtains on?'"

Jackie's a Protestant and is close to being legally blind, if he's not there already. The glasses he wears are thick as magnifying glasses.

§

Though I sometimes act like a lord's son, and could possibly play the role of one, yet I think I'm descended from working folk, for I feel guilty when I talk to someone who gets up in the morning to go to work. I feel I should be doing the same.

In truth, I'm looking forward to my teaching job now. Not only as a means to keep me away from the drink, but to satisfy my conscience.

§

I passed two little girls playing this afternoon, one of them down on her hands and knees and the other standing. The girl on her hands and knees said, "You be the mother kitten and I'll be the baby cat."

§

Last Friday night this same Jackie Hooper and I left the tavern with our money all spent and went wandering the streets looking for someone who might have a bottle to share. We had no luck, but in front of Grogan's Grill we overheard a guy say he thought there was a beach party down at the Grove, which is a small swimming spot on the Shore Road just outside town. It's about a mile walk, but it sounded promising and we weren't doing anything better at the time so we set off to have a look. It was pitch dark along that old dirt road and as we got closer we saw the light of a fire flickering in the trees.

There were three girls and about a dozen airmen around a blazing bonfire. They weren't wearing uniforms of course but we could tell an airman when we saw one and that's what they were. Jackie wanted to turn around and go back but I said we didn't walk all that way for nothing and let's see if we can't borrow a drink or two off them.

It was quite dark beyond the circle of the fire. We eased our way in and stood around for a few minutes and then started talking to several of them. We didn't pretend to be airmen, just a couple of friendly guys. I told them Jackie was a Presbyterian seminary student home for the summer holidays. He had two years of study behind him and one more to go before he became a full-fledged minister and I'd brought him out with me so he could have a first-hand look at the way people lived in the real world. I figured he should get around and mix with the people the way Jesus did.

Jackie didn't know I was going to say any of this, it was a spur of the moment thing; I didn't myself until it popped into my head. But he caught on at once. He actually looked the part, being a small timid-faced guy with big thick glasses.

He squinted at his watch in the near dark, nervously adjusting his glasses. "My gosh, it's getting late, Walt. I should be getting home."

"It's early, Jackie."

"I know, but . . ."

"The night's just begun."

"Mother's probably sitting up . . ."

"Come on! You're on your holidays, aren't you? She won't mind."

"Well, maybe, but . . ."

"What's your rush?"

You could see he was fighting with his conscience; twisting, turning, being pulled one way then the other. It was a struggle, but in the end the wild side of him won out.

"Oh, I guess you're right. What the heck!"

"See?" I said to the airmen. "That's the kind of minister he's going to be. None of this holier-than-thou stuff."

"I don't go to church much myself but I got nothing against religion," one of the airmen said. "It helps a lot of people."

"The padre at the base is a good man," said another. "I respect men like that."

"My folks are religious," said a third. "Never miss church on Sunday."

People love sentimental stuff when they get drinking.

We could hear some loud drunken swearing going on in the background and one of the fellows we were talking to hollered at them to mind their language, there was a minister present.

"Don't worry about it," I said. "Jackie's pretty broad-minded in his way. Eh, Jackie? He doesn't drink though. He told me he's never had a drink in his life, if you can believe that. He doesn't know what he's missing."

"You're right there, buddy."

"A drink never hurt no one."

"The priest at the base, Father O'Herlihy, I hear he don't mind having one. I hear he's a regular in the Officer's Mess. Over there saving souls, eh?"

"Come on, Jackie. You can't let a priest get ahead of you. It won't kill you — if it does you don't have to take another. You can quit right there."

"Here, your reverence," one of the airmen said. "Try a snort of this." He held a pint of rum out to Jackie, who backed away, like it was a serpent. We laughed, keeping at him. He went through a lot of humming and hawing, but finally gave in and took a large swallow. "Whew!" Gasping and coughing. "That's strong!"

"It's good, eh? How does it feel?"

Jackie exhaled like he was breathing fire, and said in a choking voice, "I don't know. I think . . . I guess . . . it feels all right . . ."

"See! I told you," I said. "Jesus Christ was a drinking man himself, Jackie. He changed water into wine when they ran out at a wedding. There was wine at the Last Supper too, he and the Apostles got into it. What kind of rum is that?" I said to the airman. "You don't mind if I have a taste of it myself?"

You can believe me or not, but that's what we did. The world of inebriation is not like the world of sobriety. I haven't given the whole conversation leading up to the drink, it was more drawn out and round-about, but that was the general way of it.

My minister invention wasn't only to get free drinks, but so they wouldn't put the boots to us — a couple of town guys crashing their party. I figured they'd respect a man of the cloth.

There were cases of beer lying around and we dug into those. We guzzled until an inevitable fight started, and then like ships in the night or a couple of free-loaders getting out while the getting was good, slipped away under cover of darkness.

§

My fear of time. Why is it when faced with empty hours I get restless for a way to fill them? Why can't I just sit in a chair and let them go by as they will? Is it because like many in this world I'm in a hurry, as though I had an important destination to reach, other than the grave?

Everything is in flux, on the move. There's no reason I couldn't simply sit and watch life go by. I needn't worry, there would still be change; I wouldn't turn to stone. A man changes in his thoughts while sitting still. And his body grows a little older.

You might think it's the youthful fire in me, this restlessness. That might well be if I weren't so indolent at the same time. Wanting to go and do, I go nowhere and do nothing.

So what is it about empty time that disturbs me? Do I feel if I don't fill it usefully my value as a human being depreciates? I don't like seeing myself doing nothing, for then I have to tell myself to do something and maybe there's nothing I can do to satisfy myself. And even if there is I'm probably too lazy to do it. Too lazy, or in some instances, too inhibited or fearful. I'm urged on and held back at the same time. And to escape this condition I seek diversion, the most complete and least taxing of which is drinking — which has attractions all its own, regardless of other considerations.

If I simply sat down for an hour and thought, wouldn't that satisfy both requirements – the doing and not doing? Yes, but what of the hour after that, and the one after that? From two in the afternoon, when the anxiety begins, until three at night when I go to sleep, is thirteen hours. I am incapable of just thinking for thirteen hours. I have to do something else for a good part of the time or there's a time vacuum.

A time vacuum . . . Isn't that what I'm afraid of? A vacant unknown stretch ahead and what awaits should I enter it. I have a dread, a foreboding of coming up against a blank white wall, like a movie screen, and when my last thought is projected onto it the vacuum created sucks me into a world of nothingness. And I disappear forever, annihilated.

But surely I can't be drained so readily.

In any case it's a deficient picture. A man in prison may be subjected by necessity to this same situation, month after month, and may end by being the better for it, if it doesn't drive him crazy.

And there's the monastic life. It's true monks rise early, but mornings generally speaking are the easiest to endure, and for the rest of the day they're kept busy with manual work and prayer and chanting – and they go to bed early and sleep like logs, as men do after a hard day in the fields (hayin' and prayin'). Still, they have their silence vow and their times of meditation, and are perhaps none the worse for it. In medieval times it might have driven them to drink, a habit they were notorious for, but I don't believe they've kept up the practice.

I can give others the benefit of the doubt. I don't deny the existence of people who can sit motionless day after day, in a meditative trance; I just don't understand them. They're made of different stuff from me.

My fear of empty hours . . . It's really a fallacy in my outlook, for there are no empty hours ahead of me, only some that are more filled with activities than others. Take the damn clock away with its numbers and there wouldn't be any hours. If we wanted we could call daylight one hour and night another hour. And I'd just have to get through one hour a day!

There wouldn't be a problem if I lived wholly in the present, like a dog or a cat, but I'm human and people do anticipate, and do fear the future, or there would be no anxiety and there is.

Am I afraid of a too long and thorough look at myself? Not at all. It's one of my favourite pastimes.

Reading satisfies me, but I'm too restless to read every day for more than five or six hours. Sometimes, quite often in fact, reading does the trick. But that too can feel like time wasted, as opposed to *getting things done*, which society has instilled in us is what we should be doing every day, lest the Devil make work for our idle hands.

The problem of time on one's hands is universal. It results in boredom. Witness the ennui of the idle rich, the constant reaching for distractions of one sort or another. Or the premature death of the retired man with no job to fill his day. Men need stimuli, they need to forget about themselves, get out of the confines of their own minds.

§

I didn't drink this evening, but I managed to spend two dollars and a quarter not doing it. I went to the first fifteen minutes of the movie *El Cid* and then walked out, taking my popcorn with me. That was ninety-five cents down the drain. The offal that gets on movies screens these days is something scandalous, and it all finds its way to Bannonbridge. Before *El Cid* we had *Beach Party* – "what happens when 10,000 girls and boys get together on 5,000 beach blankets!" Actually, nothing. That is, aside from a lot of bad dialogue.

After leaving the theatre I went to the poolroom and spent the rest of my money.

§

June 17. In some parts of the province it snowed last night, and everywhere the temperature was below or barely above freezing.

According to the evolutionists (I quite enjoyed Darwin's *Origin of Species* by the way) all animal life came out of the oceans and onto land, with the exception of those fish the biologists call mammals who stayed behind. And some of the species who waded ashore progressed further and took to the air, but not man who remained earthbound. Man got stuck at the second stage, still longing to sprout wings but unable to do it. The damn things just wouldn't sprout.

Every man yearns to fly like a bird and get up into the heavens. Look at how he prefers living in a penthouse to a basement apartment. He wants to be further off the ground. He *envies* the birds (not the worms and bugs and garbage they eat but everything else), and doesn't in the least believe he's got it better than they have. Birds are free as a bird, they have no traffic lights or stop signs to impede them, no baggage to carry around when they move, and neither do they sow nor do they reap for the Father in heaven provides for them. And they get to fly south every winter and get away from the cold.

I tried to put all that in a poem, but I guess it's good enough this way.

I'm not really convinced by Darwin's evolution theory. It appears to be true, but it could be like a teller in a bank handing you money. It appears he's giving you money, and you can even say he is, but of course he's not, the money is already yours; it just looks like he's giving it to you. In other words, something may be a falsely perceived part of a larger picture. For all we know the earth and the creatures on it and the sun and the moon and the stars and all the past arrived in one package and are no more real than a movie reel about them. What if what happened yesterday, never mind a million years ago, exists only in the mind? Or in the communal mind, the mind of the spirit, common to us all? Try to reach out and wrap your hand around yesterday. Try to wrap your hand around a minute ago. They don't exist outside the mind.

I throw that out for your consideration, in case you've read Darwin yourself and are feeling superior to certain of your fellows. It's no good being self-righteous and self-complacent, because the truth is, none of us knows what the hell's going on around here. Not where we came from, what we're doing here, or where we're going. We can have an opinion, but that's it.

§

I dreamt last night about a lioness and her cub being attacked by a pack of dogs. Large and mighty as the lion was, and as valiant as the little cub was, the dogs were vicious and too many in number and killed them both. I was rooting for the lion, and at first didn't think the dogs would attack an animal that large and powerful. And even when they did I thought her slashing claws and flashing teeth would drive them away. But as quick as she sent one dog down two more were back at her, fighting for her throat.

I doubt there's a moral or philosophic observation to be gathered from that. It was just one of those things that happens.

§

At the tavern last night I delivered an impromptu lecture about the absence of a cause among Canada's young men. Religion is either believed in or not, but lukewarmly one way or the other. Some people, the majority, go to church but don't think much about God; others don't go but don't think much about it either. There is little colour in politics in Canada, and most citizens are indifferent, following the party of their fathers, but not really caring. There is no mass poverty to lament.

Apathy, indifference − French Quebeckers excepted, these are the moods of young Canadians. The talk at the tavern is about girls, sex, sports, drinking, work (or lack of), but never anything of consequence. These young men are like old men already, putting the time in, lying back and lazing in the sun.

I told them that and they laughed and resumed talking about girls, sex, sports, drinking, and work (or lack of).

§

As I was strolling along last Saturday afternoon a little girl rode her bicycle onto the sidewalk and stopped in front of me. Her girlfriend stayed out on the road with her bike, giggling.

"Do you collect guns?" she asked me. She was seven or eight years old.

"Yes," I said.

"Do you want one?"

"Sure, where is it?"

She unclasped her hand and gave me a tiny green replica of a blunderbuss, probably from a bubblegum machine. She laughed, delighted with her joke.

"Oh, thanks," I said. "It's just what I need to go hunting with."

Further down the street another little girl, about the same age, was swinging on a swing.

"Do you think it will *ever* stop raining?" she said. A light rain was falling, though the sun was out.

"No," I replied.

"Do you like rain?"

"Yes, don't you?"

"I hate it."

"It cools a person off after a hot day."

"I don't like rain at all."

The rain was very pleasant, to my mind, with the little silver drops shining in the sun.

I wish the older girls were as friendly and ready to talk to me as these little ones.

§

Every evening after supper I go through two hours of useless, wilted, half-alive existence, and the heat is no help (my window faces the setting sun).

As a young boy I was very active, running all over town, taking in or taking part in every game, contest, show, exhibit that was taking place. I had friends in all seasons, friends my age, older, younger, poorer, richer – even college students were my friends; they were kind and attentive to me for I was a bright little boy (with a beautiful sister they were all after).

It seems I spent myself in my young years. Now I do nothing but lie on my bed and read and smoke and look out the window – and drink. It's true that most other young men drink, and when not drinking hang out in the pool hall or Grogan's. Some play baseball and others watch them playing. But that's no consolation to me.

Perhaps there *are* things to do, and I'm just too idle to look for them. I don't mind admitting the fault might be my own. I admit it to myself all the time. But still, I have my doubts, for if I know of nothing to do how can I know there *is* something? Does anything unknown exist before it's known? Does the proverbial tree that falls in the wilderness make a noise? Is there a tree in the wilderness to begin with? Is there a wilderness?

§

It's hot in my room. My neck gets sweaty and my shirt sticks to my back. The sun has gone down but night comes reluctantly. It's still quite bright. A lawnmower drones. Two men shout a greeting at each other and begin talking.

§

Very hot, with a hot wind blowing.

I sat by the shore for an hour after supper watching the waves splashing in. The waves were high and hit heavily against the shore rocks.

Last night I dreamt I was living on a south sea island. I had a pretty native girl for a wife and we had a brood of fifteen kids, and I felt proud as hell.

§

I got in a fight a few nights ago at Henderson's Beach. In the morning I had a bruise or two but nothing serious. We were all drunk. The guy I was fighting with tried to knee me in the privates and I threw him down and we rolled on the shore grass. He was punching me and I had one hand on his throat trying to choke the life out of him. He kept punching and I clawed at his face and next thing I knew I was out of there and on my feet and sliding around to the back of the bonfire and into the darkness, making myself inconspicuous. The guy was an airman – there were about twenty of them on the beach. I don't know if they were the same bunch Jackie Hooper and I befriended that other night because away from the bonfire it was dark as Egypt and impossible to make out faces. And as I said I was drunk. They prowled around looking for me but I hid myself in their midst like I was just another silhouette until they packed up and left. My glasses were lost but I found them later with the help of Nick Doyle's car lights. It was his car we came in, four of us. Nick got in a fight too. I have a vivid memory of him against the firelight catching a haymaker and doing a complete backward somersault off the bank that overlooks the shore.

What keeps me drunk for a string of days is too much the night before and too much the morning after. I'm no sooner out of bed than I'm into a pint of beer or a glass or two of wine, and the madness, the chain of drunkenness continues unbroken.

That first drink in the morning is the best drink there is; it's usually better than any point in the drunk the night before. It's hard to resist, if it's there, and almost impossible to stop at that point once I've had it. To stop is to slide back into torment and gloom, and to keep going is to open up all sorts of delightful possibilities.

The streets are teeming with young boys and girls newly freed from school. On every street you meet them, and from further off hear them shouting.

The wind from the west is warm and fragrant, bringing the smell of summer grass and leaves and flowers. A few flecks of rain fall at intervals. The long grass and bushes bend and tremble in the wind. I pick an orange blossom but discover I have no buttonhole in my lapel. I walk down the street inhaling the fragrance, then put it in my jacket pocket.

To the narcissist, his face is like the sunrise: though he sees it every day he is always eager to see it again the next morning.

Evening comes and the air is cooler. A cat sits on the road under a streetlamp. Another cat walks towards it, silent, stealthy, looking very intent.

This afternoon across the river the wind blew dust off an unpaved road, where the new bridge is to be built. A truck driving along the road dragged a wake of dust and then buried itself in it when it turned and drove back the way it came. There were kids swimming at the shore below the bridge site.

The tension, the suspense of it all. Will anything happen today — is it possible I'll think of something to do? At what point will the weight of inactivity and absence of stimulation burden me most? At what point will I break and head for the tavern or liquor store? Will I feel like reading and get through the afternoon dry, having suddenly found an urge to read one of my paralysingly dull books, which are all I've got left unread? Thrillers like Alfred North Whitehead's *Process and Reality: An Essay in Cosmology* and Immanuel Kant's *Critique of Pure Reason?* And be the first person in history to ever finish either? Or might I not come up with a new street to walk on, one that has remained unknown to me, despite having lived in this little town all my life? What if, outrageous hope, someone should come and visit me? What of all the contingencies in the world can happen tomorrow? You never know. I can think of nothing.

For me, this past month and a half, each day has been an adventure in boredom.

SEVEN

The night wind steals in the window in soft gusts, growing cooler as the night grows deeper; the high-pitched song of crickets fills the air. Occasionally a cat moans, a door slams, someone shouts from across the street. In the kitchen the electric clock buzzes quietly, and at long intervals the refrigerator gives a start and begins to generate and whine.

I'd have gone swimming this afternoon but my bathing suit was buried at the bottom of a crate of empty wine bottles, and the old man had the afternoon off and was lying on his bed, and his bedroom is but a few steps from mine, and I didn't want to rattle all those bottles digging it out.

Living is an art — the art of deception of self and others.

You need parts to play in order to protect yourself and satisfy others. You must learn how to act at all times and in all situations.

I'm not objecting to this fact. I appreciate the realities of life and man's fate, and do what I can to adapt. I'm constantly training myself in playing roles.

Granted, I'm more conscious of my *self* — more self-conscious if you will — than the next man (witness my lack of fluidity and "naturalness" vis-a-vis the other actors), but that only means I need to work harder. Life is, as many have noted, an art, and art requires training, self-discipline and practice. You can have an aptitude for the art (though I have little or none) but of itself art is not natural or it wouldn't be called art.

I know why people play parts. This morning I woke up feeling low, remembering a crazy letter I wrote and mailed last night – while imbibing – to Professor Jane Rowley, the pretty biology teacher at St Tim's. I felt scruffy, aimless and empty, and the thought crossed my mind that it would be nice if I could just be a mad hairy poet. Macbride, a wild eccentric who goes his way without giving a damn what anyone thinks, and of whom any strange behaviour might be expected.

I saw the comfort, the secureness of slipping into that part, where I'd be either accepted as an eccentric (which would be fine, we all like to be accepted) or rejected for being an eccentric; and if the latter, why, it's the *poet*, the character I'm playing who's rejected, not *me*, personally, the man behind the mask. And it's not just a poet I'm portraying but a mad one, so what else would you expect?

Anyone could figure that out. By the time I did I was out of bed and taking myself not so seriously.

Some more on the role of the poet. Poets have been drunks and debauchees, and yet been considered great men (usually after they're dead and not bothering anyone). So if I were a poet my drunkenness and debauchery (the latter still in the potential stage, due to lack of opportunity) would have justification. It's what poets do. Poets have been rejected by society and later recognized and eulogized; they've been lonely, and through their loneliness reached depths of insight unknown to more normal men. In all this and more I would have a positive answer to my predicament. And if I'm not acceptable in life I can delude myself I will be when I'm dead and gone, which would give a person something to look forward to.

§

Her complexion is of the Mediterranean type, naturally tanned, her face round, features slightly heavy. She has a friendly and intelligent smile, bright liquid eyes, appealing lips. When she smiles she squints a little, which becomes her. Her hands are rather strong-looking, perhaps somewhat masculine. Though at first impression she seems a bit stout, she's actually nicely shaped, her figure very much a woman's.

The trouble with this description, though it may be accurate enough, is that it doesn't convey the *complete* impression she makes, which overshadows any flaws there might be in her separate parts.

She's an extremely attractive girl. Down-to-earth, good-hearted, with just the right touch of shyness in her nature.

Or so she looks to me, from my observations.

I'm talking about Professor Jane R.

§

A man with a downriver French accent was sitting beside me at Grogan's counter tonight. We were both drinking coffee. He'd paid for his when served, which almost no one does, and from habit and without thinking Judy the waitress gave him a bill later when she was making them out.

"I already paid for mine," he said. He was about fifty, with a thick mustache.

"Oh, I'm sorry," Judy said. "I forgot. I'll give this to Walt."

"Just pass it down the line," I said.

She handed the bill to me.

"I don't want to have to pay for my coffee twice," the man said.

"No. Of course not," Judy replied, smiling.

"It's bad enough paying once. Fifteen cents for a cup of coffee!"

I looked at him, thinking he might be putting her on, but he was serious.

"It's fifteen cents everywhere," she said.

"You don't pay fifteen cents anywhere else."

"Oh, all the restaurants charge fifteen cents now."

"Anywhere else you go, down in Moncton or anywhere, you pay a dime."

"We used to charge a dime but the other restaurants raised it to fifteen cents, so we changed the price two months ago."

She spoke to him politely, unruffled by his manner.

"Fifteen cents for a cup of coffee. Tabernac! That's expensive."

"I know . . . you're right, it's expensive . . . for a cup of coffee . . ." Moving down the counter, putting some dishes in the sink. The Frenchman stomped out, still in a huff.

§

In my relations with girls I no longer think of sex as the *sine qua non*, since far too often I've ended up with the *non* part (and "far too often" states it mildly). If you're fixed on one thing and will settle for nothing less, and you don't get it, then you're left with nothing. It's wiser to be flexible and be happy with what you get. As they say in Logic class, half a loaf is better than nothing. *Nothing is better than sex, but companionship is better than nothing, therefore companionship is better than sex.* And maybe in the long run it is. In a higher sense or something.

§

July 6. Up at seven-thirty this morning to begin my first day of summer school. I'm more used to going to bed at this hour than getting up at it.

§

In the tavern last night Paul Mooney who's a high school teacher told me he'd assigned his English Composition class to write a poem about winter. "Try to use metaphors and similes – imaginative language," he told them. "Remember, it's poetry you're writing, not prose." He gave them some examples, such as this one from Shakespeare: *"night's candles are burnt out"*. "See, the poet doesn't just call stars stars, he calls them candles."

The next day he had some of the students go to the front of the class and read their verses, but his exhortations had fallen on deaf ears; there wasn't a poetic word among them. Then one student, a boy named Edward Cady, raised his hand and said *his* poem had poetic language. Mooney asked him to read it, which he did, as follows:

"In winter I go to the shed,
and look around and get out my sled,
And make cool balls when the snow is right,
and throw my balls if I'm in a snow fight."

"Of course the class roared, they thought it was tremendous," said Mooney. "He's now known as Cool Balls Cady."

§

It's Friday afternoon and I've already done my lessons for the weekend. It feels good to be a student again, with new books to read. I'm especially looking forward to *A History of the English Language,* as well as a book on phonetics.

I have a bottle of cheap Sauterne in the fridge, a mild wine as befits a gentlemanly drinker like myself, and am sipping away at it.

Dreaming last night I got myself into a position where I had to stop the dream and change to another one. The situation was intolerable: I was in the back seat of a car with a certain fellow, a local man, driving from Saint John to Bannonbridge, and I'd opened a can of pop before suddenly realizing he was going to ask me for a drink of it. He was a half-retarded individual, with huge wet lips, saliva dripping off them, and he had a bad temper. If I refused him I was afraid he'd take a swing at me.

I knew he wasn't half-witted enough not to guess my reason (that I thought him loathsome) if I gave him a drink and then said, "Keep the can, you can have it all – I don't want any more."

The can was already opened so there was no way out. So I braced myself, disgusted about the whole situation, and said, "I'm changing this dream, erasing it!" And with an effort I succeeded. It was all done quite consciously while unconscious, in my sleep.

§

I took a bath this evening and went into the bathroom after and it smelled like someone had bathed a dog. I kind of thought I needed a bath. I actually don't mind the smell of a wet dog.

If a book I read by a Dr. Peck is to be credited, that odour should attract girls, for there will be an aromatic association of me and a dog, and according to Dr. Peck women prefer men who are like dogs, simple, guileless, affectionate, trainable, leashable.

This afternoon I passed an interesting half hour watching ants. Two of them were dragging what looked like a dead wasp across the sidewalk. They kept pretty much in time with each other, working in unison, except every now and then one would stop suddenly and brace his foot making the other swing around in a full circle. Sort of a practical joker.

Once off the sidewalk the going was much less organized. The dead wasp was four times the size of both ants together and his arms tended to catch on straws and blades of grass. The ants tugged him through jungles of grass, up sliding sand hills, over and around boulder-like pebbles. To see what would happen I steered another ant of their kind (they were black ants) towards the two, and the instant he saw them he joined in and lent a hand. As they lugged their cargo closer to home more ants appeared and gave assistance until finally as many as eight were pulling, tugging and pushing all at the same time. At intervals one or another, often several, would break off and dash ahead and circle a few times and come back, perhaps scouting for enemies or more helpers.

The party ran up against any number of obstacles. Two or three times I thought they were beaten but they overcame and soldiered on. Their efforts were frantic and not always concerted: sometimes they even pulled against each other. There were a couple, obviously brighter than the others, who instead of just pulling at the wasp ran ahead and removed obstructions from the way.

I noticed one thing that happened at each of the very worst impediments, where further progress seemed impossible. Where four or five ants could make no headway at all, working together, all of a sudden another one would step up and take hold of the burden by himself and with a super-ant effort lift it clear and they'd be on their way again. I couldn't tell if it was the same ant every time but it might have been – an ant Hercules.

At times I was tempted to give them a hand and clear the path, but I refrained; I wanted to see how they managed under everyday circumstances; and they did manage – by the old ant-like qualities of perseverance, cooperation, dedication, and strength. They brought the wasp to a large ant hole that looked like a miniature cave in the side of a hill and dragged him down out of sight.

They'd brought him a long way, and with their fine sense of direction it was done all in a more or less straight line.

Just to see what would happen I dropped a small red ant at the doorstep of their cave and blew on the ground. A swarm of black ants appeared magically and one of them caught hold of the red ant and ran down a hole with him (there were some smaller holes around the main one). But in no time the red ant was back up again, and of his own will went down another hole! I can't explain what this was about. Possibly the red ant gave the black one the slip and stepped into the nearest doorway to shake him – or it could be he throttled the black ant and his blood was up and he thought he'd take on the next-door neighbour too. Red ants are supposed to be vicious. I tried the experiment several times, with different red ants, but nothing happened. Their swarming bigger cousins left them alone.

I suppose the obvious explanation for this is that the first red ant came to an agreement with the black guys and a truce was agreed on between their two tribes. Whether it was more advantageous to the reds or the blacks is to this moment clouded in mystery.

§

I was drinking a pint of Guinness stout this afternoon and fell asleep halfway through. Not because of the stout, but because I've been averaging about four hours sleep a night this week. I've had to get up early for classes but I still have the habit of staying up most of the night either out carousing or lying in bed reading.

While I was asleep I dreamt about the pint of stout, how I'd gotten drunk on it.

Guinness is hard-tasting stuff. When it rolls down your throat it tastes fine enough, like a rather sweet beer, but when it hits bottom and the taste comes up to your mouth it's bitter – really bitter. I don't know anything else quite so bitter.

I couldn't take more than a sip at a time (I mean of the one I was into while awake), drinking it like straight rum. With every sip I shuddered and shook my head and let out an oath. It was so strong it actually made me laugh. I have three more pints in the fridge and am wondering if I'll be able to get through them; maybe when they're cold, which the first one wasn't. About a third of that still sits blackly on my table.

I rather like the smell of it though.

Don't worry, I'll drink it. It's got alcohol in it.

§

Tonight I saw a fellow I know get slapped in the face by a younger guy and not retaliate.

He didn't retaliate because if he'd done so a fight would have followed and since he was much smaller he'd have got the worst of it, and then some. He obviously wasn't very happy about the situation. His pride was hurt; he'd looked weak and cowardly in front of people.

I was musing about it after, and thought, if he'd had in mind the teachings of Christ and believed it was morally good to turn the other cheek, then he shouldn't have felt bad at all. On the contrary he'd have seen his passivity as an example of putting his beliefs into practice, and rejoiced.

In theory anyway. For had he been bigger and stronger and able to beat that other guy he most certainly would have done it, and Christian principles be damned.

The subjugated Jews of old, the subjugated lower classes of all eras, the weak, the meek, the humbly situated — for these Christ gave the means of reconciling themselves with what otherwise they might think a base way of life.

However, when Christianity came into *power* . . . What emerged then was something quite different, a decidedly anti-Christian position on the subject. You can be sure in medieval times that if someone struck a bishop or a cardinal there'd have been no cheek turning — other than the cheeks and other parts of the offender as he turned on a spit over a nice hot fire prior to some fun on the rack and a good disembowelment to teach him a lesson.

It must have been hard for the Church in the Middle Ages not to *crucify* heretics and anti-clerics, since it was such a popular form of public torture and execution. But even they could see that it wouldn't have been quite the thing, Christ having gone that way and all.

It appears Christianity — real Christianity — works best for the oppressed and downtrodden of the world. The trials and sufferings of this world are then nothing for after death they'll have eternal happiness. And while they're inheriting the earth or frolicking in heaven, their masters, the rich and the powerful, will be trying to squeeze a camel through the eye of a needle so as to sneak into paradise themselves – and that's a real needle, not one of Cleopatra's Needles with a big hole cut in it; an ordinary sewing needle with an eye that a malnourished gnat couldn't squeeze through.

The new religion of Communism, on the other hand, asks from the impoverished and subjugated action rather than resignation, and promises a worldly, not an otherworldly heaven. With the decline of Christianity (and I suppose of other religions) Communism these days is in many parts of the world the people's new religion.

The charity of Christ is indisputable. He brought relief to countless men and women. Communism is charitable too, in its way, in theory. But neither Christianity nor Communism has remained what it was intended to be at the outset.

Once mankind get its hands on something watch out. Give becomes take, charity becomes greed, equality becomes privilege, humility becomes pride, and faith becomes cynical self-interest.

§

The Church holds as a doctrine that man has free choice, but it doesn't believe freedom of choice is good. It much prefers blind obedience from cradle to grave.

As a strict doctrine, freedom to choose is acknowledged, because there are people who don't follow the ways of the Church, and if it's not their choice it would have to be God's.

The important part of man's freedom in relation to God is that obedience without full choice is meaningless – or lacking in meaning to the degree that choice is not full.

This aspect, the importance of *obedience to conscience*, and the act of will which is free choice, is overlooked (or played down) by the Church because it diminishes the position and power of the Church to make people's decisions for them.

It's right for the Church to teach. But to judge and enforce is God's prerogative.

To do things like excommunicate — or imprison and torture and burn at the stake, as in olden days — is to undermine man's birthright (if such it is) of free will before God.

Enforced obedience demonstrates nothing to God.

If the Church listened to Christ and understood him there would be no Church as we see it today.

This is the way Christ's followers should act: have no hierarchy, teach the love that he taught, judge not but be tolerant and forgiving, and gather (informally, without pomp and circumstance) to worship God in communion with others, and in remembrance of Christ and the wisdom he left behind . . .

That would seem the ideal. It has practically nothing in common with the Catholic Church as it is today, in this year of 1964, and as it has been for a good many centuries.

Not that I don't like churches (with a small "c"), their architecture, the peace one finds on a quiet day within their doors; or the exaltation felt when an organ plays, or a choir is singing. But when they were a-building I doubt there were many popes and cardinals and bishops and such out at the site whipping mortar onto the stones. The common people built them with their sweat and donations, and they did it (in many if not most cases) in homage to their creator; as humble participants in something greater than their individual selves.

§

I just struck me that I no longer hear the sound of frogs singing after dark. Perhaps it's because there are none in the neighbourhood where I'm living.

I'm not talking about French people, but the little amphibious creatures who dwell in boggy dead-water ponds, the legs of which the French are said to enjoy eating.

I don't hear crickets now either. They used to join in and sing along with the frogs at night. Some people would say, "listen to the crickets", and others would say, "listen to the frogs". I never saw a cricket in the flesh, they were like little children weren't supposed to be, heard but not seen. But frogs were a common sight.

The Catholic Church – St Cecilia's, the parish – has a large farm on its property and raises cows and pigs and chickens, the purpose being to provide butter and eggs and milk and meat for the priests and nuns and the boarders at the university. They also grow vegetables and have hay fields and cow fields scattered about the vicinity of the church. One of the cow fields was across the street from where I lived as a kid, and being on the side of a hill there was a swampy area at the bottom that was ideal for frogs.

We'd hear them, the frogs, and the crickets, on warm summer nights. Families would sit out on their front steps, the grown-ups relaxing after the day's work, the kids watching mosquito hawks and pointing out the Big and Little Dippers in the sky and trying to find Cassiopeia's Chair and Orion's Belt and other exotic constellations we'd heard of but had no idea what they looked like. And always in the background the sound of frogs and crickets filling the air with their shrill familiar music.

The house I lived in has been done over and is unrecognizable now. My family has disappeared, just the old man and myself left and living elsewhere.

The large family that had the other half of our building has also dispersed, the children grown up and out on their own except for the two youngest who are teenagers now.

Of all that great world then, the world of childhood, there remains only what's in my mind, what I remember. It's saddening to think of a whole world, which our neighbourhood was, being blotted out; and for all the present and future will know might just as well have not existed.

One evening after supper we heard a Jersey cow in the field across the street bawling its head off. We looked out the front window and saw it had its horns caught in the wire fence. It must have seen some better grass on the other side of the fence, greener stuff, and poked its head through and now couldn't get it back out. It kept bawling something fierce until my mother told my father to go over and free it.

"You grew up on a farm. You can do that."

He didn't want to though.

"I'm tired, I can't be bothered with damned cows. Let someone else look after it."

She made him go though. In our house her word was law. Grumbling, he got out of his rocking chair and crossed the street and wrestled with the cow's head with the creature bellowing bloody murder until he got it free.

I was very proud of him. A deed like that, rescuing that big cow with its sharp horns, took courage and strength. None of the other men on the street had done it, they were too afraid and weak; it had been left to my father. He freed the cow and came back and sat down and rolled another cigarette, like it was nothing at all.

It was just the way I wanted him to be, the way a father should be. Brave, strong, and heroic.

§

I just made three terrific claps at a mosquito and missed him every time. Sometimes I get chasing mosquitoes or flies or moths around the room in the early hours of the morning, naked and cursing to myself, with the light on and the blind not drawn, gambling (and not really caring in my anger) that no one is passing on the street below to see me. I go springing over my bed, slapping the wall with a book – hollow resounding whacks – the frantic creature darting every which way until finally, indiscriminate in my frenzy, I kill him (naturally) on my pillow or sheet, making a bloody splotch on the white fabric.

I get under the sheets again then, panting, but satisfied, having destroyed the beast and appeased my nerves. If I've been reading I return to my book, otherwise I put the light out and try to sleep. Minutes later there comes a distinctive buzzing and another one appears, and in a silent rage I spring at him like a bugacidal maniac.

This one dives and hides under the bed and I get down on my knees and crawl under after him, lifting the bed up and down on my back to flush him. But all is silent. I see no more of the thing until I've settled down again and forgotten him altogether. And then . . . bzzzz . . .

§

Imaginary conversation between a raving lunatic and a certain pretty lady professor. We tune in as the lady says to him:

"I thought you'd talk to me."

"I intended to," the lunatic replies, "but a number of things stopped me . . . Four things stopped me. First of all, the day after you received my letter I passed you sitting in your car and you turned your head away. Maybe it wasn't you or your car but I thought it was and that you were offended. The second thing was, I was thinking of asking you to a dance at the Legion in Newbridge but before I could make up my mind my money ran out, and I had no way of getting more. That was the only place I wanted to take you because they have a bar . . . which brings me to my third reason. I didn't have the courage to speak to you the way I wanted without being half-lit, or at least having a few snifters inside me; and I knew that was a bad foot to start off on. Once begun it's hard to change the pace — I'd have to drink any time I was to meet you, otherwise a quite different person would show up in my place, one considerably less lively. And aside from the loss of self-respect this involves (having to drink to face you), I was determined about that time to stop drinking anyway.

"And now for my last reason. The night after I mailed my letter to you I got drunk – not insensibly, but not really sensibly either – and about two in the morning I found my feet had led me to your window. Your light was on, which was why I didn't pass by, but went over and stood beneath it . . . I stood there in the dark, staring at your window, on the verge of calling you to come out. I stayed on that verge, that cliff edge – a remarkable balancing feat – for more than a minute, my tongue refusing to obey my command to speak. I wouldn't have had to call loud, for your window was open.

"I saw I was getting nowhere this way, and took a walk along the side of the building, debating furiously with myself whether to make my presence known to you. I couldn't make up my mind – I was a breath away from dismissing all caution, and a bit further away from giving the idea up and going home. When I'm drinking like that I can't bear unresolved issues. From my short distance away I looked at your window, and then the light went out. That seemed to decide matters – I had to act now. So I walked firmly, almost hastily, back to your window, opened my mouth – and said nothing. I tried again, but some strange caution restrained me. I stood a long while looking fixedly at your window, waiting for you to see me perhaps. Then I got the idea you'd seen me already, and had turned the light off to leave the building and come out to me. Remember, I was drinking, drunk in fact (though well aware of my actions), and was capable of harbouring any crazy notion. And in any case, I wasn't going to leave even the most remote possibility unexamined. I went around by the door and waited. You didn't come, of course, and I walked slowly past your window, picturing your eyes on my lonely, disconsolate, retreating form – and thinking you might yet call to me.

"I went home then, cursing myself for having been so cautious, and not doubting I'd thrown my opportunity away. Telling myself you'd stayed up to such a late hour on the chance I might appear, and when the night wore on felt the vigil hopeless and turned the light off and went to bed. I berated myself for not acting, knowing how much has been lost in this world through fear of taking risks.

"The next day I got out of bed, still upset with myself, but for a different reason – not because of what I failed to do, but for what I almost did! For being such a fool in even going near your window like that. I thanked the gods for stopping me from doing worse, and determined such madness would not happen again, and accordingly was disposed to stay clear of you and let you forget I was alive.

"You see," he concluded, "there are reasons why I haven't approached you again."

A pause.

"Well, don't you have anything to say?" he asks. "Why are you looking at me like that?"

§

When I was in Montreal I dreamt several times that I'd returned home to New Brunswick and was in danger of not getting back in time for work. It was almost a nightmare the way it scared me. I had a dread both of being back in Bannonbridge and of getting fired from my job.

Then when I got home again and going to college I dreamt I'd gone back to Montreal to work – and *that* frightened me in the same way.

So perhaps I'm on the right path after all, even if my conscious mind can't see it.

§

The sun as it goes down is behind clouds, but it penetrates and colours them like a light-gold reflection on burnished metal. A light breeze stirs my curtains, the air sweet with the smell of summer.

A man passing on the street says to another who's trimming his lawn: "A great shower, eh?"

"Yes, sir!"

It must have rained while I was napping after supper, but the streets are all dry. There was time for that since I was asleep for two and a half hours. I have to sleep sometime.

I awoke to rock 'n roll music in the next apartment, with a boy and girl inharmoniously adding their voices. I felt well-rested, and didn't mind. For a while. Then I put a jazz record on to drown them out.

I've been thinking about that strange parable in the gospels, where the vineyard owner hires a man to work all day and pays him ten dollars, and hires another to work just the afternoon and pays him ten dollars, and then goes and hires another man to work only the last hour and pays *him* ten dollars. The first man is naturally outraged, and says to the owner, "What the hell's going on here? I slave the whole jeezless day in the blazing sun and that so-and-so bastard works one hour and you pay him the same money! You call that fair labour practice?" And the owner, the master, says: "Shut your goddamned mouth. You agreed to work for ten dollars and I paid you ten dollars. If I paid the other men for working less that's my business. I'm the boss here."

In other words — how the parable translates —

"I'm the boss here (I'm *God!*) and if I want to play favourites I will. I don't care whether it's fair or not, or what you think. If you don't like it you can go f**k yourself."

§

I saw a firefly tonight, on my walk. I haven't seen one of those in years. And the moths were out, fluttering around the streetlamps like snowflakes.

Today was one of the hottest we've had. My room is like a brick oven now.

I had the honour of influencing this Sunday's sermon. The parish priest, Father O'Connell, brought up the subject of "filthy magazines", and what a bane they were to society, especially the young – an unmistakable reference to the controversy I've stirred up with my letters to the Moncton Times defending Playboy Magazine.

Well, he's seen nothing yet, wait till my next letter appears. In that one I as much as defend premarital sex and the use of condoms! It's subtle but it's there.

I'm almost sure to get reprimanded not just from the pulpit but in person if O'Connell ever runs into me. I'm preparing my defense in case he does. I'll tell him I did nothing wrong, that I was only following my conscience.

I'll say: "The views I expressed aren't necessarily mine, Father, but they *are* the magazine's views, and I'm defending them on two principles: freedom of speech, and freedom of choice in personal morals even if the choices aren't ones we'd make ourselves or condone. Censorship and other forms of forced Christianity don't help the Church's mission on earth; over time they have the reverse affect. The Inquisition for example, think of the bad publicity that brought on. It still does, even to this day."

I kind of doubt he'll come round to my way of thinking, though.

§

It's raining quite hard, and across the river the sun is sinking below the horizon. I can just see the top of it, red as blood, a dark thick red, and there, just now, a long rumble of thunder overhead. The rain splashes steadily on the veranda roof, the dusk deepens, the sun loses its grip and drops away from the earth, falling to the great infinity of space beneath.

Or so it appears, but appearances are deceiving, according to astronomers. They say the sun is not falling off the earth's edge, but rather rolling *around* the earth, like a small ball held magnetically to a great one – or rather a great ball held magnetically to a small one. And it's not rolling around the earth but the earth is rolling around *it*, and in the meantime the earth is also rolling around on itself, on its axis, like a rolling ball. And it's the sun not the earth with the magnet. Imaging believing all that.

§

A light rain tonight.

That's it.

I have nothing more to say about today, other than that it was well spent: class in the morning, lessons and reading in the afternoon, one glass of Guinness stout before supper (my only drink of the day). Later out to a movie, and a quite interesting movie it was, a documentary narrated by Peter Ustinov called "Women of the World". Then to the restaurant for a coffee and cigarette. A slow walk home. And here I am.

My pretty biology professor snubbed me this morning. In revenge I smoked an extra cigarette.

And there it is, another Day in the Life.

Perhaps tomorrow I'll have more to say.

§

The King Reid Circus is in Newbridge this week and I hitchhiked up to have a look. There's a great ring of tents in a field above the tracks with the usual wheel and board games and wooden milk bottles to throw balls at and coloured balloons to throw darts at and rides like the merry-go-round and tilt-a-whirl and ferris wheel and there's a freak show and a disfigured animal show and a fire eater and a sword swallower and a snake dancer and *two* girly shows — both of which I took in. The first charged fifty cents and wasn't that great — the ladies there (one a redhead, one sandy-haired) were a bit overweight and not overly attractive. They stripped off their dresses and bras and pranced around the stage in G-strings. The high point was when the sandy-haired girl bent in front of me and put a hand on the back of my neck and buried my face in her breasts. The stage didn't project and I was lucky – or pushy – enough to get a spot up against the edge. When it comes to pageants of this type my normal good manners go out the window. I'm not shy with the elbows.

The routine of the girls, after they strut about removing pieces of clothing and doing the customary "bumping and grinding" as it's called, is to go down the line of men who are pressed against the stage and waggle their tits in their eyes and spread their legs close to their faces.

The girls in this first tent didn't have an assistant to handle the music and had to change their own records as the show went along, economizing like the second-rate spectacle they were. And the records they played (including a couple by the Beatles) were worn and scratchy. They didn't even have a picture or a name for their show on the facade out front.

The second tent, the Esquire Girls, appealed to a higher class of fair-goer, and cost a dollar. Naturally I went for the bargain first, but the cheap show just whetted my appetite, so I ran right over to the other one, without a moment's hesitation. Here the stage projected, giving three ample sides to support the elbows of the spectators.

There were two girls in this tent as well, but they were younger, in their twenties (the others were in their thirties if not older). Both had attractive figures, and their faces, for all anyone looked at them, were certainly passable. One was petite and dark-haired and had a shy appealing manner; the other – a tall blonde with large high breasts – was loud and vulgar. When she first looked out from behind the curtain to check the house, one of the men shouted, "Come on out, we want to see what you got!" And she said, "Don't worry, boys, you got a treat coming! I got a cunt like the Grand Canyon!"

When they were satisfied the tent was full, the music started and the girls emerged, first one and then the other. They were wearing frilly bras and panties, and went along the line of men spreading their legs and pulling aside the crotch of their panties, giving the men a peek at what was there. The tall blonde led off, and when she came to me she pulled her panties all the way down and fondled her (as she called it, or as Chaucer would say) — her cunt and passed her fingers across my face. This brought a great roar from the men and she repeated it several times as she moved along, raising more cheers and hoots.

For the second act of the two-part show the quiet girl came out first, wearing a tiny black G-string and nothing more. I was near where she made her entrance, and she stopped before me, legs spread, lowering herself closer, tantalizingly closer, and I could see the pubic hair on both sides of the string between her legs, a sight that thrilled me to say the least. Then she leaned to me until her breasts were an inch from my face — large full beautiful breasts waving gently before me (I'm getting horny again just writing this stuff). During the course of the show this girl made several stops in front of me. I looked up into her eyes, and saw them looking into mine in a quite friendly and intimate way, with a hint of good-natured amusement.

Then she left the stage and the tall blonde came out, bared breasts bouncing, and strode back and forth displaying herself. She was wearing what amounted to a fringed belt slung low on her hips, with *no* G-string. She stood before the men with her knees apart, holding the frills out of the way, giving them a good look, although she hardly had to do that, given the height of the stage and the angle from which she was being observed. Halfway through the record that was playing she removed the frilly belt and finished her act fully naked. And then the cute girl stepped out a moment striking a nice pose, hand on hip, and she had nothing on either.

I'd have to say the second tent was worth the money.

§

Last night I got hammered. It wasn't my intention to but Harold came by in the afternoon and we bought some wine and went to the seashore. Once started you have to keep going, so after supper I traipsed down to the tavern and didn't leave till it closed. I got very drunk and remember little of the evening's latter half.

I missed classes this morning. On my bed sheet there was a broad green and yellow stripe where I'd thrown up in the night. In the afternoon I changed the bedding and took a bath.

My spirits have been quite low all day, as happens after a drunken night and sick morning.

But I'm not going to drink anymore this week, and I hope not the next.

The sun didn't show itself today, and around supper-time the sky became very dark and it rained for a while.

After the hot sun and the mugginess of the previous few days the change was welcome. I don't think I'd mind if it stayed dark and rainy.

§

Guy in the tavern: "I see you got an answer to your latest letter in the paper."

"Yes, I saw that."

"Is that the same fellow you were writing against before, who wanted to ban Playboy Magazine?"

"That's him all right."

"When are you going to answer?"

"I'm not."

"You're not? Why?"

"What's the good of picking him apart if he jumps back together again, the same as he was before?"

"You can't let him have the last word."

"Sure I can. As far as I'm concerned he's got it – and he can stick it up his arse. I only wrote the letters for enter-tainment anyway, to shake things up. Well, not only that; I think I had a good cause. But by now anyone with a grain of sense can tell the fellow's a nitwit."

"Why don't you write a letter and put that in it?"

"Why don't you write it yourself if you're so interested?"

"I couldn't write a letter."

"Well, there you go."

That wasn't the proper answer. The proper answer was, "Then shut up about it." But I was too cultivated to put it that way. Too much the gentleman.

§

A hex must be laid on Bannonbridge: within the past week five men in town have died, one of them twenty years old. The young fellow was a passenger in a car whose brakes failed coming down the St John Street hill; it went through a stop sign and got broadsided by a pulp truck. Usually young people get killed in late-night drunken smash-ups, but this was in broad daylight and the lad was sober, which hardly seems fair. Then three men between the ages of forty-two and fifty-six died of heart attacks, two of them living across the street from each other with just a day's interval between their deaths. The last man, Teddy Ross, an amiable, clownish homosexual who was drunk most of the time, fell off the wharf this afternoon and drowned. I haven't heard the story firsthand from any who were there and witnessed it, but there would have been many, because today was hot and the wharf where he went over is a favourite swimming spot for youths of the town.

I happened to go there for a swim myself today at four o'clock, before I heard about the drowning. By that time the body had been found and taken away. A Norwegian steamer was tied up at the main part of the wharf loading pulp but at the upriver end where everyone swam there wasn't a soul in sight. I found this strange, and it did occur to me that someone had had an accident, perhaps drowned. It's not only Sherlock Holmes who can make such deductions. I didn't go in the water, but sat and smoked a cigarette, then went across to the tavern for a couple of draft, where I heard the news.

The man who drowned was a big-bellied fat fellow. When I was a kid he was a mechanic at the White Rose garage and whether he was working or not always wore work clothes and looked and smelled like the inside of a garage, a sort of grease and motor oil smell. He lost that job from drinking too much but even years later still went around in the same clothes. As a little kid I remember him saying to me, when we passed on the street, in his big fat-guy high-pitched voice, "Ah, you're a cute kid, Macbride! Do I look like an Indian to you? Do I look like an Indian to you, kid?" Followed by a flood of giggling laughter.

What he meant by looking like an Indian I don't know.

In the summers he spent a good many afternoons at the wharf, I would guess to be around the young fellows in their bathing suits, sitting in his old work pants with his shoes and shirt off, his big belly hanging out, a bottle of wine at his feet. Sometimes he went in swimming. He was legendary as the only person in town to have reached bottom off the end of the wharf. I've seen him go down and stay an amazingly long time before coming up with a handful of muck.

I can picture when he fell off, having lost his balance with too much wine in him (or having been pushed off by the kids in play, something I've also seen happen), with just time to let out an exclamation, "Uhhh!" and then the great splash, and all the lads on the wharf laughing, going to the edge to look over.

And the wait – the long wait for him to come up. Nobody worried because he never surfaced quickly. The speculation, the amazement at how long he could stay under. A couple of boys running to look round the corner of the wharf, thinking he might have swum underwater and come up there to fool them. He wasn't there but nobody doubted he'd bob up *eventually*.

"Jeez, he's been down quite a spell . . ."

By now they've stopped laughing, everyone staring at the water, the truth sinking in.

Depending on who's there someone either dives in after him followed by one or two others, or else there's indecision until one of them says they should do something — get a boat, go for the police, pull the fire alarm. A couple of boys run towards the front street for help while the rest wait, standing at the wharf edge looking down at the water. Meanwhile men are coming down the pulp boat gangway to see what the trouble is.

If the boys pushed him over no one will ever know. Even if they get found out nothing will be done about it. They obviously didn't mean to drown him so it was an accident, one of the hazards of a man being drunk and overweight and sitting on the wharf's edge with who knows what fancies simmering in his head.

§

A five-year-old girl to a girl a little older who's walking up the other side of the street: "Cindy! Tell me, is Marvin married?"

"Oh, Nancy!"

"Is he? He said he was married."

"Nancy, you're crazy, do you know that? He's five years old."

"He said he was. Marvin said he was married."

"Sure, Nancy, he's married. Sure he is."

Little kids have a nice command of language.

§

This old notebook is suffering and will continue to suffer this week. My sister Maria and her husband Edward are visiting with their four kids.

It was sweltering hot today, despite the sun being behind clouds. I went for a swim at the Station Wharf where the young folk are back swimming and lazing around again. They only stayed away a few days because of the drowning.

The water felt cold to the touch but warmed up once I got in it, as is generally the case, unless it's early spring or late fall. Besides the usual crowd of boys there were five teenage girls on the wharf, none of them what you'd call pretty. Plain-looking, would be the word. They had an inner tube for floating on, and a small stack of movie and romance magazines for reading on the wharf, and a package of filtertip cigarettes.

§

This morning I got a haircut, after going three months without one. Doesn't look too bad at all.

I'm good now till mid-September, anyway.

§

This afternoon Maria and Edward and I drove in their car to a beach near Richibucto. I met an attractive girl there, a beautiful girl who liked me immediately, as I did her. She was French and spoke no English but I talked to her anyway, and to her mother, a fat and friendly woman who did speak English. The mother told me they were from Quebec City. I splashed the girl while she stood trying to work up courage to get into the water and made her laugh. I'm sure we'd have done very well together, had the stars been more kindly configured.

When the mother said her daughter couldn't speak English, she added, "It's too bad for her, eh?"

"It's too bad for me, you mean!" I said.

She liked my reply, laughing. She was a jolly good-natured woman.

Ah, but the girl was pretty, with a gorgeous figure.

But such is my life. The afternoon ended, and with it the romantic tale of the French girl and me. We parted, destined never to meet again.

§

Lots of things to report, but no energy to report them.

Tomorrow we drive to the mental hospital to see my other sister Alice. It weighs heavily on me. I'm hardening my heart in preparation, becoming a man of steel so that I can handle it as a man should.

§

Tonight was good; indeed the whole day was extraordinary. We went to the hospital to see Alice. She's a wonderful girl but I have to forget about her. I'm just not as hard-hearted as I should be, for this life. She seemed so innocent there, like a child.

Someday I'd like to be able to help her. If I had a lot of money and a huge house and a staff of servants and nurses and . . .

Tonight, after we were back, Edward and I went to the tavern. And later at home Maria and I had a few glasses of wine together in the kitchen while Edward and the old fellow discussed the days of Prohibition in the living room. And so on. It's late and I'm too tired to keep on.

EIGHT

'Tis now the very month of August. It's been raining all day today. The schooner Bluenose II is in at the Station Wharf but I haven't been down to look at it yet. At the moment I have no enthusiasm for anything.

Maria and Edward and the kids left this morning, and with them went all life and colour from our house. Admittedly, the children were beginning to wear me down, and I longed for a few minutes' peace to myself. But without them the place seems desolate and empty.

I used to feel something like this as a small boy when visiting relatives came and left. My mother's sisters were outgoing people and brought liveliness and laughter when they visited, and took it with them when they left. My mother and father weren't getting along then, and my sister Alice was acting in scary ways, staying in bed all the time or screaming about nobody liking or wanting her and how she wished she was dead. And Maria, a teenager then, living for the day she could move out of "this mad house", as she called it.

When the happy relatives left, leaving just their empty bottles behind, I felt heartsick and depressed.

I don't so much feel depressed now as wrung out and purposeless. Talking to myself, saying things like, "So what? What do I care? What difference does it make?" As though nothing matters.

It's sad thinking about Alice. You know what I think about? Alice sitting with us in the visiting room for twenty minutes, and when we get up to leave knowing she won't see us again for another year, if that. Just as she hadn't seen us for a year since last time.

She says, "Goodbye, Walt," and her smile is the most innocent smile you can imagine, shy, unsure, like a little child's. She goes back to her dormitory and we walk out of the building and into the sunlight, saying, "My, she seems much better."

I'm really not as tough as I'd like to be.

Anyway, I'll put aside these pictures and recollections, as I've done before, of necessity. You can't let yourself go around feeling like crap all the time. There's no percentage in it.

§

This week is the last week of summer school. After that I'll have three weeks to prepare myself for teaching.

The fields are overgrown with long grass and goldenrod, and thistles with their soft violet flowers. The chokecherries are beginning to ripen; there are some now that are red on one side and green on the other.

Two young men off the Bluenose II were in Grogan's tonight. According to an interview I heard on the local radio station several members of the crew are young men selected by various yacht clubs around Halifax. Apparently it's quite a privilege to be on the Bluenose II, and these two with their well-groomed self-confident air looked privileged enough.

I suppose they learned their seamanship from cruising around the Carribean on the family yacht.

I noticed them when they played a record on the jukebox and sat at the counter where I was perched on a stool with my coffee. They began chatting with Cora, the cute waitress behind the counter, asking her about the annual folksong festival they'd heard was held somewhere around here. She said she knew little about it, and asked me.

"It's in the middle of August," I said.

"It's in the middle of August," she relayed.

"We know *when* it is," one of the fellows said.

"Well, what do you want to know?" she said.

"What is it, anyway?"

Cora turned to me again.

"It's a folksong festival,"I said, with a broad smile.

"Yes, it's a folksong festival," she laughed.

One of them grumbled. "I mean what's it like? I've been to some pretty big folksong festivals."

"It's not big," Cora said. "I think it's just some old men from the backwoods who get up on the stage drunk and sing songs nobody ever heard of . . ." She looked at me for confirmation, and I nodded, grinning at the uncertainty on the boys' faces.

They gave up on us then, thinking we were making fun of them, as yokels traditionally do to dudes and city slickers. They were still talking to each other on their own level as I finished my coffee and left.

§

Okay, so I'm biased against the rich and privileged. There should be nothing surprising about that, given my working class upbringing and the type of testy person I am anyway.

§

I learned today by mail that I'm to be pretty much the whole English and History Departments at Barker's Ridge Regional High School. I'm to teach English I, English II and World History to Grades 10, 11 and 12. There will be two Grade 10 classes and one each of grades 11 and 12. The only thing I won't be doing is teaching the Grade 9 classes because the above will completely fill my schedule.

Three of the courses are provincial matriculation courses. When I read that I laughed, thinking of my poor students, what their chances will be with me for a teacher!

It wasn't a cruel maniacal laugh, but the head-shaking helpless sort.

I know there are worse places in the world than where I'm going. Devil's Island is quite unpleasant, I hear, and the Sahara Desert in the middle of summer. And the Arctic Circle, I understand it's pretty chilly up there.

§

It just occurred to me that I haven't been in jail for a full year.

§

A fellow I met in the Quebec jail while I was there dropped in on me yesterday. His name's Dan, a rambling man, a professional bum, who hitchhikes back and forth across the country panhandling from town to town. He's an excellent story teller and seemed to me at the time, young romantic that I am, to be a fascinating and admirable individual. He's a hard drinker, and has seen the inside of many jails along the way, primarily for drunkenness, vagrancy, or soliciting people for monetary handouts.

I was surprised to see him. Not so much because I never expected to, but because he didn't look the same as I remembered. In jail he'd been washed and shaved and wearing clean jail clothes, and there'd been a jauntiness about him. Now he had a scruffy chin beard, and looked haggard and seedy. From the look of his clothes you'd think he'd spent the night in a ditch, but he said he'd spent it in the Moncton jail. He said he'd thumbed his way north to Bannonbridge and hadn't had a drink all day, even though it was almost one in the afternoon.

I don't know how old he is, it's hard to tell, but probably around forty. We talked a while and he asked if I had any money so we could get something to drink. I told him I was broke and he said, "In that case I'd better see if I can't put the arm on some of the locals." He asked me to accompany him, show him where the churches were. Clergymen were among his chief sources of income.

We set off, and on the way a curious thing happened. I stopped in at the post office to check the mail, as I did every day, and found a letter for me from Susan, Harold's friend, the one I'd spent the night with (in a manner of speaking). In the envelope was a five dollar bill.

It's hard to know why she did this. Perhaps in my drunken state I'd given her a touching story about how impoverished I was, the proverbial starving poet, and she'd been so touched (and touched is the right word) she'd actually gone and sent me money. I might have even suggested she do so (I don't remember if I did, but that doesn't mean anything) and to demonstrate her unconventionality she'd taken me up on it. There was no letter with the money so I can only guess.

Whatever her motive, it was valid currency, and Dan and I got two bottles of Hermit with it, one for each of us, and then picked up a couple of packages of tobacco and papers and came back to my room, shut the door, and got into the wine.

The old man was working mornings and evenings that week, which meant he was home, but he was in his room sleeping — when he wasn't working he was usually sleeping. Four-thirty rolled around and I had to get supper ready. I invited Dan to join us, but by now his bottle was empty (I still had about half mine left) and he said no, what he'd do if it was okay with me was take the rest of the money and go to the liquor store before it closed and get another quart which we could split. I said okay and he left.

He didn't come back. The old man went to work, and I hung around until nine o'clock. By then my bottle was finished and with Dan nowhere to be seen I went out myself to pay a call on Barbara. I guess I hadn't quite given up on her — and possibly she hadn't given up on me either, not entirely, because she let me in, maybe hoping I'd become a different person. But of course I hadn't; I was still me. We spent several hours on the living room couch while I talked and talked and got nowhere and when we'd both had enough I left.

There was still no sign of Dan when I got home. Thinking he'd found somewhere else for the night I got undressed and climbed into bed and was just falling asleep when I heard a groan. I turned on the light and listened. Another groan . . . It seemed to be coming from beneath me. I leaned down and looked and there was Dan stretched out asleep on the floor.

The old man must have been still at work when Dan returned and he'd let himself in. Our door is never locked, nobody locks doors in Bannonbridge.

I left him there, and in the morning I was awakened by his head hitting the bottom of the bedsprings as he tried to sit up, followed by a muffled "Jesus!" He slid out from under the bed rubbing his head.

I glanced at the clock. It was a little after eight.

"You sleep well?" I said.

"Not bad. As well as could be expected. The mattress was a bit hard."

I pulled my clothes on and we sat at my card table desk.

"You want something to eat? I never eat breakfast myself but I can get you something."

"No thanks." Giving me an ironical look, like what kind of question was that. "I'm a light eater when I'm on the road."

I asked him how he'd made out yesterday, after leaving here.

"Oh, you know, you start out to do one thing and end up doing something else. I bought a bottle at the drugstore and was strolling along with it in my pocket when I spotted the tavern and thought I'd pop in and have a look. I don't normally go into taverns, it's not an economical way to drink – unless you run into the right kind of people. Anyway, that's what happened. I ordered a beer and started talking to some guys and told them a story or two and they ended up buying the rest of the night. All it cost me was one glass of draft, and I didn't have to touch my bottle."

"You got a bottle at the drugstore?"

"Where did I leave it now . . . " He rooted behind some books on my bookshelf and brought out a quart of horse liniment. "You ever try this?"

"No."

"It's quite good, if you mix it right. I could use a taste right now. You wouldn't have a milk bottle I could borrow, would you?"

I got him one from the kitchen, filled two-thirds with water as instructed. Keeping the bottle slanted he poured the rubbing alcohol carefully into it, tipping it slowly up and down, allowing the two liquids to blend gradually. When the mixture was to his satisfaction he filled the glass I'd brought him to the brim.

"You sure you won't have one?" he said.

"I don't think so." The stuff gave off a sharp powerful ether-like smell. "Maybe later."

He took a drink and let out a long sigh, rubbing his mouth with his shirt sleeve. He let that work through his system, then had another one, a bigger one. The effect was sudden and pronounced. With just those two drinks he went from being reasonably sensible to absolutely plastered — and not just drunk but badly drunk, moody, incoherent and volatile. And the more of that awful stuff he drank the crazier he got.

He dug a wad of handwritten notes out of his pocket, saying he'd written a book he wanted me to edit and type and get published for him. It was very important I do this, he said. He didn't see any way out of the life he was leading unless he got his book published and became a successful writer.

"You don't know what it's like . . . tramping around . . . place to place . . . going nowhere . . . feel like jumping off a bridge . . . be done with it . . ."

It was strange hearing him say this, because in jail he'd made his vagrant life sound like a great happy adventure, a life he'd gone into with his eyes open. It was the rest of the world with their nine-to-five grind who didn't know how to live.

I had to tell him I didn't know any publishers, that all I did was write poems and I was lucky to get a few of those into scraggy little magazines that didn't pay a cent. I said I wouldn't know how to get a book of my own published if I had one, let alone someone else's.

"You won't help me?"

"I wish I could. It's not that I don't want to. I don't know how."

"I thought you wouldn't mind doing me a good turn."

"I would if I could . . ."

"Thought we were friends."

"We are, but . . ."

He emptied his glass and poured another, staring at me with moist gray eyes.

"I don't think you know who you're dealing with," he said. "I could take you . . . throw you out that window . . . like that! . . . not a man to fool around with . . . pick you up throw you out the window. . ."

It was very uncomfortable, being with someone in that condition. By way of changing the subject I told him I'd try a shot of the rubby after all, and went and got myself a glass from the kitchen. I wasn't overly eager about it; I poured only an inch or so in the glass, and holding my breath gulped it down. It was like drinking hydrochloric acid. I felt it scorch a path down my throat and for a minute thought it was going to burn right through the bottom of my stomach.

He grinned, his mood suddenly changed. "Good stuff eh? . . . smooth . . . a good year."

He finished the milk bottle and mixed another one, and before long I could hardly follow his talk at all, a disjointed repetitious drunken rambling.

At noon my father came home and I had to get the dinner ready. Dan stayed in my room while I ate. The old man returned to work, and Dan finished off the last of the rubby, and was so drunk I didn't know what to do with him. By now all I wanted was to get him gone.

He eyed the clothes rack I have behind my door, a board on the wall with half a dozen nails for hangers. He pointed at my jacket.

"Give me that," he said.

"I can't, it's the only jacket I have."

"Give it to me . . . need a jacket . . ."

"I can't spare it."

"I want it . . . Give it to me. . ."

"I tell you I can't." We kept this up for a while, until I managed a compromise. I gave him my scarf instead.

"Lend me coupla bucks."

"I haven't got a couple of bucks. I don't have a cent, we spent it all."

"Just a few bucks . . ."

"If I had it, but I don't."

"And that jacket . . ."

"I can't, I told you."

"Huh! . . . squeeze blood from a stone . . . want you get my book published . . ."

"Maybe someone else will help you."

"Thanks . . . for nothing . . . wasting my time here . . . time's money . . ."

He rose unsteadily to his feet. He put the scarf around his neck and I helped him into his old coat and he felt his way along the hall and down the stairs. From my bedroom window I watched him stagger along the street until he was out of sight.

It's late at night now, so I guess he's well gone, wherever he's going.

§

Ross Trowbridge who lives across from the Anglican manse, said he saw a drunk fall on the ice yesterday and the minister came out and took him in. The minister told Ross later that he'd kept the man overnight, sobering him up, and in the morning gave him some money and put him on the bus for Fredericton. It seems the man was on his way to see his dying mother and in his grief had got drunk and lost all his money or had it stolen.

§

I was thinking of the time Vladimir Lenin and I were fugitives from the Tsar's secret police. We were by the railroad tracks intending to hop a freight when they spotted us and we took off running. If I'd been alone I think I could have got away but Lenin was out of shape and had short legs and they caught up to us inside the deserted Exhibition grounds as we tried to scale the fence and make for a copse of trees where we could hide. They caught us and – it was a remarkable dream – I know it was because I woke up in the middle of it and agreed with myself that it was; then I went back to sleep. The second sleep continued the dream but it also washed out almost all recollection.

Somewhere else I've written down what I could remember of a dream about John Steinbeck and T.S. Eliot but I can't find it. In this dream Steinbeck was painting a picture and as I'd been doing some water colours myself at the time we had a friendly talk about painting. I found Steinbeck an engaging fellow, easy to get to know. Eliot on the other hand was aloof and pompous, and obviously took himself very seriously.

Since in reality I've never met either of them I assume those are literary judgments corporealized – insubstantially corporealized, that would be. Dream embodiments.

§

I was coming home from Grogan's tonight when I happened upon an accident at the corner of Northumberland and Astle streets. There was a small crowd gathered and a man told me a car coming from the Legion had driven through the stop sign and slammed into a new Ford hardtop.

The car that went through the stop sign was blocking most of Northumberland Street, leaving just enough room for traffic to edge by, and the man who'd been driving it was standing on the side of the street directing traffic. He was wearing a rumpled blue suit with the jacket open, the top button of his white shirt undone, and his tie loosened. He didn't look all that sober. The driver of the other car, a thick-set blond-haired young man, was standing by his car smoking a cigarette.

The rumpled man's eyes were ringed with sleeplessness. There was very little traffic and when a car came along he made a show of waving it past. His traffic directing was quite unnecessary, but he was in the wrong and like a child who's broken his mother's favourite vase he was trying to do some good by way of amends. Hoping maybe she wouldn't punish him as much.

It's not surprising he reacted like this – like a child – since when you get down to it a man drinks to slough off the cares, responsibilities, and inhibitions of adulthood. A few drinks in him and he's a kid again, at home in a world full of joys and wonders (for a while anyway).

But I doubt the law will be as lenient as a mother might be.

§

Myself and a couple of the lads were walking in the dark and the rain Saturday night, making our way from the tavern to the dance at the Exhibition Hall, and as we went along Victoria Street we came upon Corinne and her latest boyfriend sitting in a car outside her house. I could make out her face by the light of the streetlamp, and she seemed to smile, but then as though catching herself, remembering it was her duty or declared position to dislike me, she frowned.

It's quite possible with the two of us leaving town shortly and travelling in opposite directions that I'll never set eyes on her again. And that frown could be the last picture I'll have of her.

§

A sunny Sunday. The man across the street is picking twigs and scraps of paper off his front lawn, keeping the yard tidy. In his back yard, but clearly visible from the street, there are lawn chairs and a chaise longue and a lawn table with a huge red and white umbrella blooming above it.

I've mentioned before how I sometimes tentatively try out "plots" while dreaming. Last night I was watching two strangers shoot pool; there was a lot of money on the game, and I couldn't decide which one I wanted to win, and how he should do it. I tried it one way, then another, and finally settled on the shorter man banking the eight ball into the side pocket. All this was going on in my mind while the men were playing and I was a spectator with (apparently) no control over the game whatsoever. It was true I didn't have; but it was also true I did. Both were true at the same time and this seemed perfectly natural and uncontradictory.

Which might be a clue that there are more things in heaven and earth, Horatio, than are dreamt of in your philosophy. Who can say? An afterlife might have all the amazing possibilities of a dream and more (the more being less randomness and confusion).

And lots of pretty dream girls who are crazy about me and don't change their minds or disappear just when things are getting interesting, as usually happens in my dreams.

§

Our Philosophy of Education professor Mr Burns, demonstrated the either/or fallacy to us last week. "There are thinkers who say education must be either this or that, one thing or the other," he said. "But that's incorrect. What if the solution is *both* this and that, to varying degrees, and not one to the exclusion of the other? Or better still, what if it's neither?" He grinned broadly. "Eh? It doesn't have to be either one or the other. Do you see?"

We saw. Tomorrow we have an exam in Philosophy of Education and have been told by Professor Burns it's to be a "choose-one-of-the-following" type of tests. No writing is involved, all we do is check off the correct answer. Some will be multiple choice, and some true or false.

I raised my hand.

"With these true-or-false either-or questions," I said, "what if the answer is neither one nor the other, or both?"

The class took a moment to catch it — then the recollection of last week's lecture struck them and there was a burst of laughter.

Burns wasn't amused. He'll have a problem getting revenge on me however, if I pick the right answers. He should have given himself some leeway by including an essay-type question or two, and not been so lazy.

§

Went to a movie this evening. The theatre is a smelly place, it holds an odour like unwashed winter clothes drenched with sweat that evaporated into the air over the winter and remained there to ripen in the heat of summer. The theatre has no windows or air circulation system of any kind.

Grogan's where I had a coffee after is worse if anything. There's a mass of thick voluminous community air, breathed in and out until it becomes a sort of invisible fog. It has the distinct smell of a shithouse about it. You feel it doesn't go all the way down when you breathe but catches in your lung passages because of its density. I might have gagged if I hadn't gone for a leak upstairs where the air is thinner, in the rarified regions of the toilet.

On the way home tonight I saw some young pranksters at work. They were standing at the corner of Victoria and George streets and when they saw the lights of a car approach gathered around one young fellow and pretended to be tying him to the lamppost. As the car came closer they bolted, leaving the young fellow behind, and he immediately slumped to the ground as though unconscious. That was the plan anyway, but as the car slowed the young fellow lost his nerve and jumped up and ran after the other kids. I think he was supposed to wait till the car stopped fully and the driver got out.

It was a gang of girls mostly, ten or eleven years old, and their victim was a boy about six.

They're the same neighbourhood kids who've used the old wallet-on-a-string trick on pedestrians. They didn't catch me because I saw the string after spotting them hiding behind some bushes. But the old man said they fooled him. He reached down and zip! the wallet was gone.

They must have learned these tricks from their older brothers and sisters, the previous neighbourhood generation of young jokers. I remember that crew making a stuffed dummy and leaving it lying bent and twisted in the middle of the road. Another thing they did was put a noose around its neck and hung it from a tree limb by the roadside and let it swing in the wind. That was singularly effective and stopped quite a number of cars.

§

I got really drunk last night with Paul Mooney, the high school teacher, and around one in the morning we went into the college residence building and knocked on the pretty biology teacher's door. She didn't answer despite my loud and repeated knocking so I told Paul to go and see if her car was parked outside. She must have heard me then because she shouted through the door at me.

"Get out of here!"

"It's me!" I said.

"I know who it is. Get out of here now! You woke me up!"

So we got out of there.

We went to my place, to my room, and turned the record player on and began arguing about something. We were in the midst of it when the old man appeared in his underwear and told us to turn that damn record player off and quit that damn loud talk there were other people living in this building and if we couldn't be quiet get out! Get out of here!

We turned the record player off and argued less loudly, but didn't leave.

I got to bed finally at four or five o'clock, dead tired and beginning to feel sick. I'd drunk a quart of Hermit, four draft, my share of a pint of rum, and a quart of beer. Of what I could remember.

Just before noon I got up and with a remarkable show of fortitude and head hung low prepared dinner. Four aspirins made no impression on my headache. I didn't eat but went back to bed and slept till three in the afternoon.

§

Tonight I sat for a while on the veranda steps, smoking and musing as I've done so many times about the women who weren't in my life, and about the women who once were and the sexual experiences I didn't have with them.

There were some dingy clouds overhead, hiding most of the stars. A light breeze stirred the air.

From the intersection down the street I heard tires squeal and a car came rushing by with a chorus of male voices singing "Toura-loura-loura!"

It irritated me, a bunch of guys singing like that with the windows open so people would know what fine drunken fellows they were, in the best drunken tradition of good fellowship. But then I thought, am I one to judge? I've done the same myself — and I wasn't trying to impress anyone, just happy to be drinking and singing and speeding down the road in a car.

My school textbooks that I ordered came in. I can see that teaching will be a sixteen hour a day job, at any rate for the first few months. I don't know how I'll find time to manage all the preparation and homework-correcting I'll have to do.

But strangely enough, at this moment I'm looking forward to the job. Don't ask me to explain that.

One thing I'll never do is get drunk on a school night. When I got out of bed at noon yesterday I could no more have taught a class than I could have wrestled a bear – or eaten dinner which I think would have been harder.

§

Beneath a maple tree at night
sheltered by leaves
from a brilliant streetlight
leaves thin as paper
and more white . . .

I came out of the night shadows and into the light of a streetlamp and crossed the street and walked along the sidewalk. As I passed the last house on the corner I heard the voices of girls from somewhere behind me . . .

"It was sort of like jelly," one exclaimed.

"Ahhh!" several others cried in unison, laughing.

I strained my ears but they were too far off for me to make out anything else. As I continued on I could hear bursts of laughter at intervals, until finally I could hear no more.

What was sort of like jelly?

§

I saw my biology teacher at church today. She really is much prettier than I've described her. I say this in spite of the impassable gulf that lies between us now.

She informed St Timothy's bursar Father Brannigan (who's also one of my summer school teachers) of the visit I made to her door, and Friday he saw me on the street and stopped his car and called me over.

"What's this I hear about you?"

He didn't have to spell it out. I knew what he meant.

"I guess we were acting pretty wild, Father."

I was going to say "I guess we were pretty drunk", and would have had he pressed me further, but he simply said, "You'll have to stop that kind of nonsense. You'll be teaching school next year and just one incident like that and you'll be out of a job, and probably never get another one. You can easily ruin your reputation — not around here, maybe, but wherever you're going."

"I'll be reformed when I get there," I assured him. But he didn't hear me, driving off before half the words were out.

Not around here, no, I won't lose my reputation around here. He as much as said that around here I had no reputation to lose.

His lecturing me put me in a bad humour. I didn't like being reminded of my drunken antics several days after the fact, after I'd made peace with myself about them. And not only reminded but *chastised* — and given *advice*, of all the unnecessary and unwanted things. As if I didn't know what I'd done.

I smoked two rapid cigarettes, and after buying the groceries, which was what I'd been on my way to do, went to the tavern for a few glasses of beer. I cooled down once I got those into me.

I was saying, the girl is very pretty. At the end of mass I looked over her way, as I was leaving my seat, and she lowered her eyes. She'd been to communion and was staying after to say her prayers and I suppose she looked down to drive away evil thoughts before they struck. It wouldn't be right to go to communion and then wish someone would fry in Hell, meaning me. Gathering herself, praying hard, O God, you're in my soul now, and thanks for all the blessings in my life, and may I be a good girl, ever virtuous, pure and chaste, never getting laid, especially by rowdy drunks like that jackass sitting over the way there —

I hope what she really felt was guilt for turning me in. You wouldn't see Jesus do something like that. He didn't do it with Mary Magdalene, a lowly prostitute, a common disrespected pretty young streetwalker. Instead he took her home with him.

§

Alcoholic drinking, insofar as it's not biologically determined, or in as many cases as it's not, is a result which is a cause and a cause which is a result, neither preceding the other by very much, and in the end not at all.

Perhaps scientists say that in all cases alcoholism is determined biologically. I don't know what they say. But I don't think it's the case. An alcoholic may have a physical reaction to drinking that is more pleasureful and gratifying than it is to non-alcoholics, and no doubt he does, but if there were no other reasons he could still walk away from it as he would from chocolates or strawberry ice cream knowing too much wasn't good for him. It's his mind and emotions that get him hooked. The drink provides him with an ease, a self-confidence, a bright outlook, a fearless sense of adventure, a view of himself and the world that is more to his liking than what he experiences when sober.

What I mean by "a result which is a cause and a cause which is a result" is this. It's actually quite obvious. A man is dissatisfied, and he takes a drink and it relieves his dissatisfaction. But when the effects of the drink wear off not only is he back where he was before but he has the knowledge of where relief lies. He was just dissatisfied before, now he has a happier state to compare it with, which makes the dissatisfaction worse and the call to drink greater.

And then, the effects of drinking are more than a magical transformation that takes place: in the aftermath the man often feels sick and disgusted with himself. There's the money spent (when drinking he has no thought for the morrow, the carefreeness of the day being sufficient thereunto), and the time that could have been better spent wasted, and the loss of will and control, the misbehaviour, the risks to life and limb, the embarrassing things said to friends and strangers, the weight of society's disapproval . . . All this heightens his usual and ever increasing (as he builds up more reasons for it) unease when sober, and makes the call to escape into drink much stronger, and ultimately more abysmal. The term "vicious cycle" is aptly applied here.

§

One of the waitresses at Grogan's told me a minor brawl took place earlier in the night between a new posting of airmen and some local boys. It was her opinion the battle would continue at the dance, and whether it did or didn't, there would likely be an outbreak downtown after.

I wanted to hang around and see, but it meant waiting close to an hour so I went home.

The curious thing is, I like to watch fights, but I don't like to see one person hit another.

That doesn't sound very reasonable, so perhaps it's best to conclude that I'm fascinated in spite of my repulsion by two men fighting each other. My primitive side and my civilized side having different preferences.

§

On this rainy morning my summer school B.Ed. courses came to an end. I'm quite sure I passed all of them. And now it's on to studying high school Grammar, Literature and History on my own, so I can be ready for my students.

§

I've been reading the regulation Grade 12 literature textbook in preparation for teaching it in a few weeks. It's a laborious business. One poem, Milton's *Lycidas*, was exceptionally troublesome. However, I mastered it and to such a degree that I wrote an elegy of my own in the same grand style. I didn't have to look far for a subject because not long ago Russell McPhee, a sometime drinking companion of mine, got married. I give you my poem:

RUSSELLUS

Though but an unlearned wight, new to the pasture,
And bearing a green oat,
My little skill scarce enough to
Herd the sheep, and our one agèd goat,
I grab presumptuously for the laurel yet undue,
And a myrtle, and strive to blow a brave note
For the passing of my friend, Russellus,
Who was known to sing a rugged line
Down in the boxcars, over a quart of wine.

O, thou muses, aid me in my chant,
Keep the tone aloft
That I may not drift into cant.
Orpheus, break out your lute
And strum it sweet and soft
So I may be inspired from a humble mute
To declaim with fire
And fall worthily, when finished, with a pant,
The spirit of my song still rising
Like a seraphitic choir
Beyond the scrannel pipes of critics criticizing.

Not long past the lowing herd
Standing solemnly in Jardine's field
Behind the racetrack, where we sometimes drifted,
Oaten reeds in hand, and in our belts concealed

The grape of Bacchus, witnessed our hearts uplifted,
And gave ear to our inspirèd lays.
Blithe were our hearts then, and as the car
Of Phoebus moved further down the sky
We played upon our oats in praise
Of old Bacchus, and 'twas far
From the thoughts of either swain
That one would to the wedded state
Fall prey.

Weep for Russellus, O weep into your beer,
The swain who once sat that chair
Expect not to see him here
Except, perhaps, but once a month on Saturday
When Amaryllis feels he's in her hair
And sends him to the tavern for some cheer;
But what is that? . . . For Russellus, we knew
(His brother shepherds), was nightly at the door
At seven, when the shearing feast began,
And if he had ten dollars, ten he blew,
And never at a loss to bum for more,
Standing up the customers to scan
To see who'd sold a sheep today
Or what young shepherd had got his pay,
And Russellus would blow a mournful ditty
On his reed, till the man who lent his ear
Gave evidence that none since Orpheus played
A stronger note, by adding to the kitty;
For Russellus was irresistible to hear
Could wheedle and moan and pester so
He rarely walked away unpaid.
And now there comes in dire lament
One who rues the loss of Russellus,
Old Kit the bootlegger, bowed and bent,
Sheds a tear and wails for Russellus:
"O, him I lent two quarts of Hermit wine
And since have seen nor hide nor hair of him

Who said he'd pay me ere the week was gone!"
Ah, loud she keened, old Kit, and wrung her hands.
And that is just the voice of one
Who weeps for Russellus; and many more there would
Within my rough verse, as many as the sands
That make the shingle of Alpheus, but more
Would still not justice give our parted shepherd.

But Russellus, take heart, you are not lost
Though things look bad. Though you've gone
From the fields, abandoning your oat and song
And the apostleship of Bacchus, a seeming pawn
In the Devil's game of matrimony, take heart!
For methinks it won't be long
Before you're back among the meadows, striving hard
To catch up, and once more play your part,
And drink your share, and reproduce your oaten lays,
Returning to your old and carefree ways,
Thankful for the saving fact we swains
Who stayed behind have noted —
And which gives us hope in all our pains
For our lost shepherd, Russellus —
The fact your Amaryllis, unlike you, old sot,
Is working and you're not —
She'll work, she'll slave, and in a month or two
Will be sick of supporting a lump like you —
Your happy marriage will reach its end
And you'll be free as a lark again, my friend.

And now my rustic numbers crudely o'er,
And trusting that the reader's wiser than before,
I don my cape, and sheep hook under arm,
And bidding all the world go free from harm,
Stride ere it closes to the liquor store.

§

This evening I was startled out of my reading by a rapid cloppety-clopping in the street below. I looked out and saw two horses trotting by, riderless and harnessless. As I watched they turned into a yard, and a few minutes later two boys came running up the street after them. They stopped at the corner of our house, and after a consultation ran across the street and into a yard, but not the right one.

Neither horses nor youths ever came out again.

§

The fundamental reason for all art is that every man sees himself in every other man. All mankind is a family, and you can't be an artist without realizing that all people are your brothers and sisters, and the final good is the good of the family.

You may write off some of them, or even most of them if you're misanthropically inclined, but as an artist you work on the assumption that because it's a family there are people you've never met who will benefit from what you do. As for the others, you know they *could* benefit if they weren't so goddamn stupid.

(Just couldn't resist that.)

Seen from a distant perspective, you have a familial species often fighting within itself, but never getting away from the need and desire in each individual to be part of the community and do his share. It's like a great ant hill of men running every which way but all working within the boundaries of the species, and sometimes within the larger boundary of all creation.

§

Ran into Harold on the street. He tells me he's decided to go into the priesthood! I think that deserves an exclamation mark. The arrangements have been made and he leaves for the seminary next week.

He also told me our mutual friend Susan is now up in the lunatic asylum.

I was surprised. She was a little strange, certainly, but I didn't think she was that far gone. I asked him what happened, expecting something analytical and profound, and he didn't disappoint me. He said, "She flipped her lid."

§

A fine bright day today, the wind fresh and autumnal, so much so that I nearly froze in bed this morning. By eleven-thirty I had the blankets air-tight over my ears in an effort to keep the chill air out. I keep the window open and could have shut it but I refuse to because it's still summer! It says so on the calendar.

People from the country around have a twangy way of pronouncing words that's not easy to convey in print. For the writing of conversation I suppose it would be more precise to use phonetics, if everybody understood them, but of course they don't.

One of my B.Ed. courses was Phonetics. It was a good one, as was *A History of the English Language,* both taught by Father Brannigan, to give him his due.

I'm not always criticizing and belittling. I can say favourable things now and then, when the occasion merits it.

In the pale orange of the setting sun and in the darkness of the leaves and the early dusk rising from the earth, while the sky stays bright and blue . . . in all these I see the distinct beginnings of fall. There's a ripeness in the air, the rich ripe smell of autumn. It's by the smell you first know a new season is coming on.

Fall days are the most brilliant. The cooler air seems to sharpen the edges of buildings, fences, chimneys.

I notice some leaves are already changing colour. One maple tree is halfway between green and red, and there are yellowing leaves in all the elm trees.

The chokecherries are ripe. When I walked downtown today I picked a few off a tree and ate them.

I remember when I was a kid we were told by older kids — and maybe by our parents, I'm not sure — that if you drank milk after eating too many chokecherries you'd die of poisoning. Five or six cherries before drinking milk was considered safe: after that you took your life in your hands. When you ate them gluttonously, not planning on touching milk for a while, your teeth took on a brown coating and the inside of your mouth felt like it was lined with fur, and in your throat there was a "choke" feeling. Once you started eating them it was practically impossible to stop.

They were tasty, but English cherries were better by far. There were only two English cherry trees in our neighbourhood, and a few more in other locations in town. As kids we robbed them at night, climbing the tree and eating the cherries hand over fist and filling our pockets. Sweet, tangy, juicy flesh around small pits — there was nothing quite like them.

So far as I know there are no English cherry trees left in town. The last one was bulldozed to make room for a used car lot. The others, like those in my old neighbourhood, were chopped down by their owners. It was the same with the August apple trees in town. The owners got rid of them because they were tired of gangs of kids climbing their fences at night and robbing them. Since they were growing the apples they thought it would be nice to have an apple or two for themselves but to guarantee this meant an almost nightly vigil, a continual chasing off of young boys, and they evidently felt it wasn't worth the effort. So they cut the trees down and had no more worry. They had no more apple or cherry trees either, but it was one thing or the other.

I think they should have read Samuel Johnson, who had this advice to pass on: "My friend Dr. Madden of Ireland said that in an orchard there should be enough to eat, enough to lay up, *enough to be stolen*, and enough to rot upon the ground."

There was one plum tree in town, and we plundered that too, but only once. Once was enough. Plums aren't really designed for our northern climate and they were hard and sour, like certain discontented people. Not myself, who's tender and sweet, but some other people.

§

Harold predicted he would die in a matter of minutes, and he did, right on schedule. He dropped to the ground, quivering and flopping and foaming at the mouth, then lay motionless. His brother Leon and Paul Mooney were with me when it happened.

"Get some hot tea," I said. "We'll pour it down his throat, that might save him. Quick!"

They ran to Harold's house, which was half a block away, and I heard the kettle begin to boil. A moment later it stopped, and Leon and Mooney came out onto the veranda.

"We're not going to go running down the street with a cup of tea," they said. "That would look stupid, wouldn't it?"

It was too late anyway. Harold lay on his back, arms outstretched like Christ on the cross, eyes staring fixedly at the sky, dead as a doornail. As I stood over him I thought, there must be a God, because Harold had been talking to this God, so he said, and God told him he'd die in a few minutes, just as soon as he recited a verse. And he recited the verse (which I didn't catch, being too busy scoffing; it sounded like a lot of gibberish anyway), and just like that he fell down dying.

I started to walk towards Leon and Mooney, but they ran in the house, so I went back to where I'd left Harold. And he was gone!

I shouldn't have left him by the shore. The ice he was lying on had obviously melted and the tide carried him away.

His funeral was held without the body, and everyone shed a tear and mourned.

And then some weeks later I heard he was still alive and going about town in disguise! It seemed a low trick to pull, after all the hypocritical remorse he'd caused his friends. But I was glad he was alive; the strangeness of his death had bothered me. I kept having the eerie feeling I'd be next, and had been avoiding reading poetry, lest I hit a dilly like the one he'd recited.

NINE

September 2. I woke up this morning with a feeling of disbelief. In less than a week I'll be teaching school! It's madness, I thought. I can't teach school, I've never done it before, I know nothing about it. But there it was: on September 8 I'll climb out of bed and go to a roomful of unruly teenagers who won't want to be there any more than I do. My heart sank at the thought.

I pulled myself together eventually, as I adjusted to being awake. I told myself I'd be all right. I tried to picture less capable classmates of mine who were to start teaching at the same time and who'd find it even worse.

It wasn't so bad once I was up and about. It's the shock on first waking that's unnerving.

§

I walked up the railway track yesterday after supper, almost to the cement plant. On the beach I saw a seagull with a broken wing. I thought at first he was dragging a piece of stiff bark in his beak, but it was his wing, broken and hanging stiffly at his side. He saw me and tried to walk away from me along the beach but went no more than five or six steps before stopping. It was pitiful the way he looked at me. There was nothing I could do to help him; I couldn't take him home with me and I had no way of killing him (supposing I had the stomach for it). So I left him there and continued walking. When I was down the track a piece I looked back and saw him gazing out at the river, broken wing hanging by his side. After a while he took a few steps along the beach and stopped again. Another gull swooped overhead and I thought it might land near him, but it whirled away and came down on the water some distance out, where there were a dozen or so other gulls floating. The gull with a broken wing remained on the shore about a foot from the water watching them. I could still see him when I left the track by the train station.

§

A PARTING POEM

What is Bannonbridge to me
but the neighbour's pink house
framed in my window
a dull cheerless sky
a tree branch bending
over the eaves of my roof
a bottle of wine
a shelf of books
a record spinning dreams
of other places

§

This is my last night at home. Tomorrow I catch the bus for Barker's Ridge and the start of my teaching career. I meant to avoid the bottle for at least a week before leaving, but I was drunk last night, and tonight I've got a start on another one. I've discovered a new girl, an attractive intelligent Protestant girl with a sense of humour who's a friend of Harold's and so isn't put off by off-beat types. Her name is Eva and she's been out of town for several years. I told her I'd be over to see her a little later.

I can expect to awake tomorrow in a state of semi-paralytic apprehension, but it can't be helped.

PART THREE

———

*"This huge world out there, standing
before us like a great eternal riddle."*
Albert Einstein

TEN

I'm boarding at a Mrs Tuttle's house, along with a teacher named Rashid who's just over from Pakistan. He has a bachelor's degree and several year's teaching experience but will earn less than I do because the province doesn't recognize his foreign degree as being up to the standard of what's handed out at home here.

Aside from Rashid I'm the only one on the staff who has a university degree of any kind, foreign or domestic. The others, the principal included, have Teachers College certificates, and so (the principal excepted) they all earn less than the $72 a week I make, despite their years of experience.

Which probably explains the ungodly workload they've saddled me with.

Our boarding house is a large Victorian structure on a country road somewhere beyond the middle of nowhere. Our landlady, Mrs Tuttle, is a widow and a cheerful and kindly old body. She's in her seventies but shows little sign of age, not a line or wrinkle on her face.

There's an ancient barn on the property and a couple of old sheds. The barn isn't used anymore but still houses a buggie and sleigh and other horse-related paraphernalia from former times, all covered in dust and cobwebs. On both sides of the house are fields, and across the road another field rises to a steep tree-covered hill, and in the back of the property there's a field and a brook. And beyond the brook, across the valley, another tree-covered hill. The nearest house to our left is a mile away, and in the other direction there's the school about half a mile distant, and beyond the school are a few more houses and a small general store.

When I first got here and saw where I'd be for a whole year I nearly burst into tears.

§

I have to get out of this place.

§

Today, my first day as a teacher, has been one of the longest days of my life. Not because it was one of the worst, because it actually went quite well, to my surprise; but there was a lot in it, and I'm still dealing with it, preparing lessons for tomorrow.

It's strange to think that only yesterday I was willing to take almost any desperate action to get myself away from here.

My fellow teachers appear to be nice enough people, particularly the principal. Mr Gates is calm, quiet, gray-haired, friendly. The kind of man you'd ideally envision for a boss.

As forewarned, I have the heaviest workload of anyone on the staff, with only *one* free period each week. And I have three matriculation subjects.

Most of my students are girls — I gather a lot of the boys quit school at age sixteen, when they're legally allowed to, so they can go out to work. The girls are cute with their girlish ways, some of them anyway, and giggly.

It's a consolidated school, the students being bused in from a wide area around.

By the end of the afternoon I was beat, talked out, dead on my feet.

Yesterday Mrs Tuttle's house seemed like boarding in Hell. It's not quite so bad now. I'd still like to move, but there's nowhere else I can go that's within walking range of the school.

This stretch of wilderness, where Mrs Tuttle's house is, is actually called Winchester, not Barker's Ridge. It melds into Barker's Ridge somewhere down the road. Because Barker's Ridge is more or less central to the farm region hereabouts, the school was built there and got named after it.

My fellow-boarder Rashid has a heavy schedule too, almost as heavy as mine. He's teaching arithmetic, algebra, and geometry.

§

Mrs Tuttle is having a hard time cooking for Rashid. He refuses to eat anything (other than desserts) that's not heavily seasoned the way it's done in Pakistan. He says Canadian food is flat and tasteless. He gave her a list of what her cooking lacked and she asked someone who was going into Saint John to get the ingredients for her, since the small general store down the way has only a few of them. On the list were curry powder, cayenne pepper, saffron, turmeric, garlic, cloves, cinnamon, chutney – of those I can remember.

"Yes, yes, put more pepper in, Mama!" (he calls her Mama), "It must be hot! And more curry! And garlic, it needs more garlic! Ahhh . . ." (testing a morsel) "You're getting better, Mama, you're learning!"

"How can you eat that?" says Mrs Tuttle, making a face. "Doesn't it burn your tongue?"

"No! It's perfect!"

She now has to cook for each of us separately – that is, I eat what she eats, but Rashid gets his Pakistani specials. It means her cooking job is nearly doubled but she doesn't complain. She's almost impossibly tolerant and good-natured.

§

The quart of gin I brought with me is running low. I'm thinking I should have two quarts per week on hand. If that seems a large expenditure I can afford it, because there's nothing to spend money on out here. I'll have to get my supply in Sussex because there's no liquor store closer. This is fundamentalist Christian territory, the land of Baptists and Pentecostals, except for a few United Empire Loyalist aristocrats like Mrs Tuttle, who are Church of England.

I found out I'll have no heat in my bedroom during the winter. That's one of my gripes — and a major one — about where I'm staying. My room is not just a place to sleep, it's where I can be by myself. It's where I'll be doing my school work, correcting assignments and such. There are three bedrooms in use on the second floor and only two pipes running up from the wood furnace in the cellar, one in the hallway and the other in one of the bedrooms. That bedroom used to be Mrs Tuttle's but she gave it to Rashid because "the poor boy comes from a hot climate and isn't used to the cold." Unlike myself, who won't mind in the least freezing to death.

Rashid complains about even the mild days we've been having since he arrived. He said he didn't think our winters would start so soon! He's going to love it in January.

§

According to my estimate I earn fourteen dollars and some change each day. It's not quite what K. C. Irving hauls in each day, but it's better than a kick in the scrotum. It's fourteen and some change more than what I was making in Bannonbridge.

§

Teaching is a wearying job. It's ten o'clock at night and I'm still at it.

§

Once yesterday and then again today I experienced a sequence of events that I'm sure I dreamt about before —

yesterday in particular, when I knew everything that was coming. Or more accurately, I waited for every new impression and each one came as it should have.

I thought, this can't be, it's not possible, but the impressions kept coming, and I was verifying them at the exact moment of their happening, perhaps an instant before they happened (but not enough so that I could make a prediction).

Today's experience was a little different. What I had today left me with two recollections of the same event, one recent (today's), and one from the past that was vague and elusive.

I know it's called *deja vu*, and that it happens to others, if not everyone, and that it's a phenomenon no one can explain; no one other than myself, that is. What it means to me is I'm where I'm supposed to be since (a) I was either here before as a rehearsal, or (b) I wasn't, but glimpsed a rough draft of the event-to-be which the Great Author of Our Existence sketched out and forgot to destroy.

§

Just as I feared — three weeks in this place and it's boring the arse off me. If I had the strength after the day's teaching I might try writing a story or a poem, but so far I haven't been up to it. This job takes it out of a person.

As for my journal, I'm uneasy writing about real people in it, whether those at school or in the house, because my notebooks might be getting read by other eyes (are you reading this, other eyes? I'm onto you!).

I don't know what Mrs Tuttle is like in this respect. She probably wouldn't do such a dastardly thing, but I'm suspicious by nature. In her place I'm not sure I could resist poking around while my boarders were at school. We humans are curious about other humans, we want to know what everyone's up to and what they're thinking.

§

Apart from correcting assignments and preparing lessons for the next day — which I don't waste too much time on — there's little else to do in the evenings other than read or watch television.

We get both TV channels, CBC and CTV, and have some shows we watch regularly. There's my favourite, *Danger Man*, starring Patrick McGoohan as a British secret agent, and *The Defenders* starring E.G. Marshall as a lawyer; and a Canadian public affairs show, *This Hour Has Seven Days,* and the Canadian (and usually intelligent) game show *Front Page Challenge*. And on Sunday nights there's *The Ed Sullivan Show*.

This past Friday night Rashid and I watched *Mr Broadway*, a weekly drama about a press agent in New York. When it was over he shook his head in dismay.

"Disgusting. Absolutely disgusting!"

"What?"

"Didn't you see? You saw what that was about?"

"I think so, yes," I said.

"What kind of shows are these you have on television? They're all the same — sex and crime, nothing but sex and crime. Don't they have any cultural programs? You saw what that show was. That girl was fucked by her father."

"Wha-at?"

"That girl, the blonde, she was made pregnant by her father and when he found out he tried to kill her with sleeping pills."

I wondered if I was hearing right. The show was about a girl who suffered a nervous breakdown after a weekend on a narcotics binge.

When I explained what had actually gone on, he said, "Oh, oh. I see."

He said it was the Americans, the way they talked, he had difficulty understanding them. Now that I'd put the story into proper Queen's English it was all perfectly clear.

§

He's quite the dapper fellow, Rashid. He looks like a 1930s movie idol with his slim build and neatly-trimmed mustache and perfect teeth. His suits are finely cut and he wears highly-polished pointed shoes and a felt brimmed hat — a fedora, I believe it's called — and a tan-coloured topcoat. I must look pretty rough and ready standing beside him, even dressed up in my white shirt and tie and corduroy sports jacket.

Soon after we came to Mrs Tuttle's Rashid dropped into my room and told me all about himself, where he'd gone to school in Pakistan and what he'd taught, and how much his students loved him, and about the numerous women he'd enjoyed.

He's very dramatic in the way he talks, and loves to tell of his triumphs as a debater in his homeland. "Walt, I destroyed them, I simply destroyed them! They looked at me after and said, 'You have killed us, sir! We can't stand up to you.' I was like a tiger!"

Already he's made a hit with the Ladies' Committees in the county, and goes out regularly to give talks about Pakistan. He likes nothing better than standing up before a group of people and talking. He doesn't prepare a speech ahead of time, simply gets to his feet and out it comes.

§

We saw a seven-foot-tall basketball player on TV, which caused Mrs Tuttle to remark how inconvenient it must be to be so tall — or at the other extreme, really short, like a dwarf or a midget — the difficulties they'd have, what with chairs and beds and sinks and such being constructed for people of normal size.

The subject of height having come up, Mrs Tuttle asked Rashid and me how tall *we* were, out of curiosity. Rashid said he was six feet.

I snorted. "You're not six feet, Rashid, you're the same height I am, about five-nine."

He said, "No, no, I'm taller than you. I'm several inches taller."

"No, you're not."

To settle the matter Mrs Tuttle had us stand back to back, and as we were standing like that Rashid glanced at my shoulders and saw they were higher than his sloping ones. "My God!" he exclaimed. Then he gave an uncomfortable laugh. "The shoulders! The shoulders!"

Mrs Tuttle walked around us and studied us from all angles and after a good deal of hesitation — not wanting to upset Rashid — she confirmed we were exactly the same height.

I don't think Rashid was convinced though. He likes being six feet better. "Yes, yes," he said, and gave a wave of his hand as if brushing the experience from his memory.

§

It's October 6 and I've been here a month. The leaves are in colour and the air getting crisper.

As we were walking to school this morning Rashid started whistling, then after a few minutes he began singing at the top of his voice, waving his arms and making motions with his head like he was performing before an audience. It was some unearthly tuneless Pakistani song, a terrible noise.

I didn't say anything at first, trying not to laugh. But it's quite a long walk to the school and when he kept it up it started getting on my nerves. Several times I looked straight at him, making a face, but to no effect. At last I told him to shut up.

He stopped walking, startled. I didn't stop however, and he ran to catch up to me.

"You don't like my singing?" he said.

"No, I don't like your singing."

"You could have been more polite."

He said in Pakistan his friends used to tell him he was a beautiful singer. When he was at university he'd get up on the stage and sing with all his heart, and my, they would clap, oh! and say my goodness what a beautiful singer!

Why didn't I like his singing? he wanted to know.

"Okay, you're a good singer," I said. "But don't sing for me. I find it annoying, people singing or whistling."

"My goodness. Do you feel that way about everyone, Walt?"

"Just about."

"I'll have to remember."

§

Rashid talking about winter:

"I'm praying to the Lord, 'Lord, please keep back the winter!'"

And about food:

"Muffin, please, Mama. A muffin, bring it to me. Delicious! Most delicious! Oh, very nice. Very tasty . . . What's that, Mama? What did you say?"

About Beethoven's Moonlight Sonata, when it came on the radio:

"Ah, Chopin! Marvelous music, simply beautiful. A *beautiful* piece of music. Very beautiful. *Most* beautiful piece of music! Absolutely! *Ab*-sol-utely. Simply wonderful! Marvelous! Simply Marvelous! Oh my goodness . . ."

When Mrs T's service is not up to standard, as he sees it, whether in the way of food, laundering, bed-making, or whatever, he carefully spells out how he wants things done, prefacing it with "In future, Mama..."

For a while he had designs on Mrs Clark, the Home Economics teacher. She was friendly towards him in the first weeks, being a hospitable person and he a stranger far from home; but when she realized he was after her body her manner changed. Now she avoids him as much as possible, and is very cool towards him when their paths happen to cross.

He said to me, "I could give her a good time, she knows it – she's just crazy to have me. But I think her husband is jealous and she's afraid of a scandal. Well, it's her loss!"

At the dinner table:

"My homeroom students love me, they flock around me like bees to honey! . . . There's one boy who greets me every morning, 'Good morning, Mister Rashid! How are you this morning?' . . . When I left Karachi my students gave me a big party, they cried to see me leave. 'Please don't leave us, Mister Rashid, what will we do now?' . . . I was a great debater at university, did you know? I went against the best students in the country. There was one that nobody could beat, and I gave him such a blast, I killed him! 'Ah, Mister Rashid,' he said, 'you have killed me, I admit my defeat.' I left that poor fellow speechless!"

§

In Grade 11 English Literature yesterday we read a story where the author mentioned seeing a bustard, a long-legged bird found in Europe and other foreign parts. Today one of the boys in the class raised his hand and in the dry drawling voice common to this area, said, "Please sir, Bobby called me a bustard."

Bobby raised his hand. "I didn't, sir. I said he was a dirty bustard."

Here's a descriptive paragraph a Pentecostal girl in the same class wrote for a composition assignment I gave them.

The Tramp

"Yes; there goes the tramp trudging along, alone, cold and hungry. He knows no friends, maybe sometimes compassion is shown as someone gives him a crust of bread, a drink of milk or just some crumbs. His clothes are ragged, socks full of holes, soles worn or maybe bare feet blistered and swollen. Yet he marks a place in this Universe of God's."

Still on Grade 11, I gave them a History test Monday, and among the questions was this:

What was the Reichstag?

One student wrote:

"*Reichstag* was the power the Progressive wanted in France when Piedmont was Prime Minister."

§

Saturday for a change I went into Saint John, but I might as well have stayed at Mrs Tuttle's for all I gained by it. I took a room in a cheap hotel and walked the streets and had a few beers in a few taverns and later drank most of a bottle of Hermit in my room. I couldn't think what to do with myself, to get the time in, other than make a drawing of the fire escape outside my window which took up twenty minutes. All in all it was a long and boring Saturday night.

Sunday was no better. As I was wandering around I overheard two elderly bums standing in a doorway, one of them saying to the other: "I hate to see Sunday come. It's a lonely day, isn't it?"

I felt like saying, "You got that right, brother. I get that feeling too — every Sunday."

Eva, the girl I got together with in Bannonbridge just before leaving, is in Montreal now working as a nurse. We've been corresponding, and a few times I've called her on the phone, though I was sure one of my Grade 10 students, Eldon, was listening in. It's an old-fashioned telephone system out here, you don't dial but have to ring up the operator and ask to be put through. Eldon's family has the phone concession, they run it from their house, and sometimes you get Eldon's mother or one of her other kids, but usually it's Eldon.

I try to watch what I say, but I get carried away at times and either forget or don't care. Amorous feelings can do that to a young man.

Eldon and his family have to be careful too, however, because if it was known they listen in on conversations they could lose their franchise. They can't go around repeating what they hear no matter how scandalous.

§

The first week of November. It hasn't snowed yet, that's one blessing.

Looking out my window at the yard below you'd think an army of trucks and tanks and heavy artillery had passed that way.

About a month ago Rashid bought a Volkswagen "on time" from a dealer in Sussex. He had no license and had never driven a car, and expected me to teach him. I don't have a license either, but I've driven a few times without one and know how to put the clutch in and shift gears, and other basics. He thought he'd pick the skill up easily, but that's not how it went. We couldn't go on the road where I could instruct him for fear of the highway patrol, and so we drove around and around Mrs. Tuttle's house tearing up the ground and narrowly escaping colliding with her apple trees and whatever else was in the yard, including her house. It was hair-raising with him behind the wheel. It took him the longest time to get us going, letting the clutch out too soon or too late and stalling again and again. When we did manage to get moving it was to go jolting and jerking and bouncing along like we were on a pogo stick. He'd either stall it again or we'd lunge forward and take off like a runaway horse with me grabbing the wheel and kicking at his foot. "The brake, Rashid! The brake! Take your foot off the gas!"

"Oh oh oh! What is – where – Oh my!"

Mrs T finally asked us not to drive around the house, it was ruining her bushes and plants and in general making a thorough mess of the yard.

Next he recruited Mr. Shepherd, the father of one of the students, to take him on the road for some instruction, but the man gave up on it after several near head-on collisions. It was as if Rashid had a mortal defense in his head against driving a car; he simply couldn't catch on to any part of it. Every time he got behind the wheel it was like the first time. There'd be a nervous laugh, and he'd say, "What do I do now?"

His next idea was that I would be his chaufeur and drive him to school, since it was only down the road a half mile, and I did a couple of times. But then he began pestering me to let him drive the next time, and Mrs T worked herself into a state, telling us it wasn't a good example for teachers to set for their students, breaking the law, and what if we had an accident, what then? So I quit.

It was the final straw of discouragement for Rashid; he sighed and lamented and with great reluctance took his "Fawkswaggon", his beloved "Foxy", as he called it, back to the dealer. How much he lost by the transaction he wouldn't say, but he gave us to believe he whined and cried his way out of it being worse than it was.

So now he's without a car, but there's a positive side to the story. With no payments to keep up he has more money for another interest of his.

Several weekends he's taken the bus into Saint John and stayed at the Admiral Beatty Hotel and indulged himself in pleasures of the flesh. The taxi drivers there deliver the package and he brings her to his room and pays her for the night and then – since having a whore in your room is not strictly in line with hotel policy – slips her out about three in the morning.

He loves to tell me about these excursions. He says things like, "Ah, Walt, she was magnificent! I tell you, simply magnificent! I had the best of times, the best of times. For a full hour, Walt, an hour I went at her, up and down, up and down, up and down. It was marvelous! She said to me after, 'I never saw anyone who could go like you before'."

This past weekend he came back from Saint John, almost splitting his sides with laughter. "Ah, Walt! You should have seen me! It was two in the morning and I was going at her like a tiger! Oh, huge strokes. I fucked her and fucked her. The bed was shaking and the headboard was loose and every time I lunged into her it knocked against the wall. I was really giving it to her, uh! uh! uh! in and out with great thrusts, and she was moaning and I was making loud grunts with each plunge and the bed was going bang! bang! bang! against the wall. Walt, it was magnificent! Simply marvelous! Then we heard a knocking on the door and a voice saying, 'Sir, sir?' We stopped fucking and listened. It was the bellman. When I didn't answer he tapped on the door again. I was very stern. 'Well, what is it? What do you want?' 'Please, sir . . . the noise is coming out. The other guests are complaining!'"

§

Tonight we watched a television production of Henrik Ibsen's play, *The Master Builder*. Since it was aired on the CBC there were no commercial breaks. We weren't long into it when Rashid said, "I read that novel six years ago. I read it. Oh yes."

Ten minutes later: "I read that novel, *The Master Builder*."

Halfway through the show he said, "Mama, bring me milk. Bring me apple."

"What, Rashid?"

"Milk! Apple!"

"What? But Rashid, I have to watch the show. Can't you get it yourself?"

"Okay, Mama, never mind."

"I'll get you the apple, just wait a little. You can get the milk, can't you?"

"Very good, Mama. Whatever you say."

So she went to the kitchen and came back with the apple and the milk.

The minute the play was over I went up to my room, not wanting to hear Rashid's analysis. It's a waste of breath contradicting him. As I climbed the stairs I heard him saying to Mrs Tuttle, "I read that novel."

The two of them spend a lot of time talking at each other. Neither listens to the other but that doesn't bother them.

I forgot to mention that the Saturday I went into Saint John Rashid came with me. Before going our separate ways we had something to eat in a restaurant. As we were waiting for our order to come Rashid said, "Walt, here is a quarter. Play *My Boy Lollipop* and the Beatles singing *Yeah, Yeah, Yeah*! – and you can pick out two for yourself."

As *My Boy Lollipop* was playing he said, "Marvellous! Simply marvellous! The most beautiful piece of music."

"That's your favourite, is it?"

"But yes." Serious, wide-eyed, amazed someone might think otherwise. "It's simply wonderful. My goodness, it's simply marvellous."

It was after dark on Sunday when we returned, and in the darkened bus Rashid started leaning against me, calling me "dear" and putting his arm around me. I didn't lose time smartening him up on that score.

He acted surprised. "What is wrong, Walt?"

"Stop calling me 'dear'. And stay on your side of the seat."

"But we're friends. You're my friend."

"Friends don't call each other 'dear', not in this part of the world. Not unless they're fruits."

"Fruits?"

"Homosexuals."

"Oh my. I didn't know. In Pakistan we're very affectionate with our friends. I call all my close friends 'dear'."

"Well, you don't want to do it here. Someone might knock your block off."

"My block?"

"Your head."

"Oh. Then I had better not."

§

November 24. We have snow now. The first morning it snowed, about a week ago, Rashid came into my room and woke me. "Walt, get up! Look what is happening outside! Oh my!" It was the first snow he'd ever seen.

This morning the countryside was like a black and white movie, the fields white and the trees black and the sky a dull gray.

For now at least it's pleasant to be outside with the new snow everywhere. It changes the look of the world, gives novelty to the familiar surroundings.

By afternoon the sky cleared and the sun shone brilliantly, sparkling on the fields. A cat came by and sat out in the yard, sunning himself.

After supper Mrs Tuttle happened to mention a Mr Cockburn, one of her former boarders. He'd come up in conversation before, and she'd had the hardest time revealing a certain characteristic about him. "Well, he was, you know . . . he, uh . . ." suddenly tittering ". . . oh, I shouldn't . . . oh dear . . . well, you know, he was . . . you could say . . . well, he was different . . ."

Rashid: "Please, Mama! What are you trying to tell us?"

Mrs Tuttle: "Well, he didn't . . . he was a nice enough man . . . in other ways . . . but, you see, he didn't . . . well, men . . . single men, you'd expect them to . . . they like girls, normally, are interested . . . that is . . ."

Rashid: "Are you telling us he was a pervert, Mama?"

Mrs Tuttle: "Oh, I don't . . . but he . . ." tittering again. "He was . . . that kind, you know? And —

Rashid: "A homosexual!"

Mrs Tuttle: "Yes, well . . ."

And she went on to tell us whatever it was she had to tell, which was unrelated to that particular quality in the man.

Now, this evening after supper, she started to say something like: "I remember Mr Cockburn used to hate the snow, and —"

Rashid interrupted her. "That *obscene* man?"

Mrs Tuttle: "Well . . . oh my." Unable to suppress a laugh, a hand over her mouth.

"Don't talk about that obscene man, Mama. I don't want to hear it."

Rashid can be funny at times, with his vocabulary and his attitudes.

We eat in the kitchen now, where it's warmer, but I don't like it. The table is small and I find myself too close to the others. The sounds of eating and the smell of their bodies affects my appetite. And the old black woodstove with the oven open to keep Rashid warm is too hot for me. I'm too close to where the food is prepared, and too close to people, too confined and too hot. I'm so conscious of what's around me that the food doesn't taste as it should.

I know I've been getting irritable of late, more irritable than usual it seems. How much of it is the tension of teaching and the confinement of living in this place, and how much is just me and my nerves which can tolerate people for only so long at a stretch, I don't know. But I've felt close to the point of swearing at someone. I do swear at them now, but under my breath.

§

I'm almost finished the notebook I've been using for a journal. I'd like to start a new one to have with me should I decide to take a weekend trip to Bannonbridge or Fredericton or elsewhere; I don't want to have to carry two, one nearly full and one empty. What I'll do is try to finish this one off with an account of the day I arrived at Mrs Tuttle's . . .

THE DAY I ARRIVED AT MRS TUTTLE'S

When I came to this place it was a damp gray day in early September and all I'd had for breakfast was a quart of beer and for dinner at noon a chocolate bar and for a mid-afternoon snack another quart of beer on the bus. The bus took me to a small village on the Saint John highway and from there I hired a taxi to Winchester. The old man who drove me talked bitterly about politics, telling me our present premier was one of the richest men in the world and had all his money stored in banks in Switzerland.

I was apprehensive about teaching and about where I'd be boarding and the rest of it and now here I was driving into the depths of the woods miles from civilization with a man probably typical of the natives of these parts. Bible country, back-country people, hateful faces distorted with disapproval of everything that was in any way fun or pleasureful. I suppose the man smelled the beer off me because he next went off on a rant about the Robichaud government destroying the moral fibre of the people by allowing taverns and bars to open this past year —

"We got by without them for fifty years, but that wasn't good enough, no sir! They wasn't lining their pockets fast enough, they needed to sell more liquor!"

I was hoping the community I was making for was on a river. According to the map there was a river and a bay somewhere in the general area. Where there's a river (as I think I've said before) you can always find or build a raft and like Huckleberry Finn load up with provisions and sail away to freedom and adventure.

I was thinking these thoughts when we came over a hill and there it was up ahead, a broad green river! A strange-looking river, to be sure, lime green in colour, but a river nonetheless. I thought of commenting to my driver on its odd colour but he wasn't the kind to invite conversation so I didn't. And then we came closer to the river and I saw it wasn't a river but a field! I was seeing things, on top of everything else.

There was no river near the school, as I soon discovered, not unless you want to call a brook four feet wide a river.

We came to the house where I was to board and drove in the yard.

"Missus Tuttle is a nice woman," my driver said.

By this time I was in a cold sweat. I could feel the hand of doom tightening around me. The house was big, an old-style place with gables and dormer windows. Its gray paint had long since faded, and there were creepers creeping up the front. It had a veranda with no balustrade, and a small balcony on the second floor facing the road. There was a falling-down barn and a couple of sheds in the yard and weeds and long grass sprouting up everywhere. It was all so oppressive, the dark ancient house, the silence, the gray autumn sky. Nothing around but fields and forest. To complete the picture, as we drove in I glimpsed a man limping out of the yard, his body bent almost double and dragging one foot behind him.

The door of the house opened and an old woman wearing wire-rimmed spectacles stood there. She was in her seventies and I could see at once that her features were fiercely puritanical. My heart was dead inside me. I got out of the car and after paying the driver carried my things into the house.

We were in the kitchen, a country kitchen with a great black woodstove, two kettles on it, a table a few feet from the stove, some wooden chairs, a rocking chair, a sofa. The door to a large pantry was open. I acted like an amiable person, but I was anything but. My laugh was dry, my voice hollow, my words insincere.

Mrs Tuttle was stout and rosy-cheeked and talkative. She talked a blue streak but I scarcely heard her. I followed her to my room upstairs, carrying a box of books, which I didn't want to be doing, carrying those books up there, as though actually moving in – because I wasn't going to stay. The house was dark, the kitchen, the living room, the dining room, the hallways, the carpeted stairs. My room, however, was quite bright, with a large window and flower-patterned wallpaper. The furnishings were simple: a high double bed, a chest of drawers, a work table, a couple of chairs. They filled the room well enough, yet it seemed bare and ascetic. There were no prints or posters on the walls, no record player on the floor, no coats and jackets hanging from hooks in the corner, no homemade bookshelves, and no bottles hidden where my father wouldn't see them. In other words, it was not what I was accustomed to.

With Mrs Tuttle fluttering around I made several more trips, lugging up my suitcase, duffle bag, knapsack, two more boxes of books, and my typewriter.

When she left I shut the door and the heart went completely out of me. I looked at my doleful face in the mirror above the bureau and thought of my contract, my binding contract, and the long winter ahead, and the mobs of savage students lying in wait for me. A full year in this place. But it didn't even go that far – school didn't begin until Tuesday, and this was only Saturday – just the thought of spending a whole *weekend* here.

It was impossible, I couldn't do it.

Contract or no contract, I had to bolt, or I'd go out of my mind.

Hardly knowing what I was doing I went downstairs and told Mrs Tuttle I was going for a walk. She started talking, talking about the school, the teachers, the students, her neighbours. The man limping in the yard poor man he lives alone and comes by for a cup of tea and his son do you know oh you wouldn't well he did this and his brother who lives up that way and the man who boarded here last year – the words pouring out in an unbroken stream as I inched my way towards the door.

She couldn't understand why I'd want to go out after just getting in. I'd only been here a few minutes. Didn't I want a cup of tea? Supper would be ready in an hour or so. There was another boarder coming, a fellow teacher, from Pakistan.

I broke free and set off down the road at a furious pace, my mind going faster than my feet, thinking as hard as I'd ever thought, searching for a way out. I'd never dreamt it would be this bad. I cursed myself for not visiting the place before signing the contract.

Were it not for my books and luggage I'm sure I'd have left just like that, without explanation. Kept on walking, hitch-hiked to Saint John, taken the train to Montreal with its streets and crowds, taverns and clubs, bookstores and galleries.

But I couldn't leave my things behind. My typewriter, my books, my journal . . . And what would Eva think of me if I showed up at her door in Montreal having done such a thing? Left the school a teacher short on opening day – and not just any teacher, but the one designated to carry the heaviest load. I'd have reneged on my contract, chickened out. What would that say about my character? And what then, when I got there? I'd be no further ahead, still without a job.

So I turned around and went back.

§

Saturday, December 5. Looking from my bedroom window there's nothing to see but snow – snow and black trees, black ugly twisted trees, bushes, shrubs. Those close by move a little in the wind, but otherwise everything, everywhere, is still and white and black. I hear a low rumbling but don't know if it's the wind in the trees or a truck. There isn't much wind, but it sounds like wind. It doesn't come nearer or recede.

I got up too early this morning. Rashid was singing one of his heathen Pakistani songs in the bathroom and woke me. I had to piss anyway, and I figured there was likely a letter for me from Eva. When I got dressed and went downstairs Mrs Tuttle said she hadn't been able to get out to the mailbox because of the storm last night but there was mail, she'd called up the mailman to find out. So I went back upstairs and put on my fur cap and overshoes and a jacket.

"You'll freeze with that little jacket on!" she said.

The snow was deep in the yard and as I tramped out to the box I got some down the back of both overshoes. I hadn't washed yet, I'd got up prematurely, and my head was aching from last night's drinking. I wasn't in a very good mood. It was probably a fine morning of its kind, with the new snow and fresh morning air, but I was too grouchy to breathe it in and feel it. The letter from Eva was there however.

When the morning starts off on the wrong foot you always think it's going to continue that way. But it doesn't always.

I phoned her long-distance last night, after nipping for a while on my bottle. I still had a quart of Hermit left from a supply I got in Sussex. We talked for God knows how long, close to an hour, which will cost me ten dollars easily. She said she loved me and I said I loved her – even with that scoundrel Eldon probably listening. I don't know what will come of this; I seem to be getting caught up quite seriously with her. I have no idea what she's really like, since we spent only a few days together in Bannonbridge before she went to Montreal and I came to this place.

It's going to be difficult now to see her as she is, when we get together in the flesh, after spending the past months seeing her as the ideal I want her to be. Days and nights of my imagination shaping her into something no doubt unrealistic. If she turns out to be too far from my expectations then it will be hard times for me.

Still, I've learned to be more loose the past year, less inflexible than I used to be; I mean I've trained myself that way; whether I've *learned* it or not remains to be seen. But I think I can make adjustments, and at crucial points remind myself that she's human as is everyone. Were she an angel she'd be in heaven, not here on earth.

§

Mrs Tuttle has no problem with the fact I take the occasional drop. She's partial to a nip herself now and then – not in a big way, but enough that she asked me a while back to get her a bottle of "good" sherry while I was at the liquor store. She left the choice to me, and I brought her a quart of *Emu*. It comes from Australia and is twenty cents more than the *Hermit.* I tried a bottle of it myself once after my graduation, when I came into my invitation money, and found it quite tasty.

Rashid doesn't drink. He was brought up a Muslim, and I believe that lot has to wait till the next life before they can tie one on.

§

Rashid sitting in his room, his chair facing the window. His room is directly across from mine and our doors are open.

"Come, Walt! Look at the bars!"

"The what?"

"The bars!"

"The bars?"

"The water bars."

"Oh, you mean the icicles."

"Icic – ? How is that?"

"Icicles."

"Icicles . . . Hmm." Reflective, storing the word in his memory.

The first time he saw frost on his window he said, "Walt, you must see this! The window, look! The moisture is frozen on it!"

A few nights ago he was talking to Mrs Tuttle about one of the other teachers.

"All the students laugh at his hat, Mama."

"They don't!"

"Oh yes. They wait till he goes by and then they laugh."

They laugh at my headgear too, though they don't wait till I've gone by. I wear a Russian-style imitation-fur cap and they ask me things like what animal is it I'm wearing today?

"Didn't I see your hat on the road yesterday, Mr Macbride?"

"I saw it too, sir. I think it was still moving."

"It's moving now, sir, it just twitched. Shouldn't you kill it first?"

I get along well with my students. I only had trouble with two of them, a couple of psychopaths in Grade 10, but both hit the age of sixteen by late October and quit.

Well, there is another one, the afore-mentioned Eldon. He's bright but has no interest in school, other than as a place where he can act the fool. I got him to read something once, a page from a story we were doing, and he came to this line: ". . . and so he tried not to be too hard on his friends . . ." and read it like this:

". . . and so he tried not to be too *hard-on* . . ." A pause, then repeating ". . . not too *hard-on* . . ." Coughing. "Where was I?"

"Okay, Eldon, that's enough." The class of course got a chuckle out of it, and despite myself I couldn't hold back a grin myself before reprimanding him. But his disruptions became too frequent and too brazen to tolerate for long, and I took to sending him out in the hall the minute he opened his mouth. He never, not once, said anything seriously related to the work at hand, it was always to get a laugh. "But, sir, all I wanted to say was — "

In the beginning I gave him the benefit of the doubt. "Okay, let's hear what you thought you were saying. Maybe I misunderstood you."

But it would be just another sly wisecrack, a play on "screwing" or "riding" or "ass" or "cock" or the like. So out he went.

He thought it was a lark when I first did it, that he was getting himself a free period, but then he found out what all comedians come to know, that it's a lonely world without an audience — and a boring one. The only relief he got was when the principal would come along and give him a lecture or detention time or threaten to call his parents. So he's learned to restrain himself for a few classes in a row between offenses.

He's not really a bad fellow; I don't dislike him, and I don't think he dislikes me either, despite our differences. If I was one of his fellow students I'm sure I'd get a kick out of his antics. He's intelligent and could do well if he wanted, but he doesn't want to. He's fifteen and when he hits the magic retirement age next summer that will in all likelihood be the end of his schooling.

Besides being a comic he's the strongest boy in the class so I guess it's as well for me he's inclined to humour rather than violence.

He's been making Rashid's life hell, worse than with me. Rashid has sent him numerous times to the principal, but it doesn't help. With Mr Gates being from the community and having to live here he tends to side more with the students than with foreign teachers like Rashid and myself.

Rashid: "I said to the principal, 'I think, sir, that this behaviour is most unusual. That boy is not sane, I'm sure of it. He is slightly disbalanced.'"

Rashid teaches some Grade 9 classes and has a Grade 9 class for his homeroom, and some of the worst offenders are in there.

"They are absolutely disinterested. I have never seen boys like this before. Disinterested, absolutely."

He told Mrs Tuttle and me that one of the boys spit on the floor as he was walking down the aisle towards his desk. "I said to him, 'Hey, bugger, what do you think you are doing? What the hell you are doing?'" Shaking his head. "Bastard! In my country we would never stand for it, a teacher would box the boy's ears. That scoundrel would be expelled."

When he first began having trouble he was less emphatic, not wanting to admit he had discipline problems. All he said then was, "You know, Mama, they are slightly very lenient at this school."

A thing I've noticed is that the further up in grades you go the better behaved the students are.

I don't have a Grade 9, I'm thankful to say, but I was once in Grade 9 myself and know what it's like – and I have Rashid's testimony to confirm the opinion.

The Grade 10 class that isn't my homeroom class is the toughest for me. It's made up for the most part of shop boys and home economics girls who aren't remotely interested in history or literature or anything much else beyond the opposite sex and cars and engines and clothes and baking cakes.

While there are good students in my homeroom Grade 10, many of the others just want to be out playing or working. It's what they should be doing, but while they're here I have to go through the courses with them and get the required matter covered. It's not only Eldon I have to put out of the room but several others from time to time. Even so, and for all that, we manage to keep on fairly good terms. I've had to fail several of them on their exams but they gave me no choice. When they don't answer any of the questions beyond a few scribbles to demonstrate they haven't the faintest idea what the questions are about there's not much else you can do.

The Grade 11 kids have life and mischief in them, but there are no real troublemakers among them. By that stage the worst offenders have dropped out.

Grade 12 is the biggest, the easiest, and the most unpromising class. They're well-behaved and well indoctrinated in how to memorize for exams. Like Sergeant Friday they want the facts and just the facts so they can write them down and get a pass. That's the extent of their interest. Whenever they have the chance they sit in little knots gossiping with each other. I don't think there's one of them plans on going to college; what they want is to get their diploma and get out and get a job and get married — which is fine with me. A few of them are married already. They fight and argue with me over marks and if they don't get the grade they think they deserve they'll hardly talk to me. They're as serious as Grade 11 is carefree.

§

The Christmas holidays have come and gone. Eva came home to Bannonbridge from Montreal and we spent just about every minute together. I'm almost afraid to believe it but I think my life is looking up.

§

Like Eva Mrs Tuttle was a nurse in her younger days, before she married the late Mr Tuttle. She was reminiscing yesterday about her experiences.

"There were horses then, and one day a woman was brought in drunk and all covered with it."

Rashid said, "What? Covered with what?"

"With horse . . . horse manure." Hand to mouth, laughing. "Oh, it was awful."

Rashid looked puzzled. "What was that? Covered with what?"

"You know . . . when a horse goes to the bathroom. It was on the streets then, and she got drunk and fell in it."

"Oh yes, I see. Go on, Mrs Tuttle."

"I was a student nurse and we got all the dirtiest jobs. They told me to bath her. She was unconscious, with this awful stuff all over her, in her hair and everywhere. Ugh! And I had to cut her toenails." Grimacing, shuddering. "Long dirty toenails, and horse manure all over her. I had to get her ready to be put in bed. I didn't eat a thing that day. I couldn't. Oh . . ." Wincing. "I can still smell it."

§

This evening Rashid told me he'd once got a high school principal of his demoted, back in Pakistan, after he and the man had had a disagreement. This principal had only a bachelor of education degree, and one day Rashid was talking to the chairman of the school board and said, "Sir, it's a shame we don't have a man of higher education to guide us. All the teachers at our school have bachelor degrees, and it would be nice if we had a man with a masters or a Ph.D. for our principal, someone we could look up to and have respect for . . ."

Said in a conversational tone, without directly mentioning the incumbent principal, as though what he said had nothing to do with him, but was strictly a theoretical observation. But then lo and behold, not long after this the principal was demoted to vice-principal and a man with a Ph.D. took his place.

Rashid told me this, I could see, partly as a boast, but also as an indictment against *our* principal, Mr Gates, who, he observed distastefully, "hasn't even a B.A., let alone a Ph.D.!"

Maybe he's thinking of whispering something into the ear of Mr Hacket, the chairman of *our* school board.

§

Mrs Tuttle has an only son, Robert. We haven't met him, he's a major in the Army and is married and lives in Ottawa. Before the snow came I used to go for rides on the old bicycle he owned as a boy. Mrs Tuttle's face lights up whenever she talks of him; she still dotes on him, even now that he's a middle-aged man. At dinner yesterday she told us about a fiancée he once had, a gentle girl, pretty and nicely mannered. She'd have made the perfect wife for him, Mrs Tuttle thought, but then one day, out of the blue, he announced he'd left her and was engaged to another girl.

Mrs T was appalled. How could he do such a thing? And to such a sweet little girl!

"I asked him why, and do you know what he said? What he told me?"

"What?"

"I hate to say it. Oh, I can't."

"Come on now, tell us. Don't leave us hanging."

"Oh dear. Well, he said, 'That one, she wouldn't say you-know-what if her mouth was full of it!' Oh, that Robert! And such a nice girl."

"You-know-what, Mama? What does that mean?" Rashid said.

"He didn't say 'you-know-what' . . . He used another word."

"What word, Mama? Please explain."

"I can't say it. It's not a nice word."

"Tell me."

"It starts with 's' . . ."

"And ends with 'h-i-t'," I said.

"Ah! Ha Ha! I knew," Rashid said. "I wanted to hear Mama say it."

ELEVEN

The days, the weeks, the months go by; even out here they do. January, February, March, April . . . Trudging along to the last syllable of recorded time.

It's May now.

In all this time I haven't written a thing other than letters to Eva. I've been too busy with this teaching business — too mired, tired and uninspired, if you'd prefer a fancier version. I'm going to try and get back in the habit, scribble a few words down if I can. But it's hard to work at a job and write too.

A cold rain is falling. The grass seems to have turned green overnight.

I don't take leisurely walks the way I used to in Bannonbridge, looking around me and registering the things that struck me as making the day what it was, distinct from other days. I take walks, it's true, and I enjoy them, but never with an eye to writing what I see. It's actually quite beautiful this time of year, the greening fields climbing up both sides of the valley, the high rolling hills, the variety of trees coming into leaf. If you stand atop a hill you can see a bay in the distance, like the mouth of a fjord, the water blue and wide. There are farmhouses and barns and ploughed ground, and cows and calves in the fields, and sheep followed by little lambs. There are wildflowers fringing the fields and the air is filled with the sound of birds singing.

Brooks that were fast and overflowing have slowed and gone down the past few days, but today's rain will swell them again.

My year at teaching will soon be over. God knows what I'll do after that. I expect I'll spend the summer at home, to begin with. Eva will have graduated from nursing school by then and will likely take some time off before starting to work.

Teaching isn't for me. I'm too damned lazy to do any kind of good job at it. I enjoy the students, they're all fine kids, and I think they enjoy me as being more or less on the same maturity level as themselves. But there's so much work involved you either have to put everything you have into it, every minute and every ounce of energy, or resign yourself to accepting your limitations and fake it, which is what I've resorted to doing. Most of the time now I have no more idea than my students what the next page in our textbooks will be about. That's not necessarily as bad as it sounds. It could be interpreted as democracy at work, an example of equality among humans, teacher and students going through the subject together, at the same pace. Added to which it makes the traditional teacher-student competition — where the teacher acts as if he knows what he's doing and the students try to catch him out — even more entertaining.

I'm probably lucky I haven't been fired by now. I flew up to Montreal and spent the Easter Holidays with Eva, and it was heavenly — so heavenly I didn't want to come back. And I didn't come back, not right way. I wasn't in attendance the first day classes resumed, I was still in Montreal. But then Eva and I discussed it and decided that all things considered I really should return and finish the job and so I called Mr Gates. All I said was I was in Montreal and would be one more day late, having to catch a flight and all. I didn't know quite how to explain my absence, without telling him my whole life story, but he's a nice man and took me off the hook. "You were sick, were you? I'll put you down as sick."

"Yes . . . sick, that's right." It was true. Sick of teaching and living in the woods and being away from Eva . . .

"There's a flu going around," he said.

"Yes, the flu."

I suppose not a lot of teachers give one of their bright Grade 11 girl students Henry Miller's *Tropic of Cancer* to read and do a book report on. Or even *The Catcher in the Rye* with its "fuck you" line, which I had several others read. It would only take one of my students ratting on me to get me thrown out on my ear.

I try to give my Grade 11 Composition class interesting subjects to write about, such as having one half the class come up with questions for Ann Landers and the other half answer them, and then switch the roles around. The letters they wrote were full of girls getting into trouble and what they should do, and boyfriends who wanted to "go all the way", and boyfriends who said their girlfriends wanted to rape them, and other such sex problems.

Another idea I thought up was for them to write collaborative stories. There are 28 students in the class and I had each of them write one line of a story and then pass it to the student in the seat behind to continue it. When we were finished we had 28 stories each done by 28 authors working together.

There are some prim and proper students in the class, mostly girls of the Pentecostal persuasion with their dowdy hairdos and old-fashioned dresses and unmade-up faces. But if they disapprove of me and my assignments, as I'm sure they do, they've been good enough to go along with things and not report me to the authorities.

Here are a few of the stories the class wrote:

AN INTERESTING EXPERIENCE

One night not too long ago I had the use of the car . . . I took advantage of it by driving to town . . . Driving down main street I saw this cute girl so I stopped and asked her if she wanted a ride . . . She said "What kind of ride?" . . . Well! . . . I'll never tell, if you don't . . . She climbed into the car . . . She edged toward me, her breath was hot on my neck . . . Quickly I drove to the nearest lovers lane ready for "Anything", anything but what happened! . . . We got to Lover's Lane we stopped the car and were lost in each other's love . . . When we came to we were in the back seat both nude & a policeman standing looking in the window saying to get out this was a raid on lovers lane . . . We both got out and stood naked by the car . . . What was going to happen? . . . Your guess is as good as mine . . . They gave us blankets to cover ourselves with and then took us to the Police Station . . . They called our parents . . . Now what was the result going to be? . . . The suspense was too great . . . Our parents came to get us . . . Boy was they mad . . . But it was fun while it lasted! . . . We would do it again if we had the chance . . . Well the chance arose when I got out of the house without anyone knowing and met him at a party . . . We left the party for a lonely place to park . . . You guessed it we went to Lovers Lane again . . . This time we weren't interrupted and proceeded to go all the way . . . But there was something wrong with his lower intestine . . . It was unusually small and wasn't much good . . . But it worked out in the end . . .

SAM'S CABIN

Out in the clearing in the midst of a large forest stands a small log cabin . . . Behind the cabin is a well . . . The well is dry of water because it is the middle of summer . . . In the wall there were trapped animals . . . Everyone was terrified of them . . . They were nasty beasts and breeding like the devil . . . Many new kinds of beasts were invented that Adam didn't have any name for . . . So he didn't bother naming them . . . It was hard to classify the males from the females as they were different than ordinary beasts . . . But I guess this didn't matter because the beasts seemed to know which was which . . . The males were the life of the party . . . And the females the fun of the party . . . Meanwhile back at the log cabin . . . Uncle Sam is having some fun with Aunt Sarah . . . They were both 65 but with all that

*going on down in the well who cares . . . I'm sure I don't . . .
Neither do I . . . But Sarah's grandmother did! . . . She arrived
in time to see them getting up off the sofa . . . "This is awful!" she
declared. "Two young things like yourselves carrying on in this
way!" . . . "But you can only be young once" said Sarah . . . "Well
when are you two ever going to grow up" declared Sarah's
grandmother . . . "Well one thing I can say is, it isn't now" . . . .
And she laid back down on the sofa while saying, "Again Sam."
. . . So he did it again . . . Oh Sam! Why did you ever do such a
thing? . . .*

THE FISHING TRIP

*Once upon a time . . . The fishing trip went wonderful
even though no fish were caught . . . They weren't interested in
catching fish though as they wanted to be alone for a while . . .
When they were alone guess what happened? . . . He held her
tight and they did the general stuff every normal girl and boy
does . . . It wasn't a deserted spot but before long it didn't matter
how many were around . . . They layed in the soft sand and
caressed each other . . . The fishing trip was a good excuse . . .
Even though they didn't catch any fish, she caught a slippery eel
. . . It's not everyday that someone catches an eel . . . And a
slippery one at that . . . After she caught it she didn't know what
to do with it . . . What do you do about that? . . . You get rid of
the stupid thing as fast as possible . . . . (Oh Sexy) . . . What'll I
do throw it back in? . . . Naturally . . . What else? . . . . Go ahead
throw it back . . . So she threw it back . . . But boy was he ever
disappointed . . . And surprised because she never did that before
. . . Do you know why? . . . Why she had never caught a eel
before? . . . I would NOT know . . . I would . . . But she would
not . . . I guess not . . . I rather catch anything than an eel . . .*

POUNDING

He held her tightly and kissed her soothingly while saying 'I love you' . . . She said you can't leave me to go to India I love you too much . . . Let's get married . . . Oh I don't know, marriage is a very important step besides you would have to go to India and I don't think you would like India . . . India is so different . . . and the natives are always restless . . . Some night a lady native might get too restless and then what . . . That would be all the better . . . I know you love me and I love you too but that's just it, I have to go to India and you can't come with me . . . I must prove myself a real man before I marry the one I love (you) . . . He started to make love to her . . . but unfortunately they were interrupted by noisy pounding . . . Dropping her on the floor he ran out the back door . . . He looked around to see what was making the pounding noise . . . He walked behind the building and there he saw an old man pounding nails to his heart's content . . . The young man said, "Isn't that hard on the heart, hammering all those nails into it?" . . . Ha Ha Ha Ha! . . . Don't make me laugh, you young whippersnapper . . . and he continued to pound the nails . . . The young man returned and picked his girlfriend up off the floor . . . Passionately he kissed her . . . And gently laid her down on the floor again . . . Then he heard a pounding outside and dropped her in the waste can while he went out to check . . . Again he saw the old man pounding nails . . . Didn't he have anything better to do? . . . The young man left after saying he'd meet his girl later . . . He would meet her when midnight came . . . Midnight came . . . And a park came . . . And the girl came . . . And the man with the nails came too . . . So that added up to two men and one woman . . . What a time . . .

§

My classes can get a bit noisy on occasion, I won't deny it. There's a lot of bantering goes on, and more than once Mr Gates has poked his head in and glared the room into silence.

He's spoken to me in his office about "discipline", which as I think I've said, is the teacher's primary function in the education system, keeping the kids quiet. When he pops in it makes me look bad, as though I've let the class get out of control. It's my biggest problem, discipline. When I get tough and convince the kids I'm serious and want hard work and good behaviour and get them settled down I start acting the fool myself and everything breaks down again. I throw paper planes around the classroom. I draw cartoons on the blackboard. I relate an anecdote that gets them laughing and excited and jumping in with witticisms of their own.

I've told them I don't know the parts of a sentence myself, but I don't have to because my exam-writing days are over; theirs aren't so they have to learn them. After their exams they can forget them the way I did. I said if they want to speak and write good English they should read books by good writers and learn that way. I advise them to study and do well on their exams so they can go to college because going to college is easier than working. They'll have all their lives to work, I said; go to college first and have fun. If they should happen to get a degree while there it will be a bonus, icing on the cake. It will give them a better chance of not collecting garbage for a living.

I like being on a familiar footing with them, but the drawback is, with classes of 30 or so it's hard to be loose and easy without everyone speaking out and getting into the act. So it's back and forth, from pandemonium to order to pandemonium to order.

I don't want to get carried away here, but I've developed a certain affection for my students and even though it's not my calling I think it would be satisfying to be a dedicated teacher provided you could find some way to have fun in the classroom while you were at it without getting yourself fired.

In any event I'm glad I came back from Montreal. I was tired and over-extended and needed a break, that was all. I'd have regretted it if I hadn't returned, I know that.

Speaking of coming back, I don't know what they'd say if I were to re-offer my services for next year. I suppose if you take into account where the school is located and that there's no supplementary isolation pay like you get in the Arctic they might not be able to do much better than my humble self.

But that's idle speculation. It doesn't matter, they won't have to trouble their heads about it. I'll be relieving them of the decision by making it for them.

§

The hills are blue and misty, like apparitions above the bright green fields.

I'm sitting on Mrs Tuttle's little second-floor balcony on a Saturday afternoon. A robin just flew from her nest to another tree, and then to the yard below, where she's bouncing around. There – she's gone back to her nest.

A red-haired girl in a sweatshirt and shorts runs by on the road, practicing for a track meet. She's one of my students, one of the smart ones. She stops running after passing the house and walks a piece with arms dangling, head lowered, stepping with long white legs. Then she starts again.

The sun is out after a day of gray sky, and all the fields are green and gay, and the trees are budding.

The robin didn't go back to her nest after all. I leaned out and looked at the nest and she's not in it. I see her now, over on a fence in the bushes.

Ah! Here she comes, back to her four blue eggs.

One of my legs is skinned, but it could have been worse – much worse. I was walking this morning across what I thought was an empty field when I noticed a herd of animals huddled in one corner. I thought they were cows, but as I passed nearer I saw they were young bulls. When they saw me they perked up and exchanged glances, then suddenly took off in a body and came charging after me.

Playful young critters, I thought. I'll fix them. Instead of running for the fence I ran *towards* them, yelling and waving my arms, thinking it would scare them; but it didn't. They kept coming like a stampede in an old cowboy movie.

By good luck and the grace of God it was a large field and they had some ground to cover. When I saw my ruse hadn't worked I turned and made a run for the nearest fence. It was a four-foot-high wooden rail fence and I leaped and my right thigh hit the top rail and I tumbled to the ground. I looked up from where I lay, and hovering about two feet above my face were the snouts of a dozen snorting bulgy-eyed blood-thirsty bulls. Fortunately I was on the outer side and was just out of their reach.

I wasn't long scrambling out of there! My flying leap had knocked the top rail off the fence and it wouldn't have taken much pressure from that bunch to burst through the rest.

I still shudder thinking about it. If I'd waited another second before turning and running they'd have very likely ended my miserable and possibly in some ways at least in my own mind at times promising life.

§

I was going to die and there was nothing I could do about it. I'd been shot in the neck by a policeman who mistook me for a bank robber and didn't even bother to ask questions later. All he said was, "Tough break, fellow. Wrong place, wrong time."

I was no bank robber, I'd had the misfortune to be walking by the bank while several other men were robbing it, that was all.

I know we all die sometime, but in my case it was far too premature.

What bothered me was not just that I was dying, in the simplest sense, but that dying with me was all my promise and potential in life.

My feelings about what happened can be summed up in a small poem I composed as I lay on the sidewalk bleeding.

Is it true, God, then,
when it comes to us men,
that you treat us like toys,
indifferent alike
to our sorrows and joys?

If I sounded bitter I was. I'd been led to believe I'd do something of importance in life; I'd felt it in my bones ever since I was a boy, and had worked and sacrificed to prepare myself — and now look.

I felt like telling God to go to Hell, but of course that would have been ridiculous.

I got to my feet and went looking for a doctor. I thought I might be saved yet if I could find one. I tried the hospital but they wouldn't help me. They didn't care if I died or not. All they said was, "The doctors are busy now, come back tomorrow."

"But I'll be dead tomorrow!"

"Sorry, it can't be helped."

"You're a hospital! You're supposed to help!"

"We're not a hospital, we're nurses. Ha! Ha!" She gave the nurse beside her a nudge in the ribs. "Imagine, thinking we're a hospital . . . You need a different kind of hospital, buster. The cracker factory's on the other side of town."

So I came home, where I am now, and sat by the window.

I didn't feel too bad, though. "I really should feel worse than this if I'm dying," I thought. "I mean physically. But perhaps it's the shock."

Then a strange thought crossed my mind. What if the policeman's bullet had actually missed me? And this wound in my neck was — I don't know, a mosquito bite or something? A mosquito bite! I put my finger to my neck. The bleeding had stopped. I went into the bathroom and looked in the mirror. If it was a bullet hole it was a very small one. No bigger than the hole a mosquito's stinger would leave.

I've always been one to make mountains out of molehills, it's the way I am. It would be easy for me to make a gunshot wound out of a mosquito bite.

If it's so and I'm still alive tomorrow, I guess I'll owe God an apology. But he's not going to be happy with me, after what I said about him.

§

Walking around the auditorium while the students were writing their matriculation exams I tried to identify the feelings in myself that I'd remember years later when thinking back to this moment.

When something — say a piece of music or a certain aroma — reminds me of a particular time in my young boyhood I get an intense feeling of the time and place, which I actually don't remember having felt when I was there. So now, this being the last days of my first and (most likely) only year of teaching, with the sun pouring in the windows, and nothing to do but sit at the back of the room or stroll among the desks watching that no one was cheating, I tried to find the feelings that would stir me years in the future. But there were none. I didn't seem to feel anything one way or the other.

All of which signifies I don't know what.

§

Rashid isn't planning to return next year either. He's got a couple of dozen applications out, mostly to schools in Ontario, where the money is better. What he'd really like to do, he says, is be a car salesman. While he was looking in the Toronto newspapers for teaching openings he saw that car salesmen not only earn a good salary and get a commission for each vehicle sold, they're given a new car of their own to drive around in. It's a long-range ambition, however, seeing as he doesn't know anything about cars including how to drive one.

§

I'm aware I haven't recorded much about life in the classroom, but there's a reason for it. You need vitality to write, and after a full day of teaching I've not had enough left over to do anything but a minimum of assignment correcting and lesson preparation.

That is, until this past weekend, when the work year was more or less finished. I had a few easy days and a good sleep and when I woke Saturday morning I felt refreshed enough to write a little tale based on the kind of thing that goes on in a typical English class. It's the only story I've done over the past year, and it might prove helpful to those taking a scientific interest in the ins and outs of the pedagogical profession.

The teacher in the story isn't me, or is not I, as the grammar book would prefer I say. Unlike this teacher I've never been nervous in the classroom. You might think I would be, being the inward-looking anti-social type of human that I am, but for some reason it's never happened. I get nervous thinking about it beforehand, but not once I'm there. It's like acting, I believe, from what I've heard and read. Once the curtain goes up the actors throw themselves into their roles and the nerves vanish. Or as you might say, they throw up before the curtain goes up, then throw themselves into their roles.

My story is called *The Cask of Armadillo* and is so like what I've run into in my experience that in some ways it's hard to tell the difference.

THE CASK OF ARMADILLO

"Now, class, you've read the story you were assigned?" It was week two of the fall term and Charles Driscoll faced his Grade 10 class at St Ambrose all-boys high school. He was a pale young man with a nervous manner. While addressing the class he repeatedly adjusted his glasses, chewed his pen and thumbed the pages of the text as though looking for some passage in particular. It was his first year teaching.

"*The Cask of Amontillado* by Edgar Allan Poe," he said. "Does anyone know anything about Edgar Allan Poe?"

When no one responded he said, "How about you?" indicating a boy in the second row.

"Me, sir?"

"Yes. Can you tell me anything about Edgar Allan Poe?"

"Yes, sir. He wrote that story you told us to read."

"Is that all?"

"Yes, sir."

"Anyone else?"

Silence. Then another boy said, "He made horror movies, didn't he, sir? Like about ghouls and vampires and that kind of thing?"

Driscoll smiled. "Not exactly. He lived in the nineteenth century when there were no such things as movies. But you're partly right. He wrote horror stories, mystery stories, tales of the supernatural. He also wrote poetry and criticism." He dropped his eyes to his book, turned a page or two. "When he was in his thirties he married his first cousin, who was sixteen." His face coloured slightly as he glanced up. The class gazed back at him, expressionless. "And he was an alcoholic. He died from drinking while still a young man."

Still the blank faces.

He adjusted his glasses.

"Well, then. Can anyone tell me briefly the story of *The Cask of Amontillado*."

When nobody volunteered he walked down one of the aisles and stopped at the desk of a fat boy with curly red hair and freckles.

"Can *you* tell me the story? In your own words."

"Yes, sir."

"I'm waiting."

"Well," the boy began, "there was this one guy being bugged by this other guy — "

"Just a minute, now. This is an English class, you can at least use the English language."

"I am, sir."

"You know what I mean. Never mind the slang. Tell the story the way you should."

"You said in my own words."

"Pardon me?"

"Nothing."

"Don't mutter. All right, carry on."

"Well, it starts off with a festival where there's lots of drinking and things. One fellow, Don somebody, wants to take revenge on another fellow called Fontinato — "

"Fortunata."

"Fortunata. Anyway, he plans to kill him, but he wants to make him suffer before he dies. This Fortunata likes to drink wine and the other guy tells him he's got a real good wine hidden away in his cellar, called Armadillo — "

"Amontillado."

"Yeah. He's got this wine and he invites Fortunata down to have a taste of it. Fortunata is dressed up like a clown for the festival with a little bell on his cap and he laughs at the other fellow, Don somebody, I forget his second name — "

"*Don* is not the man's name. 'Don' is a Spanish title of respect, like 'mister'. The name you can't remember is 'Pedro' which is his first name, not his second."

"Oh."

"You can continue."

"Mister Pedro — "

"Call him Don Pedro."

"Anyway, this Fortunata laughs at him and tells him his wine is no good but Don Pedro talks him into going down to his wine cellar anyway. There are big barrels down there and skeletons lying all over the place and thousands of bottles of wine covered with dust. They go through the cellar carrying torches — it was a long time ago, they didn't have flashlights — and they're drinking wine all the time they're going, breaking the necks off bottles and sloshing it down right out of the bottle. Fortunata gets good and drunk and pretty soon they come to the end of the cellar where there's a big hole in the wall and Don Pedro clamps a pair of chains on Fortunata when he's not looking. So Fortunata's chained in this hole and Don Pedro begins laying bricks up the front and sealing Fortunata in for good and when Fortunata sees him doing this, laying on the mortar and building up a wall of bricks, he tries to act like it's a joke. But he sees Don Pedro isn't joking and he sobers up right quick and begs him to let him out saying he'll do anything he wants. But Don Pedro just keeps working, he puts the last brick in and goes away. And that's the story."

"Thank you. You might have given a less flippant description but the facts are there. Now, what did you get from this story? Anyone?" He pointed his finger at a boy with short hair and thick glasses in the front row. "You. What's your name?"

"Daniel Flaherty, sir."

"Flaherty. What did you think of the story, Mister Flaherty?"

"I liked it."

"You did?"

"Yes, sir."

"Why?"

"Well, there was suspense, and the characterization of the two men was good, and the descriptions was good. The atmosphere was good and I think on the whole it was a good story."

"Thank you, Mister Flaherty. The descriptions *were* good. And you might try to learn another adjective besides 'good'. Anybody else? You there, at the back. What did you think of Mister Flaherty's critique?"

"Me?"

"Yes. I'm sorry I don't know many of you by name yet . . . it takes a little while. As the days go on I'll get to know all of you. Your name is . . . ?"

"Murphy, sir."

"Well, Mister Murphy, what did you think?"

"About what, sir?"

"About what Daniel said?"

"It was okay. Pretty good."

"What did you learn from the story yourself?"

"Well . . . " Screwing up his mouth, thinking hard. "I guess how to kill somebody and get away with it."

Laughter from the class.

"You mean commit the perfect crime? Was that a perfect crime?"

"Sure."

"How do you know?"

"Well, he didn't get caught, sir."

"How do you know that?"

"Because in the old days they would've hung him if they caught him."

"And how do you know they didn't?"

"It says so, sir. He was an old man when he wrote the story. There's a picture of him."

The teacher glanced at his book.

"A picture of him? Where?"

"In the Classics comic. He's writing with a feather and he's an old man with white hair."

"Is that where you read the story, in a comic book?"

"Yes, sir. It's a Classics comic."

"You read it in a comic book? That's not what I assigned you. I didn't assign you to read a comic book."

"No sir. But it's like the movies, sir."

"What is."

"Well, the way they make movies out of books."

The teacher regarded him for a moment.

"Would you explain that?"

"Well, you know, sir, some people read the book and some see the movie."

"I see. And you read the comic book."

"Now you got it, sir."

§

It's my last day here. In a couple of hours I'll be taking the bus to Bannonbridge, never to return.

This would seem like the proper time to say something profound by way of summing up my career as an educator, but at the moment nothing occurs to me.

It still amazes me how I got away with being the teacher I was, but I guess nobody wanted to take the trouble to bother me very much about it. Mr Gates was as I've said a pleasant and easy-going man, and avoided problems as much as he could. He had stomach ulcers and that was problem enough for him. The other teachers were too busy grousing over discipline and keeping order in their own rooms to care what I was doing. Or rather, they did care to a certain extent, but not enough to do more than give me disapproving glances. They probably believed my failure to "keep good order" set a bad precedent and made things a bit harder for themselves. They grumbled, but on the whole they were nice people, like Mr Gates. Indeed if the whole world came up to the standard of this rural area it would be a good world to live in. There's nothing "put on" here, no affectations or false intellectualism.

When I was working in Montreal I would sometimes take the bus out Westmount way and I'd hear the little rich kids talking about the symphony they'd heard and how "powerful" it was, and that the third movement was "simply magnificent, very moving". Ten-year-old kids talking like Rashid.

Nor was it just the rich kids; the lower orders did it as well. I'd see classes of them in the art museum standing in front of some worthless abstract while their art teacher would say, "What significance do you see in this, now? Anyone?" And some pre-adolescent raises his hand and says, "It's mostly red, does that mean the artist's emotions were aroused?" And another says, "The colour's heavier on one side," and the teacher nods approvingly, "That's right. The artist is trying to tell us that society is improperly balanced. Do you notice anything else?" And she'll go on and talk about "tonality" and the "implication" and the "interpretation" when any fool can see the guy just dumped a bunch of paint on the canvas and stirred it around with a mop for a while before slapping a pretentious title on it.

And if it isn't art it's psychology. Kids prattling about "motivation" and "neurosis" and "self-actualization" and "anal fixation" and the rest. A different kind of bullshit from what you find in the fields around here.

§

As to the future, what lies in store for me, I have the woman in Eva that I looked so long for. I have summer holidays before me and an adventurous fall and winter after that — adventurous because I'm going I know not where. That is to say, the *place* will be Montreal, Eva and I have settled on that; but the circumstances are unknown.

It's the end of my teaching career, but not my life. I'm rather hoping now that I'll have a long life. I was thinking I'd like to become a wise old man, a friend of cats and dogs and birds and squirrels, and most other creatures that cross my path (reptiles excluded). A pensive fellow, sitting in the sun humming a quiet tune and whittling on a stick, at peace with his thoughts and memories. It's something to shoot for anyway, but like Rashid's car salesman plans, obviously a long-term project.

TWELVE

November 1, 1965
Barker's Ridge, NB

Dear Mr Macbride,
    Well here's a little surprise for you, I got your address from the new English teacher Arthur Sprague, have you ever heard of him? He says he knows you at least he's heard of you. He's boarding with Mrs Tuttle and she gave him your address for me.
    He's a lot like you in teaching, he's very smart but he's too damn likeable so we have a tendency to act up with him so it's just like old times but it's sure different without that head of hair to look at two periods a day. I squash mine down every noon hour because it gets all mussed up playing basketball so I just pull it down and let it hang.
    Hope you aren't too busy in Montreal to write back. I mean the women would leave you alone long enough to scratch a line or two, wouldn't they? All the boys in Grade 12 send their regards to you aren't you thrilled all to hell now? Chuckle. Hope you can make my writing out because I'm doing a rush order I want to get done before the fight on TV starts and it's 10:45 our time now and the fight starts at 11 o'clock.
    How are the ladies up there, giving you a hard time I suppose? (roar)

Do you remember Brenda MacKnight, the girl I was going with when you left well she went back to Grade 11 again because she didn't get her matrics and I'm alone in the big Grade 12, bugger isn't it?

In my next letter, that's if you get this one and write back, you better write because I write only one letter a year and it happens to be your name that was pulled out of the hat this time (roar! roar!). Seriously though I hope you write back, the boys in my room want to each write a note to you and put it in my letter and send it to you so I will do this in the next one, and they all want you to write one back to the class in care of me so don't you feel honoured because we haven't forgotten you.

I am doing good in Grade 12 this year how's that grab you? Different, huh.

Here's the order we sit in, in our corner of Grade 12's room. Bryden, Doug and Perley sit next to the board in the last three seats and Bert, me and Lester in the row next to them so we got a great thing going in the crazy corner this year. That's about all this time and I hope you write and don't forget all your friends down here because we haven't forgot you.

Yours very truly,

Bobby F

P.S. Hope you can read this without having to get a translator of course you're used to it if you can read your own writing ha! ha!

P.P.S. I couldn't find any writing paper but knew you wouldn't mind this sheet I tore out of a scribbler.